Kerala, K
Quite Co

Shinie Antony is the author of *Barefoot And Pregnant*, *Kardamom Kisses*, *Planet Polygamous* and *Séance On A Sunday Afternoon*. She lives in Bangalore with her husband, two children and a very hungry fish called Clementine.

Kerala, Kerala, Quite Contrary

Edited by
Shinie Antony

Rupa & Co

Copyright © Shinie Antony 2009

Published 2009 by
Rupa . Co
7/16, Ansari Road, Daryaganj,
New Delhi 110 002

Sales Centres:

Allahabad Bangalooru Chandigarh Chennai
Hyderabad Jaipur Kathmandu
Kolkata Mumbai

All rights reserved.
No part of this publication may be reproduced, stored in a retrieval system, or transmitted, in any form or by any means, electronic, mechanical, photocopying, recording or otherwise, without the prior permission of the publishers.

Typeset in
Mindways Design
1410 Chiranjiv Tower
43 Nehru Place
New Delhi 110 019

Printed in India by
Rekha Printers Pvt Ltd.
A-102/1, Okhla Industrial Area, Phase-II,
New Delhi-110 020

For Deepa
(14 Nov 1959 - 1 Aug 1989)
Sis-in-law, my star in the sky

Contents

The Leaf And The Thorn...   1
Shinie Antony

1. Odd Morning   5
   Susan Visvanathan

2. The Strange Sisters Of Mannarkad   17
   William Dalrymple

3. The Countryside   31
   M. Mukundan

4. Everyday And The Avant-Garde:
   The Evolution Of Society And Literature In Kerala   42
   K. Satchidanandan

5. Hijack   59
   Paul Zacharia

6. Stone The Sin, Not The Sinner   63
   Varkey Cardinal Vithayathil

7. Orhan Pamuk, Nair and I   67
   Anita Nair

8. The Argumentative Malayali   78
   D. Vijayamohan

9	The Night They Arrested The Moon *K.R. Gowri Amma*	87
10	A Medicine That Cannot Be Prescribed *S.S. Lal*	91
11	The Mundu Brigade *Yusuf Arakkal*	97
12	Three Men On A Train *Sheila Kumar*	105
13	Silent Cats *Omchery*	117
14	Sitrep Seventies *Hormis Tharakan*	134
15	Fort Lines *Shreekumar Varma*	156
16	Chinese Takeaway *M.V. Rappai*	167
17	The Clove *Sarah Joseph*	174
18	Music And Lyrics *Rama Varma*	182
19	Houseboat Story: A Travelogue In Disguise *Jayanth Kodkani*	189
20	A For Anglo *Stephen Padua*	196
21	A Matter Of Faith *Vinod Joseph*	201
22	My Urbanisation *A.J. Thomas*	213

23	No Sex Please, We Have Cable *Suresh Menon*	223
24	The Gift *Nimz Dean*	233
25	Building Brand Kerala *Shashi Tharoor*	235
26	Happy *Omana*	251

The Leaf And The Thorn...

Shinie Antony

Keralam. This state on the tropical Malabar Coast of south-west India, the land of the Cheras and the Keras, a ribbon of realty that Vamana wrested from Maveli.

Via which the Spice Route zigzagged thousands of years ago and the rich vein of commerce and culture from West Asia, the Far East and then Europe could be picked. Where the umbrellas come out dot on 1 June and the hartals happen round the year. What the Gulf Malayali weeps over when alone and the only place in the world that palli-muttais, kappa-meen, pazham-pori, chakka varatti, ice-proot and vepila katti taste like themselves. Where you can love one M – Mammootty or Mohanlal – and love-hate another M – Marxism.

This jade dot in tourism brochures, with its ayurvedic backrubs and backwater boat-rides, where colourful Kathakali dancers now huddle in ad backdrops and farmlands wisp into industrial smoke.

Having grown up all over India (dad being in the defence services), my most sensitive era on appearance, accent and every other superficial detail of self was spent in laborious denial, a denial eased by the 'for-holidays-only' tag hanging on hometown Kerala.

Through it all – the exclamations meant to flatter ('you don't sound/smell/look like a Malayali!'), the mandatory negation of mother and mother-tongue, and the lone scrambling for native identity amidst the debris of a neo-cosmopolitanism all the rage then – I managed to sniff the Judas on me. It was the horror of having rejected every exclusivity that 'belonging' brings along with simplistic generalisations of over-attachment to birth terrain that paused me on the path to soul-neutering. I still had to say, to prospective landladies and small-talkers when it came to roots that yes, I was/am a Malayali from Kerala.

As the melodramatic angst of teens receded, there tumbled down on me a whole new world never seen before, let alone explored or enjoyed. I had never entered, how had I thought myself exited? Aching to embrace what had always been mine and armed with a passion for folk songs, poetry and old-fashioned sayings, I locked my early twenties in feverish Malayalam.

Of all languages that accosted me, Hindi was the one I thought in, fought in, fantasised in. English followed a close second but Malayalam was always in my heart and, more audibly, on my tongue. I gathered school textbooks and learnt the alphabets; the first novel I read in Malayalam was the late Vaikkom Mohammad Basheer's *Phatummayude Aadu* (Phatumma's Goat). The pleasure of reading the original—and not a translation—proved addictive. In fact, so voluble was my bliss that my husband still calls me Phatumma when I linger over a Malayalam book.

Dangerously, over time the mood to share came upon me. For along with the delight was a niggling condescension for those who took Kerala too lightly and pity for those who saw the state through a tourism ad or bratty visitor. You know those ga-ga travelogues from vacationers sliding down India's ass, gushing over quaint old shacks along some ramshackle beach where appams (pronounced like 'apples') are served by women in saris with gold borders. For some sudden reason, Kerala came to be at the wrong end of the microscope. But what does this petite state itself see, feel and hear as it painstakingly prepares to criss-cross into the global spotlight?

There are those who think the state an embarrassment, that it encourages constant disorder in its politics and economy, but there are those who analyse the changes and comprehend that the state's tiptoeing towards a TechnoPark repute is a lesson in remorse for having missed the IT bus and a necessity now in the natural order of things.

While meandering footloose and fanciful all over non-Kerala, the one Malayalam saying that echoed ad nauseum in the private chambers of my soul involved a Thorn and a Leaf – *ilayum, mullum*. You know, the usual chastity hogwash for women in order to rein in their raging hormones; whether the leaf falls on the thorn or the thorn on the leaf, it is the leaf that's razed to the ground. But if contexts shifted away from the literally penile, what did the thorn itself make of the leaf's suicidal tendencies? This switch in loyalties—and you have to admit, Kerala *is* shaped a bit like a thorn in the Arabian Sea's side—turned me lyrical: when the rose-plucker's thumb is pricked, the thorn's throb goes unasked . . .

Kerala, I mean the whole of Kerala as a landmass with its seething mobs and paddy fields and movie posters of moustachioed men and bus-stops and student unions and coconut-oiled *kuli-medachil* wet plaits and angry slogans and moody monsoons and buses called Jo-Mol and Benny-Mon, morphed in my mind into the virginal *mullu* – the trembling thorn cowering from the *ila*s, the silly slutty leaves with their martyr 'comblex'. Many a development scheme jumped to its death on the so-called spikes of the state. Therein lies the state's real tragedy, for there's nothing more fatal than the preserving of 'innocence' against all odds or the process of growth.

Through the reflections and ripostes in this fiction-nonfiction-memoir-travelogue anthology, each author-contributor conveys her/his own personal perspective of Kerala. Yes, the song of the splashing oars is drowned out by strike calls and the drone of aeroplanes. The arecanut and the wee white fan behind the old woman's mundu are subjects of nouveau poesy. Yes, Kerala is still green, but the 'Venice of the East' now proudly presents the trash-can of Alappuzha. A river runs through every village but the little feet dangling in it are silt-shod. Yes, we have hundred percent literacy, but can alphabets be ladled into a plate? Too many catarctic eyes are trained on the sky – *my son will come now, will come now* . . . Yes, the priceless sayings still hold true, but all is lost in translation. It is, as Dickens said in a different tense and sense, the best of times and it is the worst of times.

The Malayali's love for travel and his amazing adaptability to new terrains can mostly be traced to his survival gene. North, east and west beckon him away from the lack of opportunities, let him play Columbus and nudge him towards sweet uncertainties. Education, employment and entertainment lie elsewhere, but oh how a spot of south cries wolf in his blood now and again!

Everywhere he goes, the Malayali takes a bit of Kerala with him and since the Malayalis, as the bad jokes go, are all over the place, why, that's Kerala everywhere in the world, isn't it?

– *Phatumma*
(September 2008)

1 Odd Morning

Susan Visvanathan

The Kerala Express stood empty and dank. In a little while it would be crammed with people and luggage, with porters in their swathe of beedi smoke haranguing for more money. There were 'No Smoking' signs at the station, yet everything was covered in a dull mist, with betel stains everywhere and rats scurrying among the passengers' legs. The tourists looked either like Chengiz Khan on a Pahadganj ticket to ride, or like Josephine, the displaced Empress of France, in olive green camouflage jackets. Delhi station was not like Palakkad or Thiruvalla with its clean platforms and creepers with purple flowers growing over the shiny black fences.

Don't ask me who I am; as I tell my story, you will know. Curiosity never served the reader well, that is if you are the kind who looks to the end and then you know the story even without beginning it.

I live in America. I love the popcorn and the candy. I'm the elegant Malayali cousin everyone craves for, an actress with the curls, the sleeveless shirt, the Bermudas and the twang of Malayaliness. I appear in Delhi and Kathmandu and Bangalore and Chennai and, oh, Kyoto, Paris, Timbuctoo and London. And when people ask me who I am, I always say 'I'm a Malayali'. And they all seem to know what that means.

The stage has meant everything to me. Lights, thick paint and now the costumes, which change from season to season. We never worry about costumes or sets anymore. But stage paint is back with a bang. I wish I could say that I have been influenced by Kathakali, but from where my ancestors came, we never went to temples where the gold of the flagpole gleamed and the music, the stories, the plays and dances were performed. That thick paint . . . four hours to put it on and, six hours later, taking it off was even more tiring. It did not hurt you though, and sitting still while it was put on was the most meditative thing one can imagine. All of this is hearsay though. I am a creature of the modern stage, we improvise as we go on. And thick white Noh paint is what comes most easily for us.

So the people come in. They stare at me. I look away. It is cold, my sleeveless blouse and glass earrings are quite out of keeping with the silks and the nylons that the women are wearing, gold dense around their necks and arms; the men are lean and muscular with moustaches and brilliant grins. They look charming and happy . . . soldiers and nurses, men and women going home. They talk with the grand volatility of those who have been camouflaged, on hilltops and deserts, in industrial towns and remote villages, and now have been left to themselves. I like them. They, however, look past me. My youth is of no concern to them. I am the outsider. Then I speak to them and they rivet around to look at me.

We have this thing, a common language. They suddenly love me without reason. They share their food with me – fried fish and fried chicken, rice wrapped in banana leaves. They have crisps and biscuits and orange juice and pineapples and curd whisked with salt and curry leaves. Food seems abundant. And the dirty train edges out of the filthy rat-infested Delhi station in a whorl of Malayaliness. Their lives have been hard, in the battlefields and hospitals in far-off cantonments and mining towns. They have served the country, some of them have been administrators and clerks and railway employees. But as they dust the rexine ledges, which are the bunks of their well-earned rest, they lay out bedcovers and pillows, take out multi-coloured sarongs and make themselves at home.

Three days pass without my having to exert. I lie on the top bed with the light on, reading Lee Simonsen's *The Stage Is Set*.

Probably the only drastically realistic performance that ever occurred in the theatre took place at _ in 1549 at a Jesuit production entitled 'The Triumph of Mardochnes'.... The organisers selected a criminal already condemned to death, he was flattered at being given a lead role, and also perhaps ignorant of the play's ending, docilely allowed himself to be beheaded on stage...

Fear makes my heart beat very fast and the wind rushes through my ears... it seems like my cranium is as empty as the blue sky we must have run into. I have no idea about the changing landscape. I know it by heart. There will be the dusty scrubs and the appearance of magical forts, there will be the dark earth and the cotton country, there will be the green, fertile plains and hills, there will be the rivers following rapidly one after another, and suddenly, the Palakkad gap. What season is it? Will the rivers be full? Will the crops be golden? Have the palm trees appeared? Have the arecanuts given way to the coconut palms? Is the sea here?

Are we home? And suddenly I know we are, people are getting off. We have become strangers to each other again. Those getting off are rapidly waving goodbye before being embraced in loving arms. Potato cutlets give way to bananas encased in golden fried batter. Rain is slushing on to wet green seats. New people enter the compartment. They are men and women... clean and freshly bathed, daily passengers. The women sit down together, and the men extending their legs look suspiciously at me. I jump down. They look away. The women smile and extend the banana leaf with Guruvayoor prasadam. It's nice, but I'm a Christian, can I eat it?

Pinnae, addunu enna! (Of course, what's there in doing so!)

Pashae numbillae akkuthu kettuthu illallo. (But they do not allow us to enter the temple.)

That does not interest the women, who all laugh and say, 'Go to the many places they will allow you to go. Have a bath though!'

I take out my bottle of Chanel 5; it's the perfume Marilyn Monroe wore, so common as to shock you with its smell of spice and familiarity. I comb my hair, I take out a denim shirt to wear over my crumpled sleeveless blouse from Janpath that I was so proud of. Chanel 5 gives me an air of legitimacy. The women turn away for a moment. The men take out their newpapers and start to read. America is a sodden country for them, constantly staking the Gulf and risking the lives of Malayalis. They have relatives there, but do I ever stop at Dubai? the women ask smilingly. The gold malls and souks have even come up at the airport. That shining gold. That column of gold, that metal armour of gold. No, I've got an education in the U.S. of A, but no gold.

The people who filled the compartment get off after a two-hour run. And then I am alone. The day is bright, the sun shines on the star spangled water . . . this is my home, America is the migrant's home, this is the dream. This water, these trees, these ducks and hyacinths, I can never go far away. I'm alone. The man in the next compartment looks furtively at me. There is something frightening and lascivious about him. He looks like a family man – a toothbrush moustache, a kindly air, and yet a subterranean lewdness. He looks at my body, he is someone's husband, but the flat band of ring on a hairy finger with his wife's name on it has really no meaning for him. He comes into the compartment. He sits down and continues to stare at me without saying anything. I pick up my suitcase and quickly walk down the aisle, weighed down by the things I've brought for my cousins. To my horror, every compartment has a man like him, or two, sometimes three. They all look at me, some bar my passage, some touch their moustaches . . . a station appears slowly with its yellow board in three languages. The train snakes to a halt. And then it shudders to a stop. The metal hinges groan. I'm near the sink with the clogged phlegm and the sambar leavings. The smell of urea clogs the narrow passage. There is an unknown man breathing over my neck, my suitcase creating a welcome barrier between us. His breath smells of alcohol. I jump off the train. It's beginning to drizzle. The train leaves. Startled faces look at me as I stand there — twenty-five years old, disheveled, frightened. Where on earth am I? It's an obscure village, a siding, where the train had stopped waiting for its signal.

I lived in that village where I got off one sunny tropical day, for twenty days. To tell the truth, it suited me well. The platform was empty, the red gravel road that led into the village was well maintained. There was not even a station master or a booking clerk. Only two women with green coats and brooms swept the hallway and the stairs, chewing betel nut all the while. They were clean and fragrant, and liked their job. No porters, no vendors, no passengers. Sometimes one comes across a surprising place like this. There was a resthouse though, and a kind man sat at the desk. He asked for my papers, and then gave me a room. Idyllic, just to look out at the paddy fields and the mango grove, the children going to school every morning. I memorised the lines of the play we were to produce when I return after my holiday. Food appeared . . . more fried fish than I was used to, but in a coating of chilly and turmeric, and crumbly and crisp at the same time. And it rained. It swung down from the skies endlessly. An old woman came every morning and cleaned out my room, and offered oil massages. The hot water appeared in grandiose steel buckets. Musk rats appeared, but the manager urbanely wished them away. And then, after I had completely recovered from my delirium, I waited for the train to arrive. But there was no train. The resthouse keeper shrugged and said that he had no idea when the next one was due. I must go now, I said desperately. He smiled kindly at me and asked if I would like sardines or mackerel. What was my preference for lunch?

'I have to go!'

'Madam, you have to wait for the train. It will be here soon.'

'How soon?'

'We must wait and see.'

'How can I leave the village?'

'Some Gulf people will be visiting soon. You can leave with them.'

'And when will they come?'

'After the rains.'

'But that's in September.'

'Not the monsoon rains. I am speaking of these sporadic Janaury rains. The tourists are all unhappy. And news is full of their woes. What can we do? The rains decide our fate.'

The slugs were leaving silver trails on the verandah, the fireflies had been dampened, the tarantula spiders appeared as casually as houseflies, and worse of all, the cook fell ill with Chikan-guniya. She was a large woman with bad knees, her kindness was the only thing that had kept me afloat in the many days after I had stepped off a scurfy express train. Always there, her cotton cloth flung over her huge bosom, her smile as tempestuous as lightning, her demeanour always in keeping with her servility, and below that, a compassion for helpless me who could not explain why I was there. Karpamma had known these red gravel hills since she was born. The rain made runnels in the soil, but on the other hand, the same earth was quick in growing things . . . jackfruit and rice and rubber and gourds of all kinds. The topsoil washed away to reveal a dark thick lumpen earth, in which white maggots thrive. Huge white maggots that eat dead bodies and in turn can be willing worms for catching fish with equal ease . . . one death substituted by another in a fertile organicity.

Karpamma's illness made me nervous, but she hobbled to the kitchen and put the rice on to boil before she lay down again, shrouded in the cabin in which coconuts and jackfruits were hoarded. I went to the station and asked the two sweeper women if they could cook food for me till the train came.

'We only eat rice and pounded chillies. Sometimes coconut chutney, sometimes dried fish.'

They looked well fed and they smiled. 'Alright,' I said, fearing starvation. My friends would never believe this. As the ketchup rolled off hamburgers in the street corners of New York, their leather jacket would curl at the ends when they heard my story. I went back an hour later. Karpamma had died and was now wrapped in a white cloth. I went and sat at the station, afraid to go back. I sat there the whole day, the looking-glass sky was now turning purple and black and welted and dark. The day had changed. It started to pour and I went to the rest house again. It was evening now, and there was no sign of Karpamma's corpse. Her family had come and buried her in the ancestral yam garden. There were only her blouses hanging on the decrepit line, her large long box of sandalwood powder and her frayed rubber chappals. She had only owned one checked sarong and one *thorath*, or cotton towel. She must have been buried in that.

And so I, who had died so many times before on stage, with my carefully razored legs stretched across wood on stage platforms, my clothes artistically askew, my deaths reconstructions of history and long lost battles . . . once an elephant had been brought on stage while we did a story about Hannibal, but the New York boards creaked and we had to pay a fortune in damages... I looked at the empty space among the tufted coconuts and the martially spiked jackfruit lying side by side in warriors' amity, and missed Karpamma who had put the rice to boil before dying.

On the twenty-first day, the train came. I stopped it as it was chugging slowly past, and the engine driver, in his sooty cubicle which had braved the bitter northern cold and come into a tropical sun (the rain had stopped), saw me and stopped. With unnerving kindness, the man holding the red and green flags got off the train, and helped me with my luggage. No one looked at me and I sat down next to a large kindly woman with her basket of green plantains and a checked turban with filigree gold jewellery. She smiled and asked me where I was going. And ticketless though I was, I was integrated into Malayaliness for the few hours that the train wound through the hills and woods of North Kerala. When we came to Travancore, the rules were in place again, and ticket checkers asked me for money and wrote out my receipts. They looked blankly at my previous ticket and raised their eyebrows like professors do at unkempt scholars. They had sharp long noses and narrow black eyes with neatly creased white trousers and shiny black coats with their badges in place. They spoke to me in Malayalam and when I twanged back in a nasal New York voice, they said, 'Be more careful next time, madam!' in clipped English voices.

I reached my grandmother's village after overpaying the taxi driver who kept looking at me through the mirror. He was driving far too fast, and the children on bicycles seemed to know him very well because they saw him in their rear-view mirrors, got off their cycles and waved to him as he hurtled past. Hibiscus in their hair, a desire to live, the little girls were particularly cautious. When we reached my grandmother's village, I saw that the river was gone.

Where's the river? It had always been in my mind in the heady days of work and afternoon sweat, lines forgotten, cues missed, a rent in an expensive robe, the director shouting in Cockney while we Americans fumbled in rapture and misread intent.

The river was gone. I felt a sense of dread, and then the taxi driver pointed it to me. It was above our head. I stared and stared, feeling a little sick.

Puroganam he said, with pleasure.

What do you mean, development? I asked, feeling breathless.

Now they will get water in the towns, our water goes there, in this cement trough. Grand isn't it? Modern engineering, what it can do!

In some places, the canal over our head in its cement casing leaked. The people of the village collected it in buckets, truck drivers stopped to bathe, elephants passing through the rice field to the ancient temple were washed, and in one place, the leakage was so heavy that a small pond had created a marsh with lilies, yams and a flotsam of ducks that were watched over by a man with a stick, smoking a beedi.

Aarrae kaanaan vannada? (Who have you come to see?)

My grandmother.

She's waiting for you. I can smell frying fish and duck all morning.

How is she?

All of ninety. They have a new dog in the house. A small Alsatian. Cost two thousand rupees! They got rid of the white cat. It bit the master.

But when I went into the huge glass house with the odd furniture, all very ostentatious and mosaic and marble and heavy wood, I felt the shadow presence of my great-grandfather's house. It was still there, its littleness, its charm, its thatched roof, the bare wooden furniture, the small carved wooden walls with its filigree patterns. Under the heavy and ornate new furniture on which no one really sat, preferring the old chairs and the corners of the staircase, and the lingering scented spaces of trees that still remained, my family sat waiting for me to say something. They loved me, there was no doubt of it. Their days were spent looking after my grandmother, who was the only sibling of that generation left in the clan, and her ninety years were a raiment of kinship and clan love. The ardour of blood that recognises the worth of old women when they have nothing to give but the grace of their presence, the wisdom of their smile, the constant scourge of their physical discomfort hidden from public view as their silver hair gleamed in early bright sunshine.

Vanna allo! (You've come!)

Train was late. So good to see you! What are you reading?

I prefer serials now, reading is hard for me. Do you know that there is a new baby due?

I heard. She looks pretty. How many months gone?

Just three, but missing her husband. He phones everyday, and sends her desert fruits, raw dates with people who are coming back on holiday.

Raw dates?

Show her! Show her!

I put down my luggage. The chocolates I'd carefully brought must have melted in the tropical winter, when the hottest season made the sky blue and hard and vacant, the sun like a distant orange, full and venomous. The rains were not due for another three months, and while the hibiscus bloomed in an arrogance of colour, the other plants needed careful watering. The aquaduct limped water to the next town in a dismal grey sheath of crumbling cement.

How lovely to sit down on my great-uncle's *chaar kasera*. I'd always loved him best. His kindness was an armour against petty remarks about his poverty, a scion of an old house, blood and lineage and memory with no money, no money at all.

The cattle-shed was where it was before, that had not been changed, but in building the new palatial Gulf house, my cousin had mixed up all the rooms. Where the bedroom of our childhood had given way to the kitchen, the long hall had been replaced by the pantry and dining room. The dining room of the old house had been transformed into the living room, in which the veranda had also been fused. The *arra* was hidden away now. Earlier it was in the hall, and now it nestled next to the pantry: heavy and rosewood and the sacred heart of the house. At the back were new large rooms where earlier there had been small cool sleeping rooms for the women. And now the annually replaced thatch had gone forever, and a hundred years after my great grandfather had built it, were these huge rooms on the first floor, with modern bathrooms, all tiled and gleaming. There was hot water and cold water, and foreign soap and shampoo. And I remembered my childhood, when water sloshed up the well in a bucket made from coconut spathe. It was nice that spathe, soft to the touch, wet and gleaming. And grandmother had fallen into the well in 1927 perhaps? Clung to the moss and lichen stones inside, and been rescued.

She was feeding the white kitten, which had come on its own. They had got rid of the big white cat because it had started biting everyone. My cousin just took it on his motorcycle and left it in some far off rubber field. But someone had done the same to their unwanted kitten, and here it was nestling in my grandmother's lap, with the Alsatian dog chained outside barking jealously. What is life, but a finding of home and safe haven? I sat down to eat the large meal that had been cooked for me, looking nervously at the river above my head as it snaked past above the rice fields, wondering when it would crumble and drown us.

At night my family belted out hymns, with the candles shining bright. The phone lines were down, the electricity lines were down, no one would come to fix them for three days. No one minded though. There was the occasional swatting of mosquitos and the fumes of Tortoise coil, which gleamed red in the dark. We had yams with fish for dinner and then, while we slept, it rained heavily, and the river in minutes became a torrent. The water raged over our heads, and the leak gushed so horribly, it was like a waterfall. There was thunder of the most fearsome kind, but I could hear the contented snore of my cousin as he thought of the new baby that would grow up in this house with its mother, study in the village school, drinking orange juice and eating American crunchies and raw dates, while its father spent the best years of his life slogging for a foreign oil company. The baby's father was struggling with a new job, hot under his helmet in the desert, but they would all fly in aeroplanes, buy gold, have insurance and, yes, this house would only grow grander with the years.

Prof. **Susan Visvanathan** teaches sociology at the Jawaharlal Nehru University in New Delhi and is the acclaimed author of *The Visiting Moon, Something Barely Remembered, The Seine At Noon, Phosphorus And Stone* and *The Christians of Kerala: History, Belief And Ritual Among The Yakoba*. Presented here is a short story written by her for this anthology.

2 The Strange Sisters Of Mannarkad

William Dalrymple

On the edge of the jungle lay a small wooden temple. It was late evening, and the sun had already disappeared behind the palms. The light was fading fast now, and the flickering camphor flames and the ranks of hundreds of small clay lamps lined up on the wooden slats of the temple seemed to be burning brighter and brighter, minute by minute.

The oiled torsos of the temple Brahmins were gleaming too. They nearly finished the evening *arti*, circling burning splints around the idol of the Goddess Bhagavati, as they rang bells, chanted slokas and blew on conch shells. The ceremony prepared the Goddess to sleep, in the prescribed way, with all the proper ceremonies that she expected, and her attendants busied themselves on what would be their final task of the day.

Only when it was over, and the doors of the inner shrine were sealed for the night, were they able to tell me properly about the Goddess they served. Bhagavati, they explained, was the pre-eminent Goddess in Kerala, the most powerful and beloved deity in the region. In some incarnations, it was true, she could be ferocious – a figure of horror and terror, a stalker of cremation grounds, who slaughtered demons and evil *yakshis* without hesitation or compassion, becoming as terrible as them in order to defeat them.

Some of her titles reflected this capacity – She Who is Wrathful, She Who Has Flaming Tusks, She Who Causes Madness, the Terrible One, Night of Death, etc. As the sloka went:

> *Come, come in haste, O Goddess, with thy locks bedraggled, thou who hast three eyes, whose skin is dark, whose clothes are stained with blood, who has rings in thy ears, who hast a thousand hands, and ridest upon a monster and wieldest in thy hands tridents, clubs, lances and shields.*

But in other moods, Bhagavati could be supremely benign and generous to her devotees – the caring, loving, fecund mother; and this was how her followers usually liked to think of her. For many, she was the deity of the land itself – the spirit of the mountains, and the life force in the soil; the green of the rice paddy and the nuts ripening slowly on the cashew trees; the pepper berries tumbling on the vines and the swelling gourds of the coconuts fruiting atop the palms. In this form, Bhagavati is regarded as a chaste virgin and a caring mother, qualities she shares with her sister, whose enclosure lies a short distance down the road:

'Yes, yes, the Virgin Mary is Bhagavati's younger sister,' explained Vasudeva, the head priest, matter-of-factly, as if stating the obvious.

'But for sisters, don't they look rather different from each other?' I asked. A calendar image of the Goddess was pinned up behind Vasudeva, showing Bhagavati as a wizened hag wreathed in skulls and crowned with an umbrella of cobra hoods. In her hand she wielded a giant sickle.

'Sisters are often a little different from each other,' he replied. 'Mary is another form of the Devi. They have equal power.'

He paused. 'At our annual festival, the priests take the Goddess around the village on top an elephant to receive sacrifices from all the different people. The Goddess visits all the places, and one stop is the church. There she sees her sister.'

'Mary gets on an elephant too?'

'No,' he replied. 'But when the goddesses visit each other, the sacrifice in the church is just like the one we have here – we light lamps and make an offering of neelam at a particular place in the compound. The priests stay in their church, but the trustees and congregation of the church receive us and make a donation to the temple. Each year they give some money and a tin of oil for our lamps.'

'So relations are good?'

'The people here always cooperate,' he said. 'Our Hindus go to the church and the Christians come here and ask the Goddess for what they want. Almost all days they are coming, for everyone believes the two are sisters.'

This was something I had seen ever since I had arrived in Mannarkad, a small village eighty kilometres to the south of the Kerala capital, Thiruvananthapuram. In the large courtyard of the church—newly rebuilt and enlarged around a medieval core—many of the worshippers had turned out to be Hindus rather than Christians.

'I have come here from seventy kilometres away,' said K.N. Prakashan, a middle-aged school teacher wearing a lavender safari suit of the sort once favoured by Roger Moore in the 1970s James Bond movies. 'Yes I am a Hindu, but Mary is our Holy Mother. She is your mother and my mother, too. I believe she is a powerful goddess. Every time I come, I ask her to let the sufferings go from my life.'

'And does she answer your prayers?'

'Of course,' replied Prakashan. 'It works. Otherwise I wouldn't be coming back here.'

No less surprising were all the Hindu customs that were being practised by the church's devout Syrian Christian devotees. As in a Hindu temple, donations were exchanged for prasad, and in this case, it was tins full of sweet deep fried rice, peppercorns and small white sugar sweets. A large stone-lined water tank lay to one side of the compound, just as it does in the temples of the south. The devotees coming in and out of the church proudly told me that during the annual festival of Our Lady, the pilgrims would all take a ritual bath, shave their heads and eat only strictly vegetarian food to purify themselves. They would also join processions under torches, banners and coloured silk umbrellas of exactly the sort used by Hindus in their temple processions. During the festival, the sacred space of the church also had a reputation for its powers of exorcism. The Christians too share the Hindu belief that certain rituals can rid a possessed person of bhadam, or unwanted spirit possession. In the case of the church, exorcisms took place in the shadow of the great stone cross that lies to the west of the basilica.

Yet all this was mixed up with forms of devotion usually specific to the Eastern Orthodox churches. The same booths along the side of the courtyard that took donations and gave prasad, also sold small bronze plaques of arms, legs, eyes, hearts and other body parts. These could be placed in front of a holy icon to remind the saint to cure one or the other particular ailment – something practised in Greek and Syrian Orthodox churches across the Levant. There were also small bronze cobras on sale that seemed to be charms against snake bites, and silver plaques of babies for women who wished to conceive.

The Christians I talked to seemed wholly at ease with the idea of praying alongside so many Hindus. 'I believe Mary is more generous to the Hindus than she is to us,' said Thomas Daniel as he prayed at the stone cross at the back of the enclosure. 'Often their prayers are more intense than ours. Yes, we also believe Bhagavati and Mary are twin sisters. Just as our gods have power for us, so their gods have power for them.'

'So you believe in the Hindu gods, too?'

'Yes, of course,' he replied. 'Those gods are there. I go to the temple with my Hindu friends, though I don't tell the priests. And I participate in their festivals, though I don't give offerings.'

Thomas smiled. 'This has been passed from generation to generation,' he said. 'That is why we believe. All the people of Kerala believe in all of the gods.'

Kerala is the greenest state in India – hot and humid, still and brooding. The soil is so fertile that as you drift up the lotus-choked backwaters around Mannarkad, the trees close in around you as twisting tropical fan vaults of palm and bamboo arch together in the forest canopy. Mango trees hang heavy over the fishermen's skiffs; pepper vines creep through the fronds of the waterside papaya orchards.

All around this central part of Kerala live the St. Thomas Christians – so called because they believe that St. Thomas, the apostle of Jesus who famously refused to believe in the resurrection 'until I have placed my hands in the holes left by the nails and the wound left by the spear,' came to India from Palestine after the Resurrection, and baptised their ancestors. This is not a modern tradition – it has been the firm conviction of the Christians here since at least the sixth century AD, and in all likelihood for hundreds of years before that.

Certainly, in AD 594, the French monastic chronicler, Gregory of Tours, met a wandering Greek monk who reported that in southern India he had met Christians who had told him about St. Thomas' missionary journey to India and who had shown him the tomb of the Apostle. Over the centuries to come, almost every Western traveller to southern India, from Marco Polo to the first Portuguese conquistadors, reported the same story. Indeed, the legend of St. Thomas led to the first ever recorded journey to India by an Englishmen – according to the Anglo-Saxon Chronicle,

King Alfred sent Bishop Sighelm of Sherborne 'to St. Thomas in India'; years later, the bishop returned, carrying with him 'precious stones and the odiferous essences of that country.'

The stories that the travellers brought back with them varied little in their outlines: all said how St. Thomas had arrived in India in AD 52 from Palestine by boat; that he had travelled down the Red Sea and across the Persian Gulf, and that he landed at the great Kerala port of Muziris (modern Kodungallur), the spice entrepôt to which the Roman Red Sea merchant fleet would head each year to buy pepper for the Mediterranean market. In Kerala, St. Thomas was said to have converted the upper-caste Brahmins with the aid of miracles and to have built seven churches.

Whatever the historical truth behind all this, there can be no doubt that Christianity has deep roots in the soil, stretching back in all probability to the first century AD. Over the centuries of unusually close coexistence, the Hindus and the Christians of the region have found their myths and their rituals fusing slowly together. There may be violence between Christians and Hindus in some parts of North India—especially Gujarat and Orissa—but there has never been any serious tension between the two faiths here in Kerala. Instead, to an extraordinary degree, the two have shared their sacred places and sacred stories.

As it was specifically the Kerala Brahmins that St. Thomas converted, the Christians here have always maintained a high social status in the complex caste hierarchy of southern India. Their birth, puberty and especially marriage rituals are still more or less indistinguishable from those of any other high-caste Malayalis, with their use of areca nut, rice, lemons, sandalwood paste, flowers and milk. Until recently, the St. Thomas Christians maintained full ritual purity and so were eligible for access to Hindu temples and holy precincts. Here they were traditional patrons and sponsors, and so were awarded places of honour in the great temple processions. They would march alongside the Brahmins and the elite Nayar caste, with their images of St. Thomas carried in palanquins while their Hindu neighbours pushed chariots carrying fine bronze images of their gods. The churches were allowed to borrow the temple elephants for their own festivals.

When the Portuguese arrived in India in the sixteenth century, they criticised the St. Thomas Christian clergy for the many 'pagan' practices they had adopted – the use of ritual ablutions and the codes of touch and distance pollution; the casting of horoscopes in the Hindu manner, the idea of following your own dharma and the belief in the transmigration of souls; as well as specifically Hindu techniques of exorcism, divination and dream interpretation – all of which traditions survived well into the early twentieth century and several of which are still common among the Christians of Kerala today.

The same fusion of Hinduism and Christianity is seen in the Christian art of Kerala. Every church in the region has a large stone cross in its churchyard; but these unambiguously Christian symbols rise out of lotus-shaped Hindu bases, which are invariably covered with exactly the sort of decoration that enlivens South Indian temples – lion-headed and fish-bodied *makaras* tangle between confronted cows, elephants, tigers and dancing girls. Paired peacocks are especially popular, doubling as they do as Eucharistic symbols and vehicles of God Murugan, the son of Shiva.

At the village of Angamally, near Cochin's airport, there is a seventeenth century wall painting in the church that reveals something of the complexity of the relationship between the two faiths. It is in many ways a conventional Hell scene, paired with the Last Judgement facing it across the nave; but there are many strange idiosyncrasies. The devil is made to resemble the Goddess Kali in a Kathakali headdress, with her tongue stuck out, a crown of snake heads above and a trishul (trident) in one hand.

To the side, what could be either a Portuguese Catholic priest or a moneylender—he is wearing priest's robes and holding a big pot of money—is being tortured, the floor of hell is slithering with king cobras, and a blue-skinned elephant is busy crushing sinners. One demon is in the form of Vishnu in his boar-headed incarnation of Varaha with long sabre-like tusks. Another has blue skin and holds an Indian mace; a third wrenches a brightly coloured umbrella from a Christian's hand.

Today, even if St. Thomas is no longer carried in temple processions, much of the old syncretism still survives in many of the villages in the form of shared myths and festivals. In Thrissur, in North Kerala, it is still largely the Christians of the town who perform the prestigious job of feeding the temple elephants with the white-stemmed buds of the coconut tree at the annual Pooram festival. Closer to Mannarkad, St. Thomas is the focus of a cult in the village of Putenangadi, a short distance away, where the majority of the worshippers are Hindu. They call him *Kurusaoopen*, the Old Man of the Cross.

'I come here so that I can be relieved of all my troubles,' I was told by one Hindu lady named Jaya who was kneeling at the back of the Putenangadi church. 'I believe that Kurusaoopen can do that – he has the power, the shakti. It is that faith that brings me here. If there's anything I need, I ask Kurusaoopen for it. When I have difficulties, Kurusaoopen solves them for me. Of course, I go to the temple too. But any big problem I have, I come here and I pray, and my prayers are always answered.'

'So do you believe that St. Thomas is somehow alive and looking after you?'

'For me Kurusaoopen is definitely alive,' she said. 'He's not dead. At all times he is in my thoughts and often he appears in my dreams. That's why I come here. Today I didn't really have the time, but I made the time to come. I feel very uneasy if I don't come and pray here every Friday.'

'So you've actually had a glimpse of him in a dream?'

'I have him in my thoughts always,' repeated Jaya. 'Whenever I pray to him, he comes and answers me. Every evening when I light the lamp in my home, I call to him.'

Even the story of St. Thomas' martyrdom has been fused with Hindu myth, so St. Thomas is said to have met his end in Mylapore, north of Madras, while hiding from his enemies in the form of a peacock, the vehicle of Murugan, and the sacred bird of the nearby Mylapore temple. The lance with which St. Thomas is supposed to have been martyred is also an emblem of Murugan.

In Puthupally, near Kottyam, the villagers associate St. George—the saint the English think of as their own patron and who we believe we have lying in St. George's Chapel in Windsor Castle—with the Goddess they say is his sister – the dark Kali whose temple lies to the side of the church. In the church, St. George is shown killing a dragon; in the temple, his sister Kali is sculpted slaughtering a demon in the form of a water buffalo. Both brother and sister are believed locally to be ferocious carnivores, and during festivals, both are fed the blood of decapitated chickens.

Not far away at Piravam, Shiva is locally celebrated as the travelling companion of the Three Wise Men. According to local myth, the four went on a long pilgrimage together, and became close friends during the course of their journey. When they came near Piravam they were distraught to find their way blocked by the Meenachil river. A local Nair boatman named Chalassery Panikkar came to their rescue and ferried them across. On arrival in Piravam their sanctity was recognised, and they were installed in their sacred spaces, where Panikkar's descendants still receive gifts from both church and temple during their respective festivals. In the case of the festival of the Epiphany, the Feast of the Magi on the sixth of January, the annual church procession cannot begin until a member of the Hindu Pannikar family lights the church's oil lamp to flag it off. Elsewhere, there are unexpected stories of travelling friendships being struck up between Krishna and St. Sebastian, believed locally not to be a Roman Captain of Diocletian's Pretorian Guard but instead a Keralite Brahmin who was converted to Christianity by St. Thomas.

Not that relations between Christian saints and Hindu deities are always completely unproblematic. Just as the substitution of the devil for Kali at Angamally shows a certain ambiguity about the status of Hindu divinities, so the village myths sometimes contain elements that reveal at least a measure of competition between the different faiths. In Piravam, Shiva is said to have thrown sacred tulsi flowers in the Church of the Three Magi; the Magi retaliated by throwing frankincense into the temple. On another occasion, the Magi caught Shiva stealing oil from the lamps in the church and are said to have hit him with their sceptres. There is also a story of St. Thomas and the Goddess Bhagavati having a spat, with St. Thomas chasing the Goddess to her temple at Kodangallur and sticking his foot in the door to prevent her locking him out. Even in Mannarkad, it is said that the crack in the church's bell is due to Bhagavati damaging it as its tolling was waking her up during her sleep. In retaliation, the Virgin Mary is believed to have cracked one of the sacred conches at her sister's temple.

Such myths may hint at periods of tensions between the different faiths, and certainly there are those today who frown on the extreme porousness of religious practice in the region. The Vishnu temple in Mannarkad is today the chosen place of worship for the village's Hindu revivalists of the RSS who frequent the temple at least partly because the Brahmins there do not have anything to do with Mannarkad's Christians, of whose prosperity and prominence they disapprove.

Likewise, the Christian clergy at the church of Mannarkad, while wishing to preserve good relations with their Hindu neighbours, and welcoming Hindus into the church, at the same time do all they can to stop their own Christian flock from visiting the temple, and they strongly disapprove of their congregation indulging in syncretic ceremonies. When I asked the local priest, Fr. Kuriakos, about the festival of the Goddess Bhagavati and the forthcoming visit of the Goddess Bhagavati to the church to see her sister, he made it clear that he would on no account be present to welcome the Goddess. 'The Virgin Mary comes from Jewish tradition,' he said, clearly exasperated from repeating this regularly to his congregation. 'She is the daughter of Joachim and Anna, and was from Palestine, not India. This Devi temple is a thing from Indian tradition.'

He paused looking me in the eye before resuming, speaking very clearly to make sure I understood. 'There is no relation between the Virgin Mary and Bhagvati,' he said. 'We cannot encourage this belief. It is a myth. Worse, it is nonsense.'

With the noise of firecrackers exploding, six cymbal clashers clashing, twelve temple drummers drumming, and the women of the village loudly ululating, the procession set off up the dirt track behind the temple, and off into the jungle. It was 8.30 in the morning of 6 January 2008, and the Goddess Bhagavati was setting off to visit her devotees and relations across the village of Mannarkad.

The Goddess, who had earlier that morning entered one of the priests of the temple—the *veliccappatu*, or oracle—and so proclaimed her excitement at the forthcoming trip, had shortly afterwards re-entered her silver image, and been hoisted onto the back of a wonderfully caparisoned temple elephant.

The elephant had been washed and painted and dressed up with belled anklets and an elaborate gilt headdress; the gilt of the headdress merged with the gilt of the brocade cloth surrounding the Goddess on her howdah, and topped with a thick mantle of jasmine and marigold garlands. From the top of her mount, the

Goddess looked down in silver splendour at her devotees, with her rounded skull-like face, her round eyes bulging, and her skeletal teeth and fangs grinning with pleasure.

The way had been prepared carefully in advance; after all, this was a ceremony which had been carried out annually in the village for hundreds of years. The track had been swept and the way lined with scarlet silk umbrellas. Between the umbrellas bunting had been draped from a series of bamboo posts, and shredded palm fronds streamers and red hibiscus flowers hung from the bunting.

As we walked along the village boundary, from clearing to clearing, through pepper and rubber plantations, groups of devotees were waiting for the annual visit of their deity. Outside each cluster of huts, irrespective of the faith of the people of that part of the village, trestle tables had been loaded with burning lamps and piles of offerings – coconuts and bananas, baskets of puffed rice and jaggery. Each time, the elephant would stop, offerings would be given and blessings received. Then more firecrackers would be let off—scaring the children and grazing goats—and the women would ululate, and on the procession would trundle, the drummer and cymbal clashers leading the way.

'She is the mother of the village,' explained Saraswati Amma, an old lady who was waiting on the verandah of her house for the Goddess, with all her grandchildren around her. 'She comes to give blessings. Bad spirits flee when she approaches.'

'In ancient times, this was a forest,' explained her son Anish, who was holding his youngest boy in his arms. 'We needed the Goddess to guard against bad spirits. They are still here, hiding in the forest, and we need her to keep them at bay.'

'She comes only once a year to see our homes,' added Saraswati, 'so we must give her a good welcome.'

'That is why we are gathered here – for the welfare of the entire village. That is why we are doing it.'

'Everyone in the village gives her something,' said Saraswati. 'Even if the Christians sometimes do it in secret.'

At several places along the route more elaborate sacrifices were performed. The story the villagers told me was that long ago, when their ancestors first arrived in Mannarkad and cleared a place for themselves in the forest, they angered an evil yakshi, or tree spirit, who had lived there. Furious at being disturbed, the yakshi struck down the settlers with smallpox. Only when the villagers brought an idol of the Goddess Bhagavati from her temple in Kodungallur and the Goddess fought seven pitched battles with the yakshi was the epidemic brought to an end. Today, as the Goddess patrolled the boundaries of the village she had promised to protect, her people showed their gratitude by offering special sacrifices to their Goddess at the site of each of these battles.

'Bhagavati protects the whole village,' explained Raji, who was waiting with his gifts for the Goddess to come. 'She keeps away diseases and gives grace and blessings to the families who respect her.'

'Do you fear her or love her?' I asked.

'It is both devotion and respect,' he replied. 'And a fear of displeasing her. This way everyone is safe.'

The site of the final sacrifice was located at the back of the church, in the Christian area of the village that the priests told me had originally been part of the church compound. A small platform was prepared on a swept piece of ground, criss-crossed with a grid of bamboo. Incense sticks were placed at the corners, and flowers, betel and turmeric scattered over the grid. Squares of camphor were prepared, ready to be lit.

A large mixed crowd of local Christians and Hindus looked on, waiting for the drums to announce the coming of the Goddess and her elephant. When she drew near, the priests blew their conch shells and the drummers gradually increased their tempo.

The camphor was lit, Sanskrit slokas were recited and the whole grid doused with the blood-coloured *guruthi*.

'Before we used to sacrifice a rooster,' said one of the onlookers, a Hindu shopkeeper called Raji. 'But that is stopped now.'

'From time immemorial, the sacrifice has taken place here next to the church,' said his wife, Susheela, 'where the Devi fought and defended the village.'

I asked if they ever went inside the church compound.

'I have always heard that the two Devis of the village are sisters,' said Raji. 'If you go to the temple you must also go to the church, otherwise one of the sisters will be jealous. Whatever you do to one you must do to the other. They are both powerful goddesses.'

'It's true,' said Susheela. 'They say that if you want your prayers answered, you must pray at both the temple and the church. So many people make prayers in both. They say that if you light a lamp at the temple, that light also can be seen flickering in the church, and vice-versa. The two are really one.'

'My grandfather told this story to me,' said Raji, 'and we believe it to be true.'

William Dalrymple is the author of *The Last Mughal: The Fall of A Dynasty, Delhi, 1857*, which won the Duff Cooper Prize for history and biography and the Vodafone-Crossword Award 2007 for non-fiction.

3   The Countryside

M. Mukundan

Nanu Nair arrived walking all the way with the aid of his stick to meet Gangadharan when he learned that Gangadharan was going abroad. His walk had onlookers doubting whether the stick led him or he the stick. Old age had caught up with Nanu Nair all of a sudden. He isn't old enough to lean on a stick. What people say is that the cause for this untimely aging is his daughter Prema.

Gangadharan had a premonition that Nanu Nair would visit him. Therefore, when he saw him, Gangadharan was not at all surprised. He went out into the courtyard, caught Nair by his hand and, supporting him, brought him over to the verandah and sat him down in a chair.

Nanu Nair looked around, not knowing where to put away his stick. The stick with a crooked handle, which was a support to him for so long suddenly became a burden for him. Gangadharan, who understood this, took the stick from him and put it on the stool and himself sat down on it.

'Where are you coming from right now, Nanu Nair?'

'From home.'

'Ayyo, in this sun.... Wouldn't I have come over there if you had just phoned me?'

Gangadharan became aware of his own folly as soon as he uttered the words. There is no telephone in Nanu Nair's house or in any of the neighbouring houses. A house with a telephone in this region is very rare indeed. The nearest house with a telephone where it is convenient for Nanu Nair to use the phone is Gangadharan's. That is, if Nanu Nair was to ring up Gangadharan, he had to come over to Gangadharan's house itself!

Sensing that someone had come to the house, Gangadharan's wife Latha, who was inside, donned a nightie and peeped out from the doorway.

'May I bring a drink of Horlicks for you?' she asked him.

'Give me a little rice water with salt in it.'

'For that we haven't strained the boiled rice yet.'

'Then I don't need anything.'

He was really very thirsty because of his walk in the sun. But, for him, the thirst in his gullet was not a problem at all. Because his mind was filled with a greater thirst.

Although he remained seated, he once again felt the need for a supporting stick.

Nanu Nair struggled to say something. Twice he cleared his throat, but not a word came out. Seeing Nanu Nair's suffocation, Gangadharan felt bad. Getting up from his seat, he paced up and down the verandah a couple of times.

'Have you brought the address?'

'Yes.'

Nanu Nair took out a piece of crumpled paper from his pocket. Picking it up, Gangadharan eyed it once. Would that address and phone number be correct? He felt doubtful. Even if the details are correct, how was he to find out Albie in that strange foreign land? But he didn't air his apprehensions.

'I'll do whatever is in my power,' Gangadharan consoled Nanu Nair.

Nanu Nair brought his palms together in a namaskaram and leaned forward as if to bend down and touch Gangadharan's feet in obeisance.

At the time of leaving, he needed Gangadharan's help to get up from the chair.

Looking at Nanu Nair tottering away leaning on his stick, Gangadharan heaved a deep sigh. Nanu Nair took very long to disappear from sight. He continued on his way, only after halting at many spots in between to ease his fatigue.

Like the memory of a night of drunken bout ending with fits of vomitting, the figure of Nanu Nair remained in his mind, unfading.

Nanu Nair's family was a happy one that subsisted on his daughter Prema's salary as a nursery school teacher, coupled with the proceeds from the little cultivation he did. Everything crumbled in a blink's time. All because of that Albie fellow . . .

It was just after the noon on 3 October 1988, that Albie first set foot in that countryside. He got down at the river-ghat from the ferry boat along with the schoolchildren. In the wind blowing from the river, his golden hair flew slanting towards the right. With crystal clear eyes, he looked around in wonderment and glee. The water-logged paddy fields stretching far and wide and thatched huts were rare sights for him. He got into the paddy fields along with the schoolchildren and walked. It was not an easy feat to walk along the slippery mud dykes without losing balance. The children laughed watching him taking pains to move ahead. He, too, laughed along with them. The children with heavy satchels filled with books on their shoulders ran along the mud dykes as if to demonstrate their prowess to him. On his back, too, there was baggage. On that there were tags of airline companies. He, too, began to run along with the chattering children. He was bound to fall in the pool of water in the field by slipping down or the dyke caving in. But he didn't fall down. He, too, learnt to run along slippery dykes within a few moments.

When they had passed the paddy field, the children left him one by one and soon he was alone. He walked along the countryside all alone, with an expression of wonder in his blue eyes. When dusk fell, he had a banana and a soda from the bunk-shop opposite the Panchayat Office. The thought that it was a strange countryside and night had descended and there was nowhere to retire for the night didn't seem to bother him. After walking about for a bit more, he went over to the Rural Reading Room and sat on the verandah. The street was deserted. A car or a lorry passed that way between long intervals.

He took out a sleeping bag from the big bag on his shoulder and spread it on the ground. Rubbing on his body an ointment for repelling mosquitoes and other insects, he lay down and stretched out. The light of the vehicles that passed now and then fell on him and faded instantly. When it rained around midnight he got up, opened the zip of the sleeping bag, crept into it and went back to sleep.

In the days that followed, people saw that sleeping bag in different shop verandahs, tree-bases and the meadow.

'He belongs to some good family, no doubt. Look at the grace and elegance of his face,' said Nanu Nair.

'Hasn't he come to our countryside traversing the seas? How can we permit him then to sleep in the streets like this?' Chathu Master opined.

'My barn is lying vacant. Let him rest his head there when night falls,' said Nanu Nair.

That evening, Chathu Master and Nanu Nair brought Albie over to the barn. He ate with relish the boiled rice and curried curds Prema's mother served him that night. There was no power supply in the barn. Prema could see from her upper storey room

Albie sitting and reading something well past midnight in the hurricane lamp's light.

He sat amazed, looking at Prema who, after her bath, hung her hair loose, fixed a tulsi-pod on it and proceeded to the nursery school in the morning with a fancy umbrella in her hand.

'What nonsense is this, Nanu Nair? You should at least have thought that you have a grown-up girl of marriageable age in your house. He looks like Jesus Christ, for sure. Still, I would say that none of these people can be trusted. Maybe he is into drug-peddling, who knows?' Achu Muthalali fumed.

Hearing that, Chathu Master, who was also the president of the panchayat, said, 'My dear Muthalali, will this village of ours be damned if a foreigner lives here? Have you any idea how many countries in the world have our people settled down in? Were any of them damned because of that? You say that this white youngster should be thrown out from Nanu Nair's barn. You say that he should be sent away from this countryside itself. Suppose the people of other lands tell the Malayalis living there the same thing? Have you ever thought about what would happen then? We can go anywhere in the world. We can go to Singapore, Dubai, America or elsewhere. If a white man shows up in our countryside, we can't tolerate it. We should be aware of the changes taking place in the world. Science and technology are changing our lives unrecognisably. After sometime, there won't be this difference between the Americans and the Indians. The boundaries of different countries will fade away. There'll be only one country, the earth. There'll be only one religion, the religion of humanity.'

'Damn,' said Achu Muthalali. 'I don't have the time to listen to your sermon. I have to take the copra to Vadakara before nightfall.'

Then, turning towards Nanu Nair, he continued, 'You should get that white boy out of the barn at the earliest. Or else you'll be sorry.'

Hitching up one end of his dhoti and making a creaking noise with the tyre-soled chappals on his feet, Achu Muthalali walked away in a hurry.

'What am I to do now, Master? My head is spinning.'

'Don't do anything now. After some days, the white boy will be on his way back. Till then let him sleep in the barn. Is he a problem to anyone there?'

'He is a meek soul.'

'We should mix with foreigners, Nanu Nair. The likes of Achu Muthalali think that the world ends with Korappuzha river. Their worldview must change. Like we go to foreign countries, let foreigners come to our country too.'

'Let the white boy stay in my barn as long as he likes,' declared Nanu Nair.

Albie was never a problem to anyone. He would sleep till noon. He would need a black coffee as soon as he got up. At first, Nanu Nair himself used to serve it. Later on it was Prema's mother who served the coffee. After that, he would go to the river, bathe and be gone for the day. He always wore a tattered pair of pyjamas and a crumpled kurta. He was not in the habit of shaving regularly. Still he looked like the son of a god. Food was not a problem for him. Bananas and soda would do. Wherever he went, he would return before dusk. Then he would read till dawn in the light of the hurricane lamp. Most of the books he read were detective stories, love stories or travelogues. The number of books he discarded after reading increased.

Prema, who had gone to the temple one day to offer the Niramaala Vazhipaad (offering), was somewhat bewildered to find Albie there.

'He has even trespassed into the temple precincts, shamming innocence. Is he playing with Guruvayoorappan? Tell him to cut it out,' Achu Muthalali berated Nanu Nair when they met on the way.

Everyone was blaming him. They had begun to spread scandalous rumours. Ony Chathu Master was there to support him.

'Do the gods have caste or religion, Muthalali?' asked Chathu Master. 'The gods will not be offended because a white boy has entered the temple. The gods do not have petty minds like us.'

'For the Hindus the temple, for the Muslims the mosque, for the Christians the church, that's the norm.'

'Then what about those who are not any of these? Where would they offer worship?'

'They need not worship. And I don't want to listen to your harangue. I have to reach Orkkatteri market before dark.'

Muthalali walked off with a wag of his behind; he was beset with troublesome piles.

Nanu Nair's mind was perturbed. His regard for Albie, who bothered no one, was not diminished a bit. But the people kept on pestering him. Nanu Nair shied away from them, not even daring to venture out. If Achu Muthalali happened to meet him in the street, he would snort like a tusker-boar.

Time passed. During the festival season, a lot of people and light filled the temple compound. Crowds who came to offer worship had flocked there. The bylanes were filled with elephant shit. Throughout the nights, blazing *choottu* torches were flashed. Nightlong Kathakali performances were held. One of those days, Prema's mother stood blazing . . .

Prema had eloped with Albie, leaving a letter behind.

Nanu Nair looked as if he had aged over ten years in a single day. His eyes dimmed all of a sudden. His feet ached as they touched the ground. A rasping sensation in the spine, like a rusty spring.

One day Nanu Nair got a letter. His hands quivered when he opened the envelope. It was Prema's letter, as expected.

My dear Father and Mother,

Albie and I are in love. We are visiting various tourist centres. After one month, Albie's visa will expire. When Albie returns to his country, I'll also go with him.

Father and Mother, please pardon me and bless me...

She had written that letter from a place called Gopalpur-on-Sea. It was Gangadharan who discovered that place on an old map and showed it to Nanu Nair.

Gangadharan was going abroad to participate in a seminar on near-extinct ancient art forms. His paper was on Kootiyattam. That most ancient theatre form of the world was slowly dying out. He had decided to make use of this opportunity to try and form a committee abroad for the preservation of Kootiyattam. Much earlier, he had received Unesco's offer of help for such a venture. It was the Indian Council for Cultural Relations that gave him a free airline ticket for this trip. After writing his paper in longhand, he went to the town to have it done on a word processor and get a printout. And after a couple of days, he went to Bombay to get the visa. He was to board the flight from there. Latha wiped her tears when he departed.

The seminar went far beyond his expectations. From all quarters, offers of help poured in for the preservation of Kootiyattam. A computer company in Munich offered the technical knowhow to preserve Kootiyattam performance in its entirety on CD-Rom. A private foundation in the Netherlands offered free air tickets for the European tour of a Kootiyattam troupe. Thus, it was with a lot of satisfaction that Gangadharan went to Calais, aboard Trans-Europe Express.

He had decided on taking the ferry service from Calais to Dover on purpose. He, the poet, had naturally yearned to see the white cliffs of Dover. Since it was a Friday, that small ship was full of holiday-makers going to England on the weekend. The lower deck of the ship was filled with their cars. Their revelry went on through the night. The empty beer cans and whisky bottles they hurled out floated on the sea water. As Gangadharan stood on the upper-deck looking out to the sea, suddenly, Nanu Nair and his daughter entered his thoughts.

The ship came to port at Dover at dawn. The white cliffs he was familiar with through poems and songs loomed large right in front of him, wet and gleaming in the morning sun. When the ship dropped anchor, the weekenders who celebrated the night eating, drinking, dancing and foregoing sleep, got into their own cars parked in the lower deck and drove ashore. The excitement and glee of the others were not shared by Gangadharan. In his mind were Prema's face streaked with dried-up tears, Nanu Nair's bent back and the stick he supported himself with.

Gangadharan had rung up Albie from Amsterdam airport. He had agreed to meet Gangadharan on Saturday and had given him an address in Drummond Street for the rendezvous.

Gangadharan took a train from Dover to the Waterloo Station. When he saw the station, for a moment he thought he was in Thalassery Railway Station. Both the stations were so similar.

He considered it good fortune to have got Albie on telephone. In fact, he had been sure that the telephone number Nanu Nair gave him was wrong. Even if the number was right, what was the guarantee that Albie would be there to attend it? Albie and his compatriots are in the habit of touring the world. If he wasn't there, Gangadharan would have been in a soup. He didn't have the wherewithal to stay there for more than a day, his wallet was growing thinner by the day. It was on rooms in hotels and train journies that he spent most of his money. He tried his best to cut down on all other expenses. The duty-free shops of Amsterdam airport are famous for the best chocolates in the world, available at extremely low prices. Latha loved chocolates. Yet he didn't buy any. He set aside each dollar the organisers gave him for locating Albie.

The address Albie had given was that of a pub. Men and women sitting and standing around were drinking draught beer in large mugs. Not only inside and outside the pub, people were drinking beer sitting even in street corners.

Gangadharan couldn't recognise Albie who was walking towards him quickly after parking his car. Albie shook his hand, evidently pleased.

'How did your seminar go, sir?' Bending forward, Albie hugged Gangadharan. Some fragrance wafted from his body. Albie had carefully brushed his cropped hair, shaven his face clean and worn a jacket and tie. He had a leather briefcase in his hand.

'I couldn't make you out at first. I am sorry.'

'If one goes about unkempt as one does in your country, one is sure to be picked up by the police.' Albie laughed aloud.

He led Gangadharan to a less crowded spot. Albie was obviously known to the bartender as well as to many others drinking there. They greeted each other and shook hands. Finally, Albie and Gangadharan sat facing each other, beer mugs in hands.

'Tell me, what's all the news back home?' Albie enquired.

'Prema's tears haven't dried yet.'

'Why? What is she weeping for?' Albie asked in surprise.

'She is waiting for you.'

'Me? What for?'

'She won't marry anyone else but you. She has shared your bed.'

'Yes, we had sex. Why should I marry her on account of that?'

Gangadharan didn't know what to say. Albie contined, 'The year before I came on vacation to your country, I went to Thailand. I slept with at least twelve different girls there. None of them have demanded that I marry them.'

Gangadharan's feeling of suffocation increased. A bitter-sour taste in the mouth and throat as if he had drunk castor oil.

'Didn't you get the letters Prema sent you?'

'Yes, I got them.'

'She has given birth to your child.'

'That's her fault. She forgot to take the pill.'

Gangadharan felt like hurling the beer at Albie's face. His hand that held the mug began to shake slightly.

Albie took out a pack of Marlboro cigarettes from his pocket, lit one and blew the smoke.

Gangadharan held the mug of beer in his hand, not drinking it. The beer wouldn't go down his gullet. He felt a throbbing sensation inside his head and his eyes were burning. Was it because of the cigarette smoke? He got up and walked outside to get some fresh air. Albie followed, carrying his mug of beer.

'I'll come over next year. Tell Prema.'

'*No*. You should never come to our place.'

'Mr Gangadharan . . .'

'We won't let you come.'

'Isn't that what only you say?' Albie laughed. 'When I land, the girls of your tourism department will be waiting for me at the airport, garlands in hand. Won't they?'

Gangadharan took leave of Albie without looking at his face. Though it was past nine at night, the tops of buildings and roads were dappled in sunlight. He remembered what he had learnt in school as a child – this was the empire where the sun never set.

– Translated from Malayalam by A.J. Thomas

M. Mukundan is a leading pioneer of high modernism in Malayalam fiction and winner of multiple awards, including the Sahitya Akademi Award and Vayalar Award. He has penned twelve collections of short stories, twenty novels and one book of literary theory, including *Kesavan's Lamentations*, *On The Banks Of The Mayyazhi* and *God's Mischief*.

4   Everyday And The Avant-Garde:
The Evolution Of Society And Literature In Kerala

K. Satchidanandan

Everyday, an inadequate yet useful translation of the French term *la quotidienne* contributed by Henri Lefebvre to the conceptual vocabulary of Marxist thought, refers to that which repeats itself consistently in daily life, something excluded by most philosophers of the West—from Plato to Hegel—from serious consideration. Henri Lefebvre in philosophy and James Joyce in literature explored this dimension of daily life that Marx, in spite of his orientation towards it, could not explore, completely preoccupied as he was with the domain of labour and capital. 'Everyday,' Lefebvre says, 'is a kind of screen that both shows and hides, reveals both what has and has not changed.'[1] ('Toward a Leftist Cultural Politics,' in *Marxism And Interpretation Of Culture*, London, 1988.) It is what Hegel called the 'prose of the world', something considered unworthy of study like labour before Marx or libido before Freud. The *everyday* is first a modality of extending the capitalist mode of production that once established integrated industry, agriculture, the historical city, and space and hence produces everyday life; secondly, it is also a modality of administering society.

The predominance of the repetitive here becomes a way of life, a base of exploitation and domination, a relation with the world and with the human being. Repetition masks and suppresses the fear of death, a major reason for the success of the instituting of *everyday* in the modern world. It dissimulates the tragic; this tragic period hides from itself the tragedy it lives. It satisfies the very need it produces on the one hand and on the other, provokes a malaise, a profound dissatisfaction, an aspiration for something else. Thus, the concept is not an object constructed according to certain epistemological rules, nor is it apprehended by a deconstruction of reality. It is *le vecu* (lived experience) elevated to the status of concept and to language. This is done not to accept it but to change it, for, this *everyday* is modifiable and transformable and its transformation must be an important part of any project for society. Any resolution should change not just the political personnel and institutions but the *everyday* life colonised by capitalism. Culture, too, is part of this *everyday*, at least in our time, for it is not merely a state palimpeset of texts, it is lived and active, a 'sleeping beauty who dozes not on flowers or fragrant grass but on a thin mattress of texts, quotations and musical scores under a vast canopy of books and theses: the coming of the Prince awakens her and everything in the forest comes to life along with her.'[2] (Peter Burger: *Theory Of The Avant-Garde*)

Such an awakening took place in the history of Kerala's *everyday* only in the early decades of the twentieth century. Till then, Kerala's *everyday* was impregnated with ritual, custom and code. The body was considered an extension of nature and even social codes of exploitation and dividing practices were identified with the laws of nature. Everything immediately given was considered legitimate, unquestionable, inescapabale. Caste, subcaste, landlordism and royalty were considered ordained by nature, fate or God. The city could hardly be distinguished from the village, and the machine from the tool. The oilpress and the farmer's wheel were close to the carpenter's hammer and the pulley at the well. The 'literary' in the period was dominated by the sacred and the mythical, the popular articulations of *everyday* life existing as a parallel stream dubbed 'folk poetry'.

The poetry of Ezhuthachan, Cherussery, Poonthanam or Unnayi Variyar refuses to deal directly with *everyday* though the situations and passions expressed by them do have a universal human core. A work like *Jnanappana* can only come from the observation of the ways of the world, and Sita, Yashoda or Damayanti have something prototypical about their states and fates. Kunchan Nambiar is one poet who, probably inspired by the folk, enlivens his Puranic narratives with humorous interpolations of the contemporary *everyday*. The 'author' was yet to emerge as a category, as literature was seldom recognised as 'literature' in its present sense; it was ritual, performance and entertainment.

'Literature' and the 'author' emerged as definite categories only with the formation of the public sphere in Kerala that was part of a general democratic movement of dissent, reform and awakening. This renaissance began as a self-criticism of the feudal caste society. The dividing practices that concealed exploitation and inequality behind the masks of the natural and the providential now became visible and came to be identified in their inhuman shapes. The placid surface of the *everyday* suddenly became turbulent as almost every caste was looking at itself in relation to those above and those below, trying to purge itself of evil customs and practices, to abolish or weaken the sub-caste system and educate itself in modern knowledge and useful crafts.

All castes were involved in this upheaval though the main thrust was subaltern as only the truly oppressed led by Sree Narayana Guru or Ayyankali alone were capable of thinking in terms of a casteless society which, to the 'upper' castes, would mean depriveleging and loss of dominance. Sree Narayana's success lay in his recognition of the relationship between discourse and power, his subtle reversal of significance of the oppressor's legitimising discourse through a secular reading of their sacred texts and a subversive use of their signs, symbols and images that together transformed Kerala's *everyday*, making visible the till-now invisible mechanisms of division and tyranny.

II

The formation of the Indian National Congress with its total disapproval of colonialism produced the first line of truly secular intellectuals in Kerala from 'Swadeshabhimani' Ramakrishna Pillai and K. Kelappan to K.P. Kesava Menon and Mohammed Abdu Rahman and later the first socialist intellectuals like A.K. Gopalan, P. Krishna Pillai, K.P.R. Gopalan and E.M.S. Namboodiripad. This double renaissance ushered in the second modern phase of *everyday* in Kerala's popular history – bodies were no more bound by the labours, spaces and distances ordained by caste. *Everyday* was a site of democratic conflicts and resolutions from which came up a public sphere of debate and consensus. Literature was now constituted as a specific category; the authorial institution was built up along with a new critical academy that came up with norms and standards gained especially from the Sanskrit and English classics that came to be widely translated into Malayalam in those days. Together they consolidated 'the aesthetic' as a specific realm of culture that had a mediated relationship with the *everyday* and transformed literature from the sacral to the secular.

The codification of grammar and translations, especially that of the Holy Bible, helped the growth of style in prose, original epics and verse narratives that often had an oblique relationship with reality and were complemented by novels, short stories and essays that often took off directly from the lived experience of the society. Ulloor's *History Of Malayalam Literature*, the poetical works of Vallathol and Kumaran Asan, the novels of C.V. Raman Pillai and O. Chandu Menon, organisations like Bhashaposhini Sabha and Sahitya Parishat and journals like *Swadheshabhimani, Kerala Patrika, Kesari, Mangalodayan* and *Bhashaposhini*, along with the translations of ancient and modern classics, activated the growth of the public sphere helped on by the spread of modern education and printing technology. Literature was released from its ritual use with the undermining of traditional word pictures by the basic ideology of fair exchange.

The anti-feudal struggles led by the Congress Socialists and the Communists of Kerala added a class dimension to the struggles of *everyday* as well as literature. The notion of class as applied to history, politics and culture in however primary and simplistic a way, helped re-orient the forces of renaissance towards a resurgence of the marginalised and mobilised for the first time on a non-caste basis, that of class. While it is true that Kerala's Communist Movement later developed links with pan-Indian and international working class movements, it was in itself an indigenous democratic phenomenon with its roots sunk deep in the social reform and anti-colonial movements of Kerala in the early decades of the century – a fact that explains its resilience and endurance even in the era of the confusion and collapse of international communism. The ideas of class struggle that flourished well in the already upturned cultural soil of Kerala also came to influence literature. The relationship between what came to be loosely called the Progressive Movement in literature and the overall process of Kerala's societal movement towards socialism and secular democracy is more a case of structural over-determination than of synchrony.

III

The Jeevat Sahitya movement, launched in 1937, can properly be considered the first avant-garde movement in Malayalam literature, for, like all avant-garde movements, it not only changed the modes of literary expression but tried to redefine the norms and canons of literature, ultimately questioning the very institution of literature. Its aim was to promote 'a literature that changes with the changing life to express reality in novel modes free from the burden of the mystical past and a philosophy that fights reactionary views about religion, society, sexuality, family and war'. The organisation considered 'everything that provokes a critical revaluation of systems and institutions from the point of view of the common interest of the majority of mankind' to be progressive and 'everything that drags man into inertia and lifelessness' as reactionary.

By the time the first conference of the Progressive Writers' Association was held after seven years, almost every major writer in Kerala – poets like Vallathol, Changampuzha and G. Sankara Kurup, fiction writers like Basheer, Thakazhi, Karoor, S.K. Pottekkat, Kesava Dev and Ponkunnam Varkey and critics like Joseph Mundassery and M.P. Paul besides fellow travellers and communist activists like K. Damodaran, Cherukad, D.M. Pottekkat, M.S. Devadas, Kedamangalam Pappukkutty, Premji and others had been won over by the Movement whose roots, again, were in the renaissance writers like Kumaran Asan, V.T. Bhattathiripad, K.P. Karuppan and Sree Narayana himself. The Movement captured the *everyday* in all its energy and diversity; the writers used different idioms even while they shared the same concerns. Whole sections of people sentenced to the culture of silence spoke through these writers, many of whom were liberals inspired by Gandhi and Lenin alike. Landless peasants, fishermen, untouchables, the rural poor, impoverished craftsmen, men and women forced into begging and prostitution and urban workers, all these subaltern layers of society found a place in literature for the first time after the age of folklore.

This change of content engendered a stylistic transformation. In poetry, it appeared chiefly as a replacement of Sanskrit metres by Dravidian and folk metres and rhythms and a considerable reduction of the Sanskrit element in the vocabulary. In creative prose, it meant the introduction of a strong dialectical element borrowed especially from the marginalised classes, castes and minorities and the consequent disavowal of the laboured linguistic sublimity of earlier fictional modes. In short, it privileged realism against mysticism in both content and style.

Writers like Vailoppilly, Edasseri and Uroob who stood mostly outside the Movement could not but respond to the new social and literary ferment. By 1948, the broad consensus-perspective that had held writers of various persuasions together in the Movement gave way to sectarian views of commitment to the party line. Calls for formal vigour were wrongly condemned by the champions of contentism as decadent formalism and aestheticism that finally led to a split in the Movement. The theoreticians of the Progressive Movement failed to see the relative autonomy of literature at the level of cultural formation with its own history and rules of formal evolution. They equated literature with ideology and considered it a direct expression of the author's personal ideology, thus unknowingly subscribing to the idealist theories of expressivity. They underrated the importance of the context, intent and ideology of reading that can make the work appear socially irrelevant or appropriate it for social transformation.

Their opponents too lacked self-understanding in so far as they did not recognise the radical potential of their writing. Writers like Vailoppilly, Edassery or Uroob who had a rather tense relationship with the Movement were, in fact, much more progressive than

K.P.G., Kedamangalam or D.M. Pottekkat with their explicit commitment, for the former revealed more extensively, deeply and innovatively the complex contradictions of the society in its multi-layeredness.

Industrial capitalism never made its real debut in Kerala; yet, by this time, the capitalist value systems, norms and perspectives on life and literature had begun to penetrate Kerala's *everyday*. The forces of renaissance had weakened, turned conservative and status-quoist, leaving enough space for the values of acquisition, greed and consumerism to influence life. The old life, however, remained underneath as a subterranean force, at times disrupting the rhythms of modern life. At times it evoked nostalgia as in the poetry of P. Kunhiraman Nair, at times it was built into a utopian project for an egalitarian future as in that of Vailoppilly or was caught in its morbidity, incest, decadence, anger and conflict with the modern as in the fiction of M.T. Vasudevan Nair.

The obscurantists found a rallying point in their opposition to the first communist government in the state; they feared the impact of the Land Reform Movement and of educational reforms. The emergence of the second, modernist, avant-garde in Malayalam literature roughly coincides with this period of middle-class discontent resisted alike by progressive as well as feudal forces. By the time the whole of Kerala society was on the path of 'middle classing', the land reform, education and standardisation of comforts had turned the *everyday* of the Malayali into the average of the middle-class social practice, of course, with a supra-*everyday* level lived by peasants, tribals and others. The middle classes could not identify themselves with either of these and found themselves left to float in an uncertain time-world where their identity was problematised and existence played out through alter-lives constructed in imagination.

IV

At the same time, the country and the town had become one big semi-urban continuum in Kerala. Modernism—in Malayalam fiction especially—came mostly from the Malayali diaspora in the big Indian cities. Fiction writers like O.V. Vijayan, Kakkanadan, M. Mukundan, V.K.N., M.P. Narayana Pillai, Paul Zacharia and Sethu and poets like Madhavan Ayyapath, M.N. Paloor and Kadammanitta lived in Delhi, Bombay or Madras, away from the social reality of Kerala, a sure basis for their feeling of loss and alienation. Most of them came from villages and had a past of communist activism or sympathy. The gradual deadening of progressive sensibilities, the revelations about Stalinism and the Zhadanovist dogmatism of Kerala Marxist critics had together estranged them from Marxism to such an extent that they began to identify with totalitarian tyranny. If communism was the god that failed, it was darkness also at the Congress-noon since the party was as distant from Gandhian ideals as it could be. In literature, the Progressive Movement appeared like a lost cause; naturalism in fiction and romanticism in poetry were fast losing their charm and usefulness.

The paperback revolution had also acquainted these writers with the modernist experiments in Europe in which they found models that would save them from the new aesthetic impasse. E.V. Ramakrishnan in his recent book *Making It New: Modernism In Malayalam, Marathi And Hindi Poetry* has characterised the first phase of modernism—of the late 50s and the 60s—as 'high modernism', different from the avant-gardists' modernism that emerged in the 70s.

It would be wrong to consider the early modernists, aestheticists and status-quoists since the deep despair, anger and irony in Ayyappa Panicker, N.N. Kakkad, Attoor Ravi Varma or Kadammanitta Ramakrishnan came from their skepticism regarding the system. We have to see the modernism in Malayalam as an indigenous literary phenomenon despite certain Western influences that Malayalam literature has always been under. It was unfortunate that it got interpreters like K.P. Appan who were entirely Eurocentric in their approach and mechanically applied Western paradigms and rubrics to the modernist works in Malayalam.

E.V. Ramakrishnan also seems to apply Peter Burger's distinction between the aestheticist high-modernists and the radical avant-gardists to the two phases of modernism in Malayalam with little consideration for their specific historical contexts. The difference between the two phases—both of which I consider avant-gardist—it seems to me, lies in the models and premises of their criticism of society – the first phase attempted a liberal-humanist critique while the second adopted more radical stances. Both questioned the literary institution in different ways. The black humour and irony characteristic of a lot of writing of the 60s are instruments that attempt to subvert not only the social order but the literary order too.

They were after forms that would best express the structures of their modern subjectivity. Discontinuity, the foregrounding of the signifier, use of irony and black humour, the employment of various masks, the metaphoric as different from metonymic modes of writing, re-visioning of myths and archetypes, surrealism, fantasy and experimental syntax and structuralisation were strategies employed for this purpose.

Strategies and attitudes varied from author to author and from text to text. The self-confident subject of idealistic cognition theory conceives himself as self-present and regards language as the belated embodiment and representation of a content previously present in his own consciousness, but the subject of modernism looks at language as a medium of self-discovery rather than self-expression. Literature here negates ossified linguistic and mental clichés that are the results of instrumental rationality. The asocial in art, as Adorno says, is the definite negation of a definite society. Whereas the novels of Vijayan, Kakkanadan, Mukundan and Sethu and the stories of Zacharia and M.P. Narayana Pillai negate values to the point of anarchy, the poems of Ayyappa Panicker (eg. *Mrtyupooja, Cartoon Poems*) or Kadamanitta negate the present order through irony or anger.

In another set of works like the nonsense poems of Kunjunni, M. Govindan, N.N. Kakkad and Ayyappa Panicker and the self-reflexive stories of Paul Zacharia or V.P. Shivakumar, the very institution of literature is subjected to criticism. Like the works of Dadaists in Europe, they criticise not only any school that preceded them but literature itself with its established notions of what it should be, whereas, during the period of realism, the development of art was felt to lie in the growing closeness of representation to the *everyday*. In this phase of self-criticism, the one-sidedness of this construction becomes visible. Realism comes to be understood not as the principle of artistic creation but becomes understandable as the sum of certain period procedures. Habermas' characterisation of art as a sanctuary for the—perhaps merely cerebral—satisfaction of those needs which become quasi-illegal in the material life-process of bourgeois society – needs like the 'mimetic commerce with nature' and 'the happiness of a communicative experience not subject to the imperatives of means-end rationality and allows as much scope to imagination as to spontaneity of behaviour' may well explain the playful element in the modernist Malayalam writing of the first phase.

The writers were reacting to the 'flat, opaque and prosaic nature of our public speech where the practical end of communication spoils the quality of expressive means' (Clement Greenberg, *Avant-Garde And The Kitsch*). The function of their new, often dark language was at once therapeutic and cathartic in respect to the degeneration afflicting common language. They were also the first to respond adequately to the complexification of the *everyday* experience in Kerala's society, react violently to the sexual repression characteristic of the Malayali psyche, and to take up the ontological—rather than metaphysical—anxieties and uncertainties that confront contemporary existence. Modernism in Malayalam grew directly out of its own pre-modern writing (eg. K. Ayyappa Panicker is impossible without the poets before him from Kunchan Nambiar to Vailoppilly, or O.V. Vijayan without Basheer and Uroob). Its angst was not derivative but was deeply rooted in the perplexities of Kerala's intelligentsia confronted with the issues of subjectivisation, the crisis of idealism in national life and the repression of desire.

The works of libidinal-political fiction of the sixties are stammering attempts to articulate some silenced aspects of Malayali middle-class life in the background of their political uncertainty and doubt; their apparent ahistoricity is a call for the historicisation of these deeper aspects of existence suppressed by or unrepresented in the era of progressivism, and their sensuous language that glows with desire is a tool to express the complicity between politics and sex or desire and transcendence. The paradigmatic texts of modernism like Vijayan's *Khasakkinte Ithihasam* (The Legends Of Khasak), Mukundan's *Delhi*, Sethu's *Pandavapuram*, or Kakkanandan's *Ushnamekhala* (all novels), Zacharia's *Oridathu* (Somewhere), MP Narayanapillai's *George Aramante Kodathi* (The Court Of George VI), TR's *Nee Jassokkine Kollaruthu* (Don't Kill Jassock), N.S. Madhavan's *Choolaimedile Savangal* (The Corpses of Chollaimedu) – all short stories, N.N. Kakkad's *1964*, Madhavan Ayyapath's *Maniyara* (The Bridal Chamber) poems, Ayyappa Panicker's *Pakalukal, Ratrikal* (Days, Nights) or Balachandran Chullikad's *Ghazal-*(all poems) reflect this complex conjucture of social awareness, ontological doubt, repressed desire and internalised violence that together transform the political into the private and the personal.

V

What the radical avant-garde of the 70s did was to foreground the political implied in the writing of the liberal-humanist avant-garde of the earlier decade. Writers like Pattathuvila Karunakaran, M. Sukumaran, Kadammanitta Ramakrishnan, K.G. Shankara Pillai and Satchidanandan, trained in the modernist strategies of expression, tried to retrieve from amnesia the leftist aspirations of the progressive period through a double critique of the hegemonic ideology and of the existing Left. It was an attempt by a section of the radicalised middle class to redefine its relationship vis-à-vis the state and the nation.

They also developed a critique of form as they were unhappy with the earlier progressive literature that followed the romantic mode in poetry and the naturalistic mode in fiction. They were equally unhappy with the solipsistic and monologic tendencies of the modernism of the 60s. The attempt was to develop more open and dialogic forms that would capture the spirit of social struggles. Irony, counter-metaphor, counter-myth, allegory, parable and surrealistic imagery were employed to create a futuristic idiom that reflected the mood of the radical left.

A critique of *everyday* that turned the historical time into reflected time in the circles of home and of fellow-radicals, an expression of the middle class intellectuals' sense of guilt and self-ridicule, a direct criticism of the upper-class institutions and mentalities and a mediated articulation of the torments and dreams of the lower classes, a satirisation of the complacent old Left that seemed to have compromised; such were the orientations of the writing of the 70s that also had built into it, a critique of the liberal humanist modernist avant-garde of the 60s.

The paradigmatic avant-garde texts of the 70s like *Allopanishad* by Pattathuvila, *Thookkumarangal Nhangalkku* (Gallows For Us) by M. Sukumaran, *Bengal* by K.G. Shankara Pillai, and *Pani* (Fever) by K. Satchidanandan. '*Samkramanam*' (Transformation) by Attoor Ravi Varma and *Santha* Kadammanitta have *everyday* built into them and transformed into the site of historic struggles. The radicals inspired by the ideas of a third-world revolution represented an internal critique of modernism, in an era of the increasing commodification of life and literature, and of the colonisation of the popular unconscious by pulp fiction, commercial cinema, television soaps and advertisements that resolved contradictions among the people and fulfilled their wishes by easy, imaginary means. *Everyday* was coming increasingly under the grip of the culture industry whose invisible *Weltanschauungs*, hyper-real images and stereotypes had penetrated deep into the perceptions of *everyday*. The popular film and fiction sought to divide the world into a public space dominated by men and a private space reserved for women. Women increasingly became the show-piece and the object of desire. Even employment and the unitary family have only made women's lives more helpless and leisureless. They not only continue to be under-represented in democratic bodies but continue to be assigned roles in public life that are only extensions of their domestic work.

This also coincides with the onslaught on environment by various agencies from the timber mafia to the tourist trade. The neo-rich culture of opulence without content, the spread of alcoholism that cuts across classes, the rapid increase in sexual, communal and political violence and the high rates of morbidity and suicide also seem to be the symptoms and products of a larger social malaise generated by unemployment, loss of identity, economic uncertainty and social discontent prompted especially by the new disparities created by money from abroad. A society where class mobility is decided by sheer chance rather than by intelligence, industry or efficiency is the ideal earth for irrationalism, fantasy and surrealism.

The magical and the grotesque that dominate Kerala's literary sensibility today are perhaps an indirect reflection of Kerala's bizarrely comic reality on creative and critical imagination. No wonder Marquez, Borges, Calvino, Kafka, Kundera and Rushdie find a ready and unsurprised clientele in Kerala. Arundhati Roy's *The God Of Small Things* honestly reflects this synthesis of the comic and the bizarre in Kerala's life and imagination.

This complex and contradictory reality of *everyday* in contemporary Kerala seems to have made a monolithic avant-garde impossible and inadequate in its literature. The struggle is no more on a single front, but is transversal and multi-faceted. While the old 'progressive' avant-garde continues to bring forth new talents, it has lost its monopoly over commitment as radicalism is no more confined to the class front alone. Today's avant-garde appears to have more than one organising principle. The most significant of them is gender. Women's writing in Kerala seems to have come a long way from Lalitambika Antarjanam, K. Saraswati Amma and Rajalakshmi.

While Madhavikutty (Kamala Das) still continues to be the finest exponent of the feminine psyche with its long-borne scars and unfulfilled longings, the new generation of fiction writers like Sarah Joseph, Manasi, Ashita, Gracy A.S., Priya and Chandramati appear almost self-conscious in their effort to fight the 'phallogocentric' social order. So are Sugata Kumari, Vijayalaksmi, Savitri Rajeevan, V.M. Girija, Rose Mary and others in poetry. They are after a new libidinal economy and a counter language, a 'mother tongue' that is capable of transcending male rationality. Some of them indulge in revisionist myth-making that attempts a deconstructive reversal of the patriarchal logic of status-quoist myths. Sarah Joseph in short story and Vijayalakshmi in poetry have taken up situations from the Ramayana and the Bible along with popular legends for a feminist reinterpretation. Women's writing in Kerala appears more like a wish-fulfillment than a reflection of reality since the actual state of women at home and in the workplace remains unchanged or has even become worse if one goes by the increasing number of gang-rapes and export of women for flesh-trade. While the women's movement continues to be weak and fragmented, the old canons of life and literature continue unchanged. Even the aggressive treatment of women as mere objects of desire in some paradigmatic modern novels like the *The Legends Of Khasak* has not been sufficiently interrogated; this is also true of the actual treatment of women in social life. Still the women writers seem to be the only collective avant-garde in contemporary Malayalam literature.

However, there are many individual writers who have taken radical avant-garde stances. Anand, ever questioning history and reality from the victim's gray margin, and N.S. Madhavan who reacts intensely to the morbid, the schizoid and the rapidly communalised aspects of outer and inner life are two such writers who continue to interrogate reality and art in innovative modes and metaphors. K.G. Shankara Pillai's anti-colonial stance and that of Attoor Ravi Varma in poetry with its ecological and regional political implications is another instance of individual avant-gardism. The post-cognitive and ontological questions about the self and the world, and the confrontation of different worlds that seem central to post-modernism are yet to be taken up seriously by the majority of our writers who seem to stop at the surface of the *everyday* and not to see its seething insides. However, literature today seems to concern itself more with the micro-politics of *everyday* than with the macropolitics of the state taking up questions of identity, gender hegemony, eco-fascism and the communalisation of individuals and institutions. In political terms, the axis seems to be shifting from the commitment to a one-dimenstional revolution to an anxious concern for all forms of structural oppression and a faith in micro-revolutions waged simultaneously on a hundred fronts. The polyphonic textuality of the new literature is possibly a product of this multi-dimensional engagement with a hydra-headed reality.

Dr. K. Satchidanandan, poet-critic and former secretary of the Sahitya Akademi, is the author of *Ezhuthachan Ezhuthumbol, Satchidanandante Kavitakal* and *Desatanam*. He is the recipient of multiple awards and accolades, including the Sahitya Akademi Award. The piece used here was originally a paper for an international seminar on 'Kerala: Culture And Development', 1996, Delhi, and published in *Encounter*.

5 Hijack

Paul Zacharia

'I have hijacked this plane!' shouted Thomas, holding aloft the hairbrush wrapped in his handkerchief.

It was Thomas' fifty-second birthday. He was flying in the city shuttle that leaves from Delhi for Mumbai in the morning. Thomas' full name was Thomas Devasia IAS. A high-ranking official in the Home Ministry, he was going to Mumbai with an emergency message for Bal Thackeray. The aeroplane was just entering the stretch of sky above the mud-flats of Rajasthan, having left behind the wheat-fields of Haryana. The air-hostesses were getting ready to roll the breakfast trolleys down the aisle.

Thomas was perspiring badly. Straightening his necktie with one hand, he raised his voice a bit more and said in English, 'Please listen, I have hijacked this plane. This thing in my hand is the latest grenade of the Indian Army with a very high strike power. I have yanked its pin.'

The Gujaratis, Punjabis, Maharashtrians, Tamilians and the white men in the plane shuddered. They gazed at Thomas without blinking. Some chanted the name of god. One or two women wept. The faces of the air-hostesses and stewards plunged into thought.

'No one must move,' Thomas said.

He walked to the cockpit with the raised kerchief bundle. The plane heaved and surged into a pressure pocket. The sign indicating the fastening of seatbelts flashed.

Since his was a last-minute ticket, Thomas got a seat in the 'Y' class. On his way to the cockpit, when he entered the 'J' class, parting the curtain, Thomas's customary co-travellers—high-ranking officials, industrialists and businessmen—looked at him and smiled. One said, 'Hello, Mr Thomas. You got a seat at the last minute, didn't you? Will you return today itself? One round of our golf remains!'

Passing through them, Thomas reached the cockpit door and turned around. Then he raised the kerchief-parcel and repeated the words he uttered earlier.

The additional secretary, the MP, the TV channel magnate, the air vice-marshall and the chairman and managing director shivered. The film producer, the car dealer, the ad company chief and the financial expert gaped at Thomas.

Thomas' raised hand was beginning to feel fatigued. After getting his IAS, he had never held his hand so high for long. What use was golf?

In the cockpit, Thomas repeated the words to the captain. Captain Minocha and co-pilot Dutta recalled the procedure they followed in the event of a hijack. They told Thomas, 'Sir, we will do exactly as you say. We pray that you do not cause danger to the passengers.'

Thomas said, 'This plane must immediately be redirected to Kuravilangad.'

The captain said, 'Sir, where is Kura . . . ?' He was unable to pronounce the place's name in full.

'Ku-ra-vi-lan-gad,' said Thomas.

'Where is this airport, sir?' the captain asked.

'What? You don't know?' Thomas asked, shaking the hand that held the hairbrush. 'Where was President K.R. Narayanan born?'

The captain said apologetically, 'I don't know, sir.'

'Uzhavoor, in Kerala,' said Thomas.

'Oh, Uzavoor, Uzavoor! Thank you, sir,' Minocha said.

'Kuravilangad is the main town near Uzhavoor. Redirect the plane to that place,' commanded Thomas.

A brave air-hostess stuck her head into the cockpit and said, 'Excuse me, sir.'

Thomas regarded her.

'Sir, may I serve breakfast to four or five passengers who are diabetes and hypertension patients?'

'Serve breakfast to all passengers. Breakfast is not the problem.'

The air-hostess genuflected before Thomas, thanked him and left.

Captain Minocha said, 'Sir, pardon my question. But who are you?'

'I am Thomas Devasia IAS. Head of a secret department in the Union Home Ministry. Call Delhi immediately and inform them of my demand.'

Minocha and Dutta were startled. Thomas waited, listening to the captain calling Delhi and informing them of the developments.

It was with some unease that the captain ended the conversation. Pensively he told Thomas, 'There is no airport called Kuravilangad in Kerala.'

'What?' asked Thomas. 'No airport in Kuravilangad?'

'No, sir,' said the captain. 'We made extensive enquiries.' He did not, however, say that the nearest airport was Nedumbasserry.

'Not only that, sir,' the captain continued, 'we do not have enough fuel to fly as far as Kerala. It is not possible to have a long flight without refuelling at Mumbai or Delhi.'

Thomas did not hear any of these. He was standing as if he got an electric shock. 'Then why did I hijack this plane at all?' he asked of no one in particular. 'Alas, there is no airport in Kuravilangad! I have been yearning to go back to Kuravilangad ever since I left it twenty-seven years ago after my selection to the

IAS. But... my Gujarat cadre... my wife, a Gujarat cadre IAS officer... children... Sikkim... China... Emergency... Blue Star... Indira Gandhi's assassination, the massacre of the Sikhs... Shilanyas... Rajiv Gandhi's assassination, ISI, foreign training... Kashmir... Babri Masjid... Mumbai... Coimbatore... Bihar... today is my fifty-second birthday. My mother is eighty-four. Today is the feast day in the Deva Matha Forane Church at Kuravilangad. Though I tried to go to Kuravilangad, even risking my life in the process, I have failed.'

Minocha and Dutta watched unconvinced as Thomas wept silently.

'We are very sorry, sir,' they said, following every step of the hijack-managing drill. 'We are ready to help you in any which way possible.'

'Let the plane proceed towards Bal Thackeray,' Thomas said, wiping his eyes with one hand.

'Bal Thackeray, sir?' Captain Minocha asked.

'Yes, Bal Thackeray,' Thomas said.

'That means Mumbai...' the captain said, hiding his surprise.

'Yes, Mumbai,' Thomas said, taking the hairbrush out of the kerchief-wrap and looking at the gray hair stuck in it.

— *Translated from Malayalam by A.J. Thomas*

Thiruvananthapuram-based **Paul Zacharia**, a recipient of the Sahitya Akademi Award, is known for his unorthodox and non-conformist writings. His books include *Reflections Of A Hen In Her Last Hour And Other Stories* and novellas *Praise The Lord* and *What's New, Pilate?*

6 Stone The Sin, Not The Sinner

Varkey Cardinal Vithayathil

'Love' is no longer a happy word, having corrupted into fickle longings and quick satiations. Love demands deep commitment, a discipline rooted in the grammar of God. Misguided westernisation in the name of modernism is taking its toll even on the Malayali Christian. I admit with a heavy heart to the rise in requests for annulments among the newly-weds in Kerala. At the bottom of all malaise lies mistrust – in God. Love for God, the purest form of love there is, is sadly shrugged off as a cliché.

Still, the entire mission of the church can be summed up in that one word – love. This involves helping the poor and asking why the poor remain poor. I am not talking only about the economically weaker, but about the spiritually bankrupt as well for man doesn't live by bread alone. We serve people because they are images of God and the icons of Christ among us. No country or culture can shut out Christ; it is a great pity to see him as a 'foreigner'. Christians remain only 1.8 percent of the population, it is evident we don't believe in artificially hiking numbers.

The soul has a deep sense of God. This sense is at its best in silence but, alas, in today's hectic rush, silence is a casualty. It is easier to turn to the 'silence' of disco music or the hustle and bustle of bars that purportedly take the edge off. But stress is only intensified this way and soon the individual is drowned out without the anchorage of faith.

Then, scandals happen but the church has a tradition of converting bad news into good news. Look at Judas; God gives the grace to step over sin. Even the recent crisis in priestly celibacy cannot be considered in isolation. The ills are symptomatic of serious sexual indiscipline and moral chaos in general. Marital fidelity and eternity vows are in jeopardy, monogamy itself is in danger of being extinct.

I am also saddened to see the church splintering in the name of Christ and his Gospel. It is the church that carries the Bible and the Bible cannot be understood without the church. Today there is a Pentecostal upsurge all over the world. I don't disagree that it may be emotionally satisfying, but it separates from the true church. Perhaps it is attuned to the contemporary consumer culture that seeks to reduce the Gospel to a health and wealth manual. This is the new Gospel of Prosperity which shrinks God to a commodity. The church and the liturgy preach the Gospel in its totality, taking care to keep pastoral concerns personal rather than institutional. Emotional nourishment is of utmost priority.

Twenty percent of Kerala's 30 million people are Christians. The Syro-Malabar Catholics who claim St. Thomas as their father in faith are about 3.5 million in number with 13 dioceses, a large number compared to the Mar Thoma Christians whose church is in communion with the Anglican Church (also known as the Church of South India – CSI), Latin Catholics who originated from the Portuguese period of evangelisation in the coastal Kerala, Orthodox Christians who are split into two at present and the Syro-Malakara Christians who are reconverted from Orthodox Church to Catholic communion.

However, there is a strong ecumenical bond among the different churches, especially the Episcopal churches. The three ritual churches within the Catholic communion function with one Episcopal conference and take common decisions on issues.

I would also like to explode a pet myth — that Syrian Christians in Kerala were originally Brahmin converts. I doubt there were Brahmins in the first century in the Malabar Coast. Historically speaking, the chances were dim. But why was this theory invented? It may explain a history of the existence of Christians in a highly caste-ridden milieu. Even today, Indian society suffers from caste issues. The meaning of such a myth lies not in its surface content but the underlying structure, which is the ultimate ground of representation. For the record, Syrian Christians were never considered low-caste people, but came from respectable stock such as traders and farmland owners.

The church has not yet given sacred ordination to any woman, which means there are no female priests. With Christ's respect for women spectacularly recorded for posterity, this is no silly gender bias. It is just that all twelve Apostles were men and one hesitates to interfere with such syntax.

As for the Divine Retreat Centre in Kerala, it is a retreat centre within my archdiocese serving millions. Due to a high-court judgment based on an anonymous letter—later set right by the Supreme Court—a lot of harassment was meted out to the centre. This is a place where people, irrespective of religion, flock to for solace. Where there's a crowd, it is easy to create mayhem and easier for vested interests to use situations to their advantage.

However, the power of prayer continues to move. In Kerala, churches burst at the seams during the Holy Mass. I am happy to report that, come rain or sunshine, the modern Malayali is in a mood to pray.

A Cardinal of the Roman Catholic Church, Varkey Cardinal Vithayathil studied Canon law at the Pontifical University of St. Thomas Aquinas, Rome. He was appointed Major Archbishop of Ernakulam-Angamaly for Syro-Malabars by Pope John Paul II in 1999, and was part of the Papal Conclave that selected Pope Benedict XVI. This piece is based on an interview by Shinie Antony.

7 Orhan Pamuk, Nair and I

Anita Nair

Unnithan sensed a couple edge into the seats behind him. He straightened. He mustn't be seen slumping. What would they think?

The seats were only just filling up. He had expected a full house. In fact, he had expected a great deal ever since the morning he received that call from the Literary Forum.

It had been a Friday morning. He had just finished reading that first line from *My Name Is Red* by Orhan Pamuk: 'I am nothing but a corpse now, a body at the bottom of a well.'

It had drawn forth all the ire that resided in the base of Unnithan's skull.

Now Unnithan's medulla oblongata was a rather peculiar thing. In the rest of the human population, it looks like the swollen tip to the spinal chord and is in charge of involuntary functions like breathing and digestion. However, with Unnithan, as it is in alligators, the medulla oblongata was enlarged. As big as a tennis ball, may be. And it caused a certain aggressiveness that in the alligator's case manifested as wanting to bite the limbs off a human or attacking cattle. In Unnithan, it expressed itself as a bilious attack that the poor soul had no option but to spew on papers.

Unnithan read the line again. This fellow, Orhan Pamuk, he had thought, studying the bespectacled serious-looking author's photograph, ought to know better. How can a corpse talk? Let alone think?

Unnithan didn't need to read any further. He had already made up his mind. The rest of the world may rush to deify this fellow Pamuk, but he was not so easily swayed.

Unnithan took a sip of his tea and opened page 146 randomly: 'There was no one in the street, not even cats.'

There, he knew it. Unnithan's medulla oblongata almost hissed. 'And this is what they gave him the Nobel Prize for?' it demanded.

Unnithan now knew there was nothing to do but show the world what an imposter Pamuk was. He had only 250 words to do it in but if he didn't, no one else would. All self-indulgent literature ought to be dealt with. And who better to do it than him?

That was when the phone rang. To pick it up immediately would show the caller that he was hanging around waiting for the phone to ring.

Unnithan no longer had the weekly 1,000-word column in the literary supplement of the paper he used to work for. But it didn't mean he was any less busy or important. He saw his daughter Indu walk towards the phone. 'Don't,' he barked. 'Let it ring and I will then pick it up.'

She had murmured under her breath, 'How do you know it is for you?' and sauntered away.

Unnithan picked it up on the eighth ring.

'We are calling from the Literary Forum.'

Unnithan sat up. The Literary Forum was the most important literary body in all of Kerala. He had heard there was some talk of his name being put up for this year's award for literary criticism. 'Yes,' he said, remembering to modulate his voice into a deeply ponderous tone.

'As you know, we have an annual award for various genres of literature. We are extremely pleased to inform you that you are one of the winners this year for your book *Laboured Lightness*.'

The voice had droned on about date, time, the mundane details culminating in the Golden Leaf coming to rest in his hands.

Unnithan leaned back in his chair, pleased. Not merely pleased. Ridiculously pleased. True, for many years he had criticised the Literary Forum, questioning their choices. The Literary Forum championed writers like N.S.Madhavan, Mukundan and Zacharia. God knows what they must be thinking of. In fact, they veered towards lightness and Unnithan didn't approve of that. Literature, Unnithan was convinced, had to lie like a brick in the pit of your stomach. Inviolate, insoluble and heavy with incomprehensibility. He liked to see the effort worked into the narrative. That was literature with gravitas. Lightness was a crime as much as accessibility. If everybody were to understand every word that was written and the complexities of the plot, what was the role of the intellectual? What was he to intellectualise?

Nevertheless, they were perhaps finally veering towards literary worthiness by recognising his work. Finally after all these years, he was being recognised for being who he was – the custodian of literature in Kerala. The trouble with the literary world was that there were too many people writing and all of them like this Pamuk fellow who made a virtue of lightness. And none more so than B.A. Nair.

'Indu,' he called out. 'Come here.'

His daughter came into the room, holding a book. When Sarada, Unnithan's wife died of a cardiac arrest two years ago, Unnithan had to invite his daughter and husband to come live with him.

'This house will be yours when I am dead. Besides, I can't devote myself to literature if I have to worry about whether the electricity bill is paid or if there are enough groceries in the kitchen.'

Sandeep, his son-in-law, had risen from the chair in one swift motion. Where was he rushing to? Unnithan wondered. But Indu held Sandeep back by his arm. 'That's fine, *Achcha*, I will run the house for you. But on one condition, you are not to ever question what we do – what we eat, what we drink, who we meet and especially what we read.'

Unnithan was relieved. If Indu hadn't agreed, he wondered what he would have done.

'Have you read this new book by B.A. Nair? It's brilliant!' she said, caressing the book as if it were a pet cat.

'Throw it into the waste-basket. That's where it belongs!' he snapped in irritation. Then unable to suppress his excitement, he said proudly, 'I've been given this year's award by the Literary Forum.'

'I am so pleased for you,' she smiled and went to sit at his side. 'Have you told your friends yet? I am going to make payasam. I am sure all your friends will be here soon to congratulate you and we need to offer a sweet.'

Unnithan felt a flush of happiness. He knew his daughter didn't very often agree with his points of view. But even she couldn't fail to be proud of her father now.

'What is the award for?' Indu asked suddenly.

'For my book *Laboured Lightness*.'

'But that was such a vicious attack on B.A. Nair's writing. How could they?' Indu whispered, her hand going to her mouth.

Unnithan frowned. He hadn't expected this, a traitor in his family.

'I don't care. I like him. I will continue to read him no matter what you think or what the Literary Forum believes,' Indu said with a belligerent tilt to her head.

Unnithan shook his head in sorrow. Like that fraud Pamuk, B.A., drew a certain kind of person's devotion. Philistines. That's what they all were. That's what she was. He had named her Indulekha after Chandu Menon's novel. He had nurtured her in an almost rarefied air of literature, but she in her headstrong manner still preferred the likes of B.A. Nair. And Unnithan believed literary ambition had to be made of sterner stuff.

Unnithan snapped out of his reverie when the music began. He recognised the tune, and each time he heard it, his medulla oblongata sizzled. If he could, he would have bitten off the arm of the man who had inserted the CD into the player. It was a song from a movie made from one of B.A.'s books. Why were they playing this song?

Unnithan detested many things. He detested dogs and English vegetables, women with their hair loose on their backs and men on motorbikes. He couldn't stand cinematic dance or cooking programmes on TV. He disliked the actor Sreenivasan and his films. But most of all he detested B.A. Nair and the unbearable lightness of his being. Actually that Kundera was one of his pet hates, too. But B.A. Nair was in his face and aggravated his bilious attacks more than anyone else.

'But *Achcha*, why do you dislike him so much?' Indu had remarked after reading a vitriolic diatribe once. Those days he had had his 1,000-word column and Sarada was alive to fuel his life and venom.

He had come home to discover that Sarada had forgotten to make the *aviyal* she had promised to cook for lunch that day. Instead, she served him a beans and carrot *thoran*, saying without the faintest trace of apology in her voice or manner, 'I was engrossed in this new novel by B.A. Nair. Once you start his book, you can't put it down... That man is a delight to read even after all these books he has written. There isn't a single trace of fatigue.'

That evening, Unnithan had one of his bilious attacks. And it was this that Indu was referring to.

Unnithan didn't reply. He wondered how to phrase that tumult of emotion B.A. raised in him. It would involve a confession that Unnithan was reluctant to make.

Unnithan had begun work on a novel when B.A.'s first book appeared. Unnithan was working then in one of the literary weeklies. The editor had asked Unnithan to interview him. 'He's being hailed as the next Thakazhi,' the editor said. 'I would like to see what you think. By the way, he's from your part of Kerala.'

Being the methodical journalist he was, Unnithan read the book carefully, pausing at every word and full-stop. Then he tore up his own novel and literary ambitions.

Everything Unnithan had hoped to make his very own, B.A had colonised. The bastard had poached his territory. The little village and the tea-shop, the hills and *pala* trees, the river and paddy fields, the yakshis and the gandharvas and the old decrepit houses in which ancient crones sat pounding their arecanut and chewing their betel leaves. Thakazhi had made the fishermen and coir workers his. Basheer had his Muslims and Mukundan had his Mayyazhi . . . O.V. Vijayan had created a Khazak out of Palakkad, but Valluvanad where Unnithan had his childhood familiars to draw from was available and this was the literary landscape he had chosen, and B.A had usurped that as well. What was left for Unnithan?

That was the first time Unnithan had intimations of his medulla oblongata's special powers. Thus was born the literary critic Unnithan.

He deconstructed B.A.'s novel with the same application with which he had read it. And then he slaughtered the novel. But in one of those quirks of fate, the book went into a reprint almost instantly. And it seemed that with each new book, B.A.'s reputation only grew while Unnithan marvelled at the idiocy of the reading world that devoured all of what B.A. produced. Self-indulgent fluff masquerading as literature.

Unnithan tried to introduce who he thought were stalwarts to the reading public. But they, fools that they were, wanted none of his brick and mortar. Instead, they were enchanted by only lightness. Unnithan couldn't speak of this to his daughter. He couldn't explain to her the moral indignation he felt to see a man violate all rules of literature and get away with it.

And there was something else. Unnithan couldn't understand that either. That B.A. wore his content like a layer of blubber. Not a crease, not a wrinkle seemed to gouge its way into that blubber. Over the years, Unnithan had routinely attacked each one of B.A.'s books, exposing them for the silly vacuous stuff they were. And such was the power of his pen that his wrath had influenced some of the other eminents of the literary establishment too. They had joined hands with him in telling the world about what they thought of B.A.

A few months ago, B.A.'s most recent book had been translated into English. Such was the long arm of his wrath that he had been able to prevail upon critics in Bombay and Delhi to attack the English translation.

He had chuckled, holding the English newsweekly pages and reading the dismissive review.

'What is so funny?' Indu had asked, surprised to see laughter in her father's otherwise grim eyes.

He thrust the magazine into her hands. That should show her. She always condemned him for being vicious about B.A. There were others who thought the same.

When she finished reading the review, Indu had flung down the magazine with a snort. 'I don't understand it! This is B.A.'s memoir! Why would he write about anyone else? This isn't a treatise on literature. These literary biddies! It seems to have completely missed them.... I guess it is resentment that's surfacing, not literary criticism. In fact, Sandeep thinks all of you are jealous of B.A. Nair's success. I agree with him,' Indu accused.

Unnithan frowned at the mention of his upstart son-in-law. What did he know of literature? Just because he read a book a week didn't make him anything more than a mere reader. What did readers know of books? Leave literary criticism to the likes of him.

Nevertheless, Unnithan had to have the last word. So he pushed his glasses up his long bony nose, flicked aside an imaginary fly from the surface of his cooling tea and muttered, 'Me jealous of that strutting self-conscious idiot? You must be out of your mind.'

Unnithan then buried his nose in a new book that had been sent to him to review to signal end of discussion.

Unnithan took a deep breath and glanced at his watch. Soon it would be his moment of triumph. He had heard the chief guest was to be M.F. Menon or Bhanumathi Devi. Now they were writers that Unnithan admired from the bottom of his heart. Each word of theirs stayed with you like a rock. No matter how you tried to crack it, it remained impenetrable and Unnithan glowed, thinking only that he had been able to actually understand their minds and literary vision. Meanwhile, the collar of the new shirt cut into his neck. He had bought a new shirt for the occasion.

'About time,' Indu had said when he asked her to go with him to choose the shirt. 'Why do critics have to look unwashed? Would a decent dress sense make you look any less intelligent?'

There was a rustle in the hall as the audience craned their necks. Unnithan turned as well. He watched appalled.

He had expected a car to be sent to pick him up. Instead he had been told that taxi fare would be reimbursed. He had expected the committee to receive him with full honours. Instead a preoccupied volunteer had led him to a front row and asked him to choose a seat for himself. (Out of sheer perversity, Unnithan sat himself in one of the reserved rows.) He had expected to see other literary heavyweights like himself there and had found a sparsely occupied auditorium and a bawling baby.

But here they were laying out the red carpet for someone. He heard the *panchavadyam* from outside, the music rising to a crescendo . . . Were they expecting a minister? The organisers were milling at the door and a bunch of girls with too much make-up on their faces and wearing cream coloured saris stood flanking the aisle. The *thalam* in their hands glowed from the little lamp that sat at its centre. The TV crew with wires and cameras walked backwards, capturing each second of the arrival.

Who was it? Unnithan wondered. Then he caught a glimpse of the curly head towering and felt a blow to his medulla oblongata. Not him. Not that popinjay B.A.!

The corpse rose from his well with a grin slashed across its face. So Mr Literary Critic, it asked with a leer, now you know what Pamuk meant when he wrote: 'I am nothing but a corpse now.' A corpse can think, too!

Unnithan sank deeper into his chair. The evening sped. A prayer. Poetry recitations. A new journal unveiled. Several short speeches. Lightness everywhere. Only in Unnithan's soul, a darkness, a heaviness, a brick that wouldn't budge.

Then it was time for the awards. And as each name was called out, Unnithan's spirit slowly revived. It seemed B.A. wasn't nominated for anything. So what was all that kerfuffle about? He probably paid for it, the tennis ball at the base of his skull sent a coded message to his brain.

He heard his name being called. He saw one of the girls come to his side to lead him up the steps. He felt the hushed air of appreciation in the audience. Unnithan smiled.

'What's wrong with them? How could they?' A loud whisper.

Unnithan started. Then he saw B.A. on the stage and knew who it was meant for.

'Exactly! What's wrong with them? How could they?' He wanted to turn and shake hands with the owner of that whisper.

B.A. smiled at him. A blubbery smile, Unnithan thought smugly. He must be crying within, Unnithan gloated. This was the last award of the evening and B.A. had been given none. Even that Pamuk had been awarded a prize for best foreign fiction.

'I call upon B.A. sir to address the audience before he gives the award to Shri Unnithan,' the MC gushed.

Unnithan cringed. Didn't they ever stop? This adulation . . . and why was that fool being asked to give him the prize? I suppose they had to give him something to do . . . Half of Kerala worshipped at his feet and they would boycott the forum otherwise.

B.A. cleared his throat. 'Unnithan and I go back a long way. Our literary lives have been intertwined in a peculiar manner. In fact, my first book and Unnithan's birth as a critic happened at the same time. Over the years, I have read each one of Unnithan's critiques of my books carefully. In fact, if he doesn't review me, I feel my book has been a failure and that my readers won't appreciate me . . . For he leads my readers in the direction of what to look for in my writing.'

Here he waited for the laughter to die down and then continued.

'The book *Laboured Lightness* is not just a treatise on literature, it is a work of imagination. Any reader who reads it will sense the depth of feeling Unnithan has written it with. Especially when it comes to my writing.'

More laughter.

'Such is the scope of imagination that one of the jury members wished to award it the prize for Fantasy Writing.'

Ha ha ha. . . .

Unnithan looked up suddenly. Was he being mocked at?

'Unnithan is a true literary critic. Literature is very serious to him. Over the years he has been literature's truest handmaiden.

They say that behind every successful man is a woman. I would like to change that to "behind every successful writer is a critic". In my case, it is Unnithan.

'However, this award is not for literary criticism. Instead, this is a new award for a Work of Faction and it gives me great pleasure as the president of the jury to hand over the Golden Leaf to him for his book *Laboured Lightness*.'

That moment, Unnithan felt the brick in his belly budge. Perhaps B.A. wasn't such a bad person after all. Half of Kerala did worship at his feet. And B.A. himself was acknowledging his contribution . . . Probably now the man would write better books.

Two mornings later, B.A., sitting in the Intercity Express from Kozhikode to Kochi, read a brief report written by Unnithan. It was all about the Literary Forum prizes, the long friendship between Unnithan and himself and world literature finding its truest voice in Pamuk. It was titled 'Orhan Pamuk, Nair and I . . .'

B.A. smiled. A quiet smile that bespoke of the contempt he felt. Then B.A. turned the page.

Anita Nair is the bestselling author of *The Better Man*, *Ladies Coupe* and *Mistress*, which was longlisted for the Orange Prize. Her Kerala connection, apparent in all her books, is especially celebrated in *Malabar Mind* and *Where The Rain Is Born*. Her book *Goodnight And God Bless* is a collection of literary essays.

8 The Argumentative Malayali

D. Vijayamohan

A team of businessmen from Europe visited Gangadharan Pillai, a leading cashew producer and exporter from Kollam in Kerala, a few years back. As Kollam was the only place in the world where cashewnut was processed by hand at that time—now there is a second place, Vietnam—the delegation wanted to see some of the cashew-peeling factories.

Pillai took them to a couple of factories. The delegation got an idea of how cashew was processed and was very happy to witness the neat and clean packaging system. But in the evening, the leader of the delegation asked Pillai, 'Sir, what is the role of the United Nations in these factories?'

Pillai was taken aback by this query. 'Nothing,' he said. 'How come the UN comes into the picture? What prompted you to ask this question?'

'Sir, we saw the flags of so many countries in front of all the factories. Definitely, the UN must be doing something here,' said the leader.

Pillai could not control his laughter. 'They are not UN countries' flags. Those are flags of our various trade unions. We have so many of them, you know.'

Welcome to God's own country. A state so famous (or infamous?) for political awareness. Everything is political in Kerala. As a newsperson, I still remember a press statement by a political party that stunned me. I was a correspondent with the leading Malayalam daily, *Malayala Manorama* in Kollam during the late eighties. Normally, Kollam is not a news centre. Occassional rallies by political parties, export of cashew, a rare visit by some VIPs . . . we were satisfied with our news bites. But that calm was shattered one day by the arrival of two whales in the beach. They were so huge that the entire activities of Kollam beach came to a standstill. The fishermen were afraid to go to sea, fearing an attack from them. Visitors started surging to the beach to have a glimpse of these sea wonders. The local pages of our newspapers were full of stories about these visiting whales.

After three days, when there was no sign of the whales going back, I got a press release that baffled me. It was from the local leader of a revolutionary party. The press release squarely accused some imperialist forces for the arrival of the whales. It said these were not mere whales, but sea giants fitted with technological devices to forage details about the Arabian Sea and the Indian Ocean. For a moment I was not able to make up my mind whether to publish it in the paper or not. But the next moment it went into the dustbin. The absurdity and ridiculousness of the argument struck me though.

This incident depicts another aspect of the state – every Keralite is fighting against an invisible imperialist force everyday. The imperialists have nothing else but one job – to destroy Kerala.

I am not sure whether Kerala is 'God's Own Country' (the ad agency and the IAS officer who coined this phrase were clever – God is never going to issue a denial or confirmation). But to me, an outsider as far as my state is concerned, being a *pravasi* who left the state for employment, Kerala is a land of controversies and paradoxes. Land of controversies because there is nothing in Kerala that cannot be a subject matter for controversy. You open the papers daily to land into one. You issue a harmless and prosaic statement, but somebody will catch it and make it into a controversy. It is a land of paradoxes because Keralites have the unique habit of opposing everything first and then after some time accepting it without any hesitation.

If you think I am exaggerating, please look at the late 1960s. The second Communist-led government came into power in 1967. The industries portfolio was handled by T.V. Thomas, the veteran Communist leader. He was with the Communist Party of India (CPI) at the time. He took a bold decision to go to foreign countries and invite industrialists to Kerala. T.V. was a visionary and he could very well make out that without foreign direct investment (FDI), industrial development in Kerala would remain a pipedream. But there was opposition to his foreign trip from everywhere. Even the Communist Party of India-Marxist (CPM), the leading party, did not support him. T.V. visited Japan but could not achieve much because back in Kerala there was a very strong move against any foreign capital coming into the state.

Look at the paradox now. Every chief minister—whether he is leading Left Democratic Front (LDF) or United Democratic Front (UDF)—goes to foreign countries and tries to woo as many industrialists as possible. Now every chief minister considers FDI an essential ingredient for the state's growth.

The Malayali, who boasts of being intellectually superior to others, has made some of the biggest historical blunders. I remember a strike against tractors when they were introduced in paddy fields. Almost all political parties opposed it, saying that it would make the labourers jobless, and lead to more unemployment and poverty. Tractors receded into oblivion but the Malayali realised his folly only after some years. Now when paddy fields are being converted for purposes other than farming and there is a shortage of farm labourers, the Malayali looks at Tamil Nadu or Andhra Pradesh for rice. There was no strike against tractors in Tamil Nadu or Andhra Pradesh, so they happily produced rice and sold it to their Kerala brethren. I won't be surprised if Malayalis start buying coconuts from Tamil Nadu as coconut pluckers are shrinking in Kerala.

Malayalis, though one of the most migrant set of people in the world, are somehow opposed to any kind of modernisation in their traditional areas. I would say that the trade unions of the Left-wing political parties are to be blamed for this. They opposed the mechanisation of the coir industry in the sixties. That was a period when western countries were showing keen interest in coir products. But the trade unions raised the same objections, that it would lead to large-scale unemployment. Many coir factories were closed. Some of them were shifted to Tamil Nadu. The realisation that the coir industry needed modernisation to compete with the carpet industry came much later. Now there is even an institute for studying modernisation in the coir industry that was started by the LDF government. The paradox continues.

The most hilarious hue and cry was raised against the introduction of computers in Kerala. When the move began to introduce computers in government officers and banks, trade unions opposed it, saying this was a hidden agenda to cut the workforce. The CPM, which spearheaded the movement, campaigned against computerisation in every field. The most interesting sight was on the Ashoka Road in New Delhi where the CPM party centre was functioning at that time. There were computers in the office and often strike calls against computerisation were typeset and printed on those computers! How computers changed the railway reservation system is known to everybody. But the younger generation may not be aware of the difficulties faced for getting reservations when there was no computer and all work had to be done on paper. Needless to add, the opposition to computerisation melted away and nobody noticed when precisely computers entered party offices.

The word 'privatisation' was anathema to the CPM for a long time. Any project started by private participation would attract opposition. When the state government—of course, it was a UDF one—mooted the idea of an airport with public and private partnership in Nedumbassery in Kochi, the CPM was hostile. One prominent CPM leader in Kochi declared that this airport could be built only over his dead body. Work began on the new airport and it soon became operational. By then, there was a change in governments and the LDF came to power. The CPM leader who had vehemently opposed it and was even ready to lay down his life against its creation, became the director of the airport body.

The politicisation of each and every issue is so deep and disturbing that it is not the project but the people who bring it that matter. If a project is brought forward by the UDF government, then the LDF opposes it. If it is a project conceived by the LDF, then the UDF thinks itself duty-bound to oppose it. The casuality, of course, is the development of the state. A perfect example is the proposed expressway from Thiruvananthapuram to Kasargode that will connect one end of the state to the other end. When this proposal was mooted by the UDF government, there was widespread opposition from the Left. Without knowing the details of the project, there were campaigns crying themselves hoarse that this road would divide the state into two and that people on one side would not be able to cross over to the other side. Another interesting question raised by one leader was how a girl on one side of the road can have a love affair with a boy on the other side? It is surprising to see such foolish arguments being sold to the people of a state that brags of having hundred percent literacy. Recently, the LDF government approached the centre for constructing this expressway – a move they should have considered two years ago. Kerala leaders should go and see states like Gujarat where expressways and toll roads have done wonders for connectivity.

Amartya Sen wrote a book called *The Argumentative Indian*. Malayalis are the most argumentative on issues that are non-issues. That is how they debated for nearly three years on whether pre-degree education should be delinked from colleges and added to schools. All over India the plus-two system was accepted without a murmur. But Kerala begged to differ. As the Pre-Degree Board suggestion was brought in by the UDF, the LDF had no choice but to oppose it. Finally, the plus-two system has started functioning in the state.

The CPM once started an agitation against the conversion of farmland for other purposes. In fact, V.S. Achutanandan pioneered this struggle when he was in the opposition. His comrades started destroying whatever was cultivated in such paddy fields. This was known as a clear felling agitation. When the CPM in Kerala was doing this, the CPM government in West Bengal was allotting 2,500 hectares of farmland to the Salim Group, another 1,000 hectors to Infosys and yet another 1,000 acres to the Tatas. This same CPM could not find fault with big community halls and mega-multiplexes coming up on paddy fields in Kerala. Some of them were inagurated by CPM leaders.

A reputed hospital chain in the US was interested to start a super-speciality hospital-cum-research centre in Kerala. They approached the government for land and relevant permissions. Suddenly, the Kerala government realised the possible imperialist threat in this, so they rejected the proposal. The US group was happily welcomed by Haryana, and given land, water and power on concessional rates. So when a Chinese company quoted for the construction of Vizinjam Port, the LDF tried its best to get it sanctioned. But the centre rejected it on security grounds as the same company was building a port in Pakistan.

When Microsoft founder Bill Gates visited Delhi a few years back, he invited the chief ministers of major states for discussions on starting new projects. Only two chief ministers were absent from the invitee list – Bihar's Rabri Devi and Kerala's E.K. Nayanar. Nayanar decided not to go because there were protests by the state CPM against Gates' visit. But the most interesting thing was that Buddhadeb Bhattacharjee, the chief minister of West Bengal, a CPM-ruled state, found no problem in going to Delhi and meeting Gates.

What happened to the Asian Development Bank (ADB) was even more ridiculous. The ADB offered a loan to Kerala for administrative reforms. They also offered loans to city corporations and municipalities for improving infrastructure. The LDF opposed it immediately. Their argument was that the ADB was interfering in the internal affairs of the administration. Also, that there was some hidden agenda somewhere in the loan to drag Kerala into perpetual indebtedness. When the ADB team visited Kerala, there were demonstrations against them. The agitators were unaware of the provisions in the loan pact. After a while, the same LDF accepted this loan and the agitation fizzled out quietly.

One should say with all fairness that both the UDF and the LDF are the same when it comes to mud-slinging. The LDF government introduced peoples' planning (Janakeeya Asootranam) in local bodies. There were studies done by experts on the working of the system. The controversy started with a dissident section in LDF 'seeing' a US hand behind the plan's implementation. The UDF took over. M.N. Vijayan, a reputed intellectual who was with the CPM earlier, spearheaded the campaign against Richard Franke and Thomas Issac. The issue has not reached any logical conclusion. Meanwhile, allegations continue to fly.

Malayalis are most obsessed with their own controversies. In fact, they love them. If Mahasweta Devi visits Kerala, it is controversial. If a CPM leader's son gets admission in a US college, it is a controversy. If fifty years of a landmark book is celebrated, it is a controversy. If threshing machines are used for paddy-harvesting, it is controversial. Even if paddy is destroyed by the rains, nobody is bothered — there should be no machines!

Then there are the sex scandals that flash up every now and then. Some are political, some are not. Young girls are lured by false promises of acting chances in TV serials and films. Fake godmen are also part of it. After all, it is 'God's Own Country'; fake godmen also have a place in it.

It was E.M.S. Namboodiripad, the leader who taught Marxism to Malayalis, who invented a new system of governance and agitation clubbed together. He ruled the state in 1957 but found that the centre was not at all helpful to the state's demands. So he coined the phrase of governance and agitation — governance by the LDF and agitation against the centre. The centre soon became an escape route, with both the LDF and the UDF governments in Kerala making it the scapegoat for everything. If projects are delayed, it is because of the centre. If Kerala is not industrialised, it is because of the centre. If Kerala is facing a foodgrain shortage, it is again negligence by the centre. If farmers in Kerala are not getting remunerative prices for their produce, again the blame is on the centre. For LDF it was very convenient as the centre was ruled by successive Congress governments for a long time. But the situation did not change even during the time of non-Congress governments at the centre supported by the Left parties like the V.P. Singh or Deve Gowda or I.K. Gujral government.

Kerala cannot take development without controversy. During the time of Dr. Manmohan Singh's government, the Vikram Sarabai Space Centre (VSSC) and Indian Space Research Organisation (ISRO) decided to start a space research institute in Kerala. Any other state would have grabbed the project by offering land and other facilities. But in Kerala, a controversy started about the land preferred by ISRO authorities. The project was not shifted to some other state only because of the Malayalis who were in key positions in ISRO and the Prime Minsiter's Office (PMO).

Sitting in Delhi, I have serious apprehensions about the bargaining power of Malayalis in the central government. There never was a time like now (2004-09) with Malayalis occupying key positions at the centre. Two cabinet ministers and one state minister, the prime minister's principal secretary and the national security advisor are from Kerala. Even the Chief Justice of India is a Malayali. But Kerala still struggles to get projects sanctioned, schemes approved and grants cleared. Something is wrong somewhere – is it the collective bargaining power? The political will? The bureaucratic initiative? Or is it sheer callousness?

When will Kerala move from this vicious circle of controversies? If one looks at the pace of development in neighbouring states, Kerala is definitely lagging behind. You can blame the political leadership for that. You can blame the administration for that. But the million-dollar question is – will Kerala change?

D. Vijayamohan is the Delhi bureau chief of the *Malayala Manorama* newspaper.

9 The Night They Arrested The Moon

K. R. Gowri Amma

There are nights that go on endlessly, with no morning in sight. When life is a six-by-six cell and the whole earth narrows down to four concrete walls that press down on the chest, when even the moon is under arrest so that the darkness that descends on you seems to pierce right through your soul.

These were two years of solitary confinement in Trivandrum Jail. I had only a cat for company in those twenty-four long months. But the cat met someone on the sly. She had her kittens, that cat.

Jails remind me of romance too. T.V. Thomas, whom I was yet to marry then, was in jail with me once. He would throw a stone over the wall to tell me that the coast was clear for me to throw my letter to him. The prisoners were allowed a walk around the courtyard at a prescribed time and that was when he tracked me down and wooed me thus.

My very first arrest was at the Cherthala Police Station. At night, they put me in a room where I was allowed a bed and food from home. The policewomen there behaved well with me, so did Inspector Ramankutty Nair. However, I was beaten up in the Central Jail. While being taken from one ward to another,

I heard cries from the ward where male comrades were locked up. When out of curiosity I ran towards that cell, the policemen beat me up badly. I bit a policewoman's wrist and then they all climbed on my stomach and stamped on me with boots. I fought back till all went black. They dragged me unconscious back into the cell. It was only much later at night that I came back to consciousness. This was the day that Mohamma Aiyyappan was killed by police violence in Central Jail Trivandrum.

I was in hospital for a long time after that. My lungs were shaded and TB suspected. But later, the doctors diagnosed it as bronchitis. Though I was thin then, I was very healthy.

Demanding that action be taken against those police personnel who beat me up, I went on a hunger strike. Rumours spread that I had died. In Alleppey, people were protesting then. At least 2,000 people marched towards the Alleppey North Police Station and did not disperse easily. In that police firing, Comrade Janardanan died. For seventeen days I fasted; I was very stubborn as I had been so humiliated. Finally they took me to a hospital. Blood clots did not allow transfusion. Minister Annie Mascrene later visited the jail. She told the doctor that if anything happened to me, he would be suspended. That evening the jail superintendent promised me in writing that all my demands would be met. I withdrew my hunger strike. But the promise was not kept.

What was the case? I was accused of *rajadroham*, being a traitor to the country. They kept extending my sentence by six months each time. I was my own lawyer. Without formal charges, I was put under police custody. I was released only in 1951. Ironically, my family status helped me tremendously during my days in jail. Better treatment was meted out to me because I was the daughter of Kalathiparambil Raman. Women wardens and jail inmates were fond of me. Jail supritendent George was transferred out only because they thought he gave me preferential treatment.

In 1948, the Communist Party was banned. But how can you ban communists? After I came out of jail, I started organising conventions for the party. Comrades T.V. Thomas and Vaikkom Chandrashekaran Nair were with me. While leaving the Convention Hall in 1950, the police surrounded us and took us into custody. I was released immediately after the elections in December 1951.

Most of our candidates fought elections from the underground — in jails or in hiding. M.N. Govindan Nair and T.V. and many others . . . all of them stood for elections that way. Out of 108 people who stood, 32 comrades, including me, won. I drove out of jail in my elder sister Devaki's car. The party was very fond of *Chechi* . . . her house was their hub.

Those days, the Communist Party was focused entirely on social upliftment of the poor. We had a tradition of protests. The Nadar weaver women in southern Travancore started wearing bras (rowka) though, like Nair women, they were not permitted to cover their breasts. The Maharani prohibited the rowka for Nadar women. This brought about the famous Nadar uprising. British intervention saw the Maharani withdrawing her directive. It was quite natural for a social worker like me to be attracted to the Communist Party, which had pitched a war against just such atrocities. The Punnapara Vayalar uprising, followed by police firing on people carrying only bamboo sticks hastened my entry into politics as a proud comrade of the party.

In 1964, in the days of party splitting, T.V. (my husband by then) took me out for a play – *Kadamuttathe Kathanaru* – where we were welcomed by the audience with claps as well as cheers. For that he bought me two saris of silk in white, for he loved white. He also bought me flowers, which was a first. Even for my marriage, I had bought my own sari and jasmine combs!

Yes, he loved me. It was the vested interests of certain people that came between us. I firmly believe he loved me till the last.

When I met him in Bombay (where he was being treated for cancer during his last days), he had tears in his eyes. He didn't say anything but it was obvious what he felt for me.

K.R. Gowri Amma, who at almost ninety is the oldest contributor to the anthology, has a unique place in the history of the Indian Communist movement and Kerala's political canvas. She was the Revenue Minister of Kerala in 1957 and the lone woman in the first ever Communist government in the world brought to power through free ballot. She joined the newly formed Communist Party of India-Marxist after the Indian Communist Party split in 1964. Expelled from this party in 1994, she put together the Janathipathya Samrakshana Samithy, which later joined the United Democratic Front. A former Agriculture Minister of Kerala, she has the distinction of piloting the revolutionary Land Reforms Bill, which turned millions of landless tenants into landowners overnight.

— *This memoir is based on an interview by Shinie Antony.*

10 A Medicine That Cannot Be Prescribed

S.S. Lal

'See you again, granny.'

It was the fourth or fifth time that Balan was bidding her goodbye. Everytime he tried, she tightened her grip on his hands. Somehow, he did not feel like forcefully freeing his hands. Caught between the reluctance to let go and the reluctance to move away, the atmosphere was growing tense. Nalini aunty was mopping her swollen eyes and Chandrika aunty's face was slowly turning red.

Softly freeing his hands from her convulsive grip, he whispered, 'I will come and visit you every year, granny.'

'Don't f . . . forget to worship at the temple on the way,' she stammered, wiping her tears with a feeble hand.

Balan and his family slowly walked towards the gate, followed by a retinue of kith and kin. On the steps he stood and cast back a last glance. Granny was still on the verandah, staring unblinkingly at the crowd that was about to disappear from her sight.

At the temple, Siddharth got down with Balan from the car. After his prayers, Balan moved towards the temple pond. He looked at the waters where memories of decades lay stagnating. He went down the stone steps towards the placid waters. Siddharth followed him. The steps were dilapidated. The devotees and the temple committee have almost wiped it from their memories, this relic from the past. With the petro-dollars flowing in from the Gulf, the temple has managed a golden flagpost with the names of the donors etched in bold. And the temple pond? Well, who needs it now, especially as a swimming pool has come up with ultra-modern facilities nearby?

Sensing unfamiliar human presence, the fat frogs that held sway over the steps panicked and dived into the moss-tipped water between the steps. Disturbed by the sudden commotion, a rat-snake gazing lazily at the world around it, slid into the water and disappeared. A bird flapped its wings and flew away, a fish in its beak struggling. From the branches of a banyan tree that spread its huge canopy over the pond, a crow was pecking at the flesh of a frog. Poor crow! Should not somebody teach it the sacred customs of the temple?

Finding a dry step, Balan sat down. Siddharth joined him.

'What about my question, papa? You did not say anything.' Siddharth was a bit cross as Balan continued to look aimlessly at the passing clouds. He didn't want his son to see his moist eyes.

'What medicine did your granny ask, papa? Why did you not write it for her?'

'You are too young to understand that.' Balan was again evasive.

The cow was mooing plaintively. Balan, in the recess of the decrepit wall, saw that old, old, old bundle of bones. The wrinkled skin on its neck hung loose, the udders were empty. Even the butchers had orphaned it. Balan could not take his eyes off the cow. He looked at it and heaved a sigh. The wrinkled face of his granny flashed through his mind. . . .

'Papa, your granny is ninety years old, isn't she?' Siddharth shot his next query.

Balan nodded his head in affirmation. His eyes again wandered aimlessly through the clouds and the sky.

Nothing else stirred in his consciousness, save the memories of his granny. She is ninety-two. Most others from the older generations had left the earth. The last was Gomathy granny, younger to her by a decade or more, who left four years back. On the days of the funeral and customised obsequies, granny took control of everything. She exuded an air of being least bothered about death.

But the truth was different. The only thing that granny ever feared was death. Balan was a privy to this secret from childhood. How many medicines and how many concoctions had granny over the years consumed? From the first day of Balan's entry into medical college, she was constantly asking him for a medicine that could ward off death. . . .

Though granny was free of the usual old age maladies like blood pressure and diabetes, she still wanted medicines so that she would not die. It was usual for granny to hold Balan's hands close to her chest and request, 'With these hands, write out the best medicines for me. I do not want to die. I want to see everything before I go.'

Granny weaved her dreams around Balan. There was no dearth of people who loved granny. She, too, loved them back. But it was doubtful if she was able to love anyone more than she loved Balan. When Balan was a toddler, she wanted to see him in school. When he joined school, she wanted to see him in college. Her one fear was that she may die before that. When Balan joined college, she wanted to see him as a medical student. All her prayers centred on that. No rituals that astrologer Chakrapani prescribed were ever ignored.

When Balan joined medical college, she had new dreams. She wanted to see him as a dashing young doctor. When he became a doctor, she wanted to see him married. And when he got married, she wanted to see his offspring... granny always had a thousand reasons why not to die.

'Papa, granny's memories are so sharp even now. Her sight is perfect. And she can hear everything.' Siddharth brought a stop to Balan's chain of memories.

Balan again nodded. Perhaps, granny's problem was that. She can see and hear everything. She remembers everything. And she understands everything. With what sharpness she said even today morning, 'This is Chingam. How many more days are left for the Uthrattathi star in Kanni? Do not forget to do the rituals on your birthday. But then you will be in America at that time. Are there any Devi temples there? How can there be?'

He had noticed some changes in her. She was now worried about Balan's lifespan.

Though the house was full of relatives, granny was not happy. Her countenance reflected that. And many of the relatives... she plain ignored.

For Onam it was customary for all the relatives to assemble at the house. Some years before, after the Utharadam feast, relatives were busy preparing for the next day. Granny was standing near the well. She slipped and fell. Nobody noticed her lying there helplessly. It was traumatic for her. She fractured her backbone. And then began a series of medicines, prayers and rituals. After coming back from weeks of hospitalisation she still had hopes. She was just looking forward to the treatment from Pankajakshan, the village ayurvedic doctor. She strongly believed that she'd be able to walk after that. She even took comfort from the fact that though her backbone was fractured, she was still alive. She did not forget to request Balan to bring from America the medicines that would ward off death.

And hidden in that request was a new desire to keep death at bay. Her new wish was to see Balan's daughter who was born in America. Two years have passed since. Now even that wish had been fulfilled . . .

But granny had changed now. The ayurvedic physician had washed his hands off her a long time back. Not only the physician, even others had washed their hands off her, complained granny. The relatives and the neighbours, who used to compete with each other to give her company during her heydays, were not to be seen anymore.

Crippled, granny's life got confined to a wheelchair. The axis of her life now rotated with the axis of the chair. The boundaries of her world shrank to the space accessible to it. She learned to eat and sleep on it. She did not try to push it anywhere. The boundaries of her desires, too, were crippled. The sounds of the old pendulum clock helped her to distinguish between night and day. But there were worse things. For her defecation and urination, she had to depend on the whims of other. Those who are unable to walk are a real load for the earth, she had told him today.

'If I had died in that fall, they would have suffered only for a few days. I heard Nalini and Chandrika saying this to each other. They thought I was sleeping. Then I continued to feign sleep for a long time as I did not want to hurt them.' Granny was in tears when she recounted this to Balan.

'You went to America to make money. And the rest of the boys left for Dubai. I was disowned even by the gods.'

Tears sketched an imponderable design on the floor before granny could rub them away with her upper mundu. Granny, who desired only to live and live, was now weeping like a child. . . . She took Balan's hands and pleaded with him, 'Will you prescribe a medicine for me?'

'Why not! Your craving for medicine is still not over, granny? What medicine do you want?'

She brought her head close to his ears and whispered, 'Will you prescribe for me a medicine to die?'

A tear dropped on the handle of the wheelchair and splintered into a thousand droplets.

'Dad, which medicine did granny want you to write?' Siddharth was asking with his childish curiosity

'It is a medicine that papa doesn't know how to write. Come, let us go. Ma and your little sister are waiting in the car. Going to the airport is a long drive.'

Balan started up the stone steps. Siddharth followed him.

– Translated by Dr. Babu Gopalakrishnan

Dr. S.S. Lal, is with the World Health Organization since 1999, and is currently stationed in Geneva. A former editor of the Indian Medical Association's monthly health magazine *Nammude Arogyam* (Our Health), he also presented a weekly health-show – 'Pulse' – on Asianet, a Malayalam TV channel, from 1993 to 2003. His short stories and novels have been published in several Malayalam periodicals. This story first appeared in the *Kerala Kaumudi*, 2006.

11 The Mundu Brigade

Yusuf Arakkal

'Kuttiye (child), go out and draw something. Don't waste your time here.'

These words of my mathematics teacher Subhadra Varasiar still ring in my ears. I was pretty bad at math. Just managed to pass the exams, courtesy my teachers' kindness. I was known for a lot of things in high-school, like being the junior football team captain and goal-keeper, nicknamed after the famous Olympian Peter Thankaraj, literary association secretary, editor of a handwritten magazine, etc. But I was best known as an artist; hence the concession from the math class. I used to win prizes for my school in painting competitions. Apart from these, my knowledge about art was next to nil. I had vaguely heard of the name Raja Ravi Varma and read something about one Michelangelo in a magazine. I have seen framed pictures of gods and goddesses by Ravi Varma at my friends' homes. At that time I did not realise they were the popular oleographs. They are produced by an elaborate process of creating pixels by hand for each colour and printed by the lithographic method. Sadly, most Malayalis, with all their proverbial ability for knowledge and intelligence and proclaimed aesthetic sense, considered Ravi Varma only as a painter of gods and goddesses.

My understanding of Ravi Varma's works began in Bangalore with my first art teacher Jaya Varma. He was from the Ravi Varma clan. An accomplished portrait painter who studied at the Royal College in London, he was a strict teacher and stickler for details. He was over seventy years when he taught me the nuances of European Academic painting. It was from him that I learned more about Ravi Varma's works and his technique.

During my art college days, I began to study more about Ravi Varma's works and realised the importance of the great painter who was the pioneer of oil painting in India. But Ravi Varma's importance does not stop there. He was also probably the first Indian artist to bring a synthesis in his work between Indian and western aesthetic sensibilities. Anywhere in Europe he would have been worshipped as a master at every turn of the corner. Unfortunately, we failed to understand him and even called him a calendar painter. Not discounting the importance of calendar painters, I wish we understood the aesthetic integrity of Ravi Varma. Is it because we are good at ignoring great things and holding on to petty ideas? Today Ravi Varma is a collector's dream and they are running all over to get hold of originals. Almost a century later, his work has been recognised and the price has skyrocketed, bringing in the inevitable 'fake' industry into play. The funny thing is that those who called him a calendar painter are now singing a different tune altogether.

This reminds me of an incident in France. End-eighties, I painted a series at a tiny village perched on the slope of a hill thirty kilometres away from the famous porcelain city of Limoges in Limousine terrain. Villa ra Joush had hardly fifteen houses, mostly French. An American photographer and a Czech farmer complete the village population. My friend and French collector Regis Richards has a lovely holiday home in this village. He transformed the wooden-clad first floor into a makeshift studio for me. In these parts of France the light is tremendously alive and inspiring. Remember the starry-starry nights of Van Gogh? The nights are equally beautiful with thousands of shimmering stars in the clear sky. I painted one of my most colourful series there – *The Kites*. Richard went back to his place at Le Havre and I was left to paint in peace with plenty of canvases and materials that he had organised. Initially, the villagers ignored me. But when they realised that I was an artist, there was a remarkable change in their attitude towards me. I began getting admiring visitors in the evenings. They came with friends for a drink, sat and chatted with me. Often they brought excellent home-brewed wine, fine cheese and other French delicacies. They prided in introducing me to their visiting friends as an 'artist friend from India'. I basked in their affection and admiration. Often I presented them with drawings and sketches. They would frame it at the earliest and invite me and their friends to dinner to show off this work.

Would this happen to me in my native place? I very much doubt it. The sad fact is that the pretended intellectualism and preached intelligence just linger on the surface. Does it mean we are not intelligent? On the contrary, we are so intelligent that we tend to think others stupid and treat them that way. We do not accept them into our territory. Outside Kerala we are ever ready to embrace other cultures and their traditions. Are we sincere about it? In most cases it is a survival trick for which we are famous. When in Rome, do as Romans do! How expertly we have cultivated this idea and turned it into a fine art.

Today we have a lot of youngsters who fuse Western and Oriental aesthetic sensibilities together in their work and bring out a universal appeal, which, in fact, has caught the attention of the world and is making Indian art countable. (That the marketing forces are exploiting it to the hilt is another story.) This brings us to the Malayali content in the Indian contemporary art today. A long list of younger generation Malayali-origin artists thrive on hard work and modern thinking. Their success and influence is so tremendous that in some parts of the country they are nicknamed the *Mundu* Mafia. Here we are talking about the hardworking Malayali. But that is when he steps out of the borders of Kerala.

In Kerala, one Malayali expects the other to do all the hard work. This has created a scenario where we have workers from neighbouring states thriving in the state as they do all that we are reluctant to do. But we are extremely good at sloganeering and lingering on issues that are at times non-existent. In art, we are very good at creating installations and decorations with flags of various hues representing political parties. These will make even the great installation artist Christo feel ashamed of himself. We put such skill into creations that do not serve any purpose other than littering . . .

When I look at the tremendous success that artists from Kerala who live outside the state have achieved, I feel elated. But the irony is that it would have been impossible to get anywhere if we had not gotten out of our homes. We are great talkers and make speeches that would astonish the great Cicero and his kind, but when it comes to constructive work we do not show that kind of enthusiasm and try to shove it on to someone else's head.

One of our great writers who tried to talk plain and pointed out some hometruths about the Malayali is Vaikkom Mohammad Basheer. Having read a lot of his work, I am a great admirer of his from my younger days. It was in the nineties that a cherished dream came true and I met the Sultan of Letters at his place in Beypore and spent a lot of time talking and photographing him. He was not in the best of health and died two years after our meeting. I began a series of paintings based on his characters and him. I exhibited these works in Kerala and received tremendous response from the press and audience; the legend of Basheer spurred that enthusiasm. But when I proposed that these works be housed in some museum or libraries, the official enthusiasm suddenly waned. As a result I had to give this series to a private collector. Later he sold it to other collectors. Most of those paintings travelled out of the state.

The contemporary art scene in Kerala is interlinked with the Madras Art School and in general the Madras Art Movement. K.C.S. Panikker pioneered the new art movement in Madras and, under his tutelage, a generation of today's well established artists were born. Haridasan, Jayapal Panikker, Nandagopal, V. Viswanathan, Akkitham Narayanan, Gopinath, M.V. Devan, Namboodiri, Kanayi Kunhi Raman, Balan Nambiar, Anila Jacob and many others form the Malayali landscape. A majority of these artists prefer to stay outside the state or the country where they thrive in a competitive and creatively energetic atmosphere.

There are many Kerala-origin artists who are not connected with the Madras Art Movement. Prominent among them are A. Ramachandran, Achutan Kudallur, K. Radhakrishnan, Surendran Nair and others. Jitish Kallat, Bose Krishnamachari, T.V. Santosh, Shibu Natesan, Riyas Komu, Baiju Parthan, Jastin Ponmani, Asiz T.M., John C.F. and more. This younger generation, already established nationally and internationally, stays out of Kerala and pursues its vocation in peace as they do not have to burst eardrums listening to slogan-shouting or get bogged down by hartals and bandhs.

But many of the artists who prefer to stay in Kerala mostly stagnate and live off their past glory. Exceptions to this may be Babu Xavier, Murali Nagapuzha and a few other younger-generation names. Some of the artists living in Kerala are unduly glorified by the press and the officialdom for their own convenience. The fact remains that these artists have not achieved anything substantial at the national or international level. While the Malayalam media is very alive and aware of contemporary issues, it has taken a soft stand of appeasement towards these self-glorified artists.

Once in Kochi I happened to read about an artist in a Malayalam newspaper – 'A new movement is born in the world art scene'. The article continued with choice phrases and quotes from world-famous names, equating this artist to their achievements. Impressed with what I read, I was immediately appalled at the sight of the works, which can be described only in one word – bad! Unfortunately, when I talked to this artist, he seemed to be in complete agreement with what was written about him. He was an example of the mediocre who believed in what's written about them by the equally mediocre. When I see such mediocrity paraded, trumpeted and felicitated all across the state, I begin to doubt my pride in my Malayaliness. Are we a lot who take pride in showcasing our own mediocrity?

While Malayalis show great leadership abilities in many fields, we are equally vulnerable to a mob mentality. We show this tendency in day-to-day life and in politics, too. A great flow of young Malayali artists to institutions outside the state began at a particular juncture. While it certainly helped the art scene and produced a few artists of national and international repute, a lot of them became blind followers of their teachers and other influential artists.

Most artists get influenced by great names. It is a part of continuity. Such influences have to be positive, beneficial for the individual's growth and help develop his own personality. Positive influence is life-giving, but mere imitation of the masters is creative death. Many of the young artists are tempted to become clones of the greats, adding to the confusion already reigning.

This reminds me of an incident that became a personal milestone in my artistic life. I passed out in 1972 from the CKP College of Art. Soon after, I was given a scholarship to study at Shantiniketan in Kolkata by the Karnataka government. I was probably the only student to get it after Venkattappa who was sent to Shantiniketan by the then Maharaja of Mysore. Any art student would have taken that with great happiness and pride. But I decided to refuse the offer, which in everybody's eyes became an act of rebellious foolishness. While I regard Shantiniketan as one of the greatest institutions in the world and respect it with great humility, I was very well aware of the kind of great personalities associated with that august institution. Including the great Ramkinker Baij and Binod Bihari Mukkerji, an array of stalwarts taught there. I was aware of their reputation and would have succumbed to it at an age when my experience and resistance power to temptations were very low. In short, I would have come back with a tag 'Made in Shantiniketan'. This frightened me and I had to take that decision, which in retrospect I believe was a turning point in my life.

Even today, scores of young artists leave Kerala in search of greener pastures. Is it because of the economic situation or wanting to exit an atmosphere where sarcasm and backbiting takes upper hand at times? It may just be the knowledge that better things are happening outside that drives the young out. Whatever it is, many want to leave and go out looking for better appreciation for their work.

During my travels around Kerala on an invitation from the state tourism department, I did a number of sketches and paintings. One early morning I sat on a beach near Kappad sketching a fishing boat lying on its side in the sand. I sort of finished the drawing and was contemplating further enhancement. My thoughts were interrupted by someone tugging at my T-shirt. It was a young child with distinct Arab features.

'You only draw boats?' The innocent voice was almost drowned out by the roar of the sea.

'Well, I do sketch other things, too.' I showed him my sketchbook. He looked curiously at some of the faces I had drawn and then looked convinced that I could do 'faces'.

'Will you please draw me?' he asked in an unsure voice.

A few more children gathered. 'Draw him, please,' they joined the chorus.

The Malayali persistence for getting things done! So I sketched him.

'Exactly like him' was the general consensus.

'But his eyes are not that slanted,' said a dissident voice typical of a Malayali.

Whatever the shortcomings in us, I love to be a Malayali in any corner of the world. But it has to be some other corner of the world!

Bangalore-based artist **Yusuf Arakkal** is originally from Kottakkal in Kerala. His repertoire takes in drawings, paintings, sculptures, murals and prints, bagging him honours like the Lorenzo De Medici Gold Medal, the Karnataka Lalit Kala Academy award and a National Award in 1983.

12 Three Men On A Train

Sheila Kumar

Kerala's backwaters sparkled, washed golden in the gloaming. The river was running swift here, at Valiyaparamba, to the far north of the state. It was what a travel writer stuck for a descriptive term would call a balmy evening; what's more, there was a pleasant breeze blowing.

Some distance ahead lay my destination, an island hemmed in thickly by palm groves. There was a motley crowd waiting at the jetty for the half-hourly ferry, almost all locals. Clad in my regulation jeans, camera and cellphone cases slung separately around my neck, jhola constantly slipping from one shoulder, I clearly stood out, the outsider. And I was getting the Kerala looks, too. The Malayali is the world's most efficient starer; you could get stared to death in this state. The looks were a characteristic admix of avidly curious and curiously blank. It had been some years since I had last encountered such intent, purposeless ogling and I was hard put not to react in some way, any way.

Whatever was my magazine doing, sending a Malayali into the Malabar hinterlands? Most of us, alas, suffer from the Kerala double whammy – a surfeit of natural beauty back home, the kind you soon take for granted, and an ingrained, therefore automatic, sardonic reaction to anything and everything. Factor in some intrinsic cynicism, the inclination to seek and find hornets in paradise, and what you get is not exactly the gushing travel writer, word-challenged or otherwise.

Then again, the whole area here was admittedly suffering from a surplus of pulchritude, even for the regular Kerala landscape. Navy ribbons of road, red-tiled houses made of laterite brick, topography in all possible shades of green, the emerald of the trees complementing the parrot-wing hue of the paddy fields. Skies that seem to have lent some of its smoky blueness to the distant wall of the Western Ghats. The thing is, I have to say it, at some stage of travelling in Kerala, you become convinced the journey is more fun than the destination.

Back at the pier, it was not that I was staring but I'd noticed her a while ago. She was clad in a burqa, which had the most delicate embroidery at the hem and cuff, something I was keen to take a closer look at. The veil had been thrown back, exposing a singularly sweet face. She was young and surrounded by a gaggle of children; I counted three girls of varying age and height, and a baby tucked at her waist. Every time I caught her eye, she'd smile and I'd smile back. How long before one of us made the first move?

Soon enough she decided this exchange of smiles was not enough. Sauntering over, kids in tow, she asked if I understood Malayalam. Her delight was evident when I said I was from Kerala. After which began a rapidfire interrogation, with me on the receiving end for a change, equal parts amused and bemused.

It was some time before I could get an oar in. Finally, I managed to ask a few questions of my own. Her name was Khadija, she said. She was all of twenty-two years old, her husband worked in the Gulf, as what and where she couldn't quite remember now. And yes, the four children were hers. I kept my face carefully expressionless but Khadija must have seen something there. 'What to do?' she said, shrugging in a resigned fashion but not in the least defensive. 'Three turned out to be girls. I had to keep trying till I got a boy.'

Was the baby perched on her hip a boy, I asked with some trepidation.

'Yes,' she beamed. 'Now I will try to have two more boys,' she added. 'I am young and I have the health for it.' She sounded like some advert for the opposite of family planning, but this time, I was successful in keeping my face blank.

Khadija was nothing if not completely, totally, utterly artless. Over the years, I have met a lot of people across the social grid and most of them usually have some amount of native smarts. Not this one though and I found myself both attracted to that as well as alarmed for her. She told me she stayed with her mother-in-law. You mean, your mother-in-law stays with you, I asked. No, she said, they all stayed in the older woman's house. Her mother-in-law, Khadija further informed me, with all the air of one imparting good news to a caring friend, now treated her well since she had broken the jinx and delivered a baby boy. A couple of years ago, she had accompanied her husband abroad for a while but city life had somewhat scared this semi-educated, quasi-literate girl. 'I am happy here among the palms, by the waters,' she smiled as I scanned her face. Was Khadija for real, in these days of the World Wide Web, Skype and Western Union remittances? Well, she was. The known evidently calmed her, the unknown alarmed her, that much was evident.

Khadija was fascinated by my presence there that evening. She kept asking why my man wasn't with me, once she'd affirmed that I was indeed married. She asked her questions with all the simple directness of one who knew nothing about concepts such as privacy or indeed the invasion thereof. Why did I need to go out and earn a living, was my husband not earning enough? The idea that women would want to work was alien to her and, of course, what she couldn't grasp, she wouldn't understand. This was turning out to be an evening where clichés came alive, and as clichés usually did, holding in them a lot of truth.

Journalists were an unknown breed to her but writers she knew, especially Kamala Soraiya, the Hindu-turned-Muslim poet. Soraiya's ancestral home was near here, Khadija informed me. I simply couldn't resist the question. Did Khadija have any opinion on whether the writer was a good Muslim? Khadija gave me a blank look. Writers write from their homes, she told me and it took me a full minute to realise she had left the topic of Kamala Soraiya. Actually, Khadija's subtext was only too clear. She followed it up in a more direct fashion. Why was I leaving my children at home to write about Kerala's trees and rivers, she asked. How come my mother-in-law permitted such doings? My carefully formed sentences made no sense to the young girl. Never had I felt so inadequately unequal to the exchange, I who wielded words for a living. All I could do was retreat into the comfort of helpless smiles.

All too soon, the ferry arrived and we climbed aboard. Conversation on the boat was impossible because of the press of people and the attendant noise. The waters seemed split into two colour zones. From where I sat near the prow of the boat, the waters caught the sinking sun and glowed gold in the twilight evening. When I turned, it was as if I had left behind another body of water altogether, a stormy grey one. Khadija and her children got down at the second islet the boat stopped by, all of them waving enthusiastically at me. And then they disappeared from my life. I watched them go with a sense of loss that seemed a bit unreal.

That night, back at the hotel, I opened my VAIO to find in my inbox an article on the growing resurgence of the feminist logic in the media. I read it with particular irony. Khadija's face kept blurring the newsprint.

That was a couple of years ago. I wonder how Khadija is faring. I wonder if her next child was a boy.

This time, I was heading into the deep south, to Konni, where mammoth black boulders sprouted from the red soil and rubber took over the hillsides with all the eagerness of lantana weed. Luckily, the compartment was only half-full. However, I got to share my two-tier AC cabin with three men.

They were all Malayalis, you could tell at a glance. A glance which naturally, had to take in starched *mundus* (with thick broad lines of scarlet, green and purple, respectively), cotton *jubbas*, (kurtas) the ubiquitous beard and moustache combine and yes, the swagger.

One was tall and balding. The second was short and stocky. The third was green about the gills. I'd heard about people being car-sick, but train-sick? And before the train rolled? Probably a terrible job of the morning shave. All three gave me a lookover, the famed Mall-look, which I survived by the simple expedient of ignoring it and them. To further strengthen my position, I pulled out my spectacles and book. The loss of interest was palpable, if not too flattering.

Baldy opening proceedings, he told his comrades a joke that seemed singularly unfunny to me. Luckily, it was not risqué, but plain unfunny. 'I'm not feeling too well,' said Green Gills, almost in response to the joke. This didn't surprise me one bit, considering that he really looked 'off'. The train blew its stentorian horn; for the life of me, I could never call it a mere whistle. I stared up at the AC vent, willing it to open and send forth some cool air.

'Nonsense,' said Stocky in a bracing tone, bringing my startled gaze back to eye level. 'It's just that you have already started missing this place.'

The logic of that stumped Gills as it did me, and he lapsed into a morose silence. The whistle blew, the train started pulling out of the station with uncoordinated jerks, rather like the rolling gait of a racing camel, or so I fancied. This could be because I was staring at the front page of a Malayalam newspaper held up by the man opposite me; after much painful peering and reading without synchronised movement of lips (that would have attracted unwanted attention from the trio), I decoded the headline of the second lead. It was about children serving as camel jockeys. I had thought that particular storm had blown over. Maybe news sometimes was recycled to test a perceptive Malayali's intelligence. Interesting concept that.

Just as the train gathered momentum, just as I pondered whether putting my toe-nails (polished a carmine red, I must inform the reader) on show by propping my feet up on the seat opposite would be something I could pull off safely, other feet thudded on the platform. A head appeared at our window, a hand thrust something through the bars. 'Please, post this when you reach Shoranur,' a voice panted, seeming not to synchronise with the face running alongside us.

The train gathered speed, the face dropped out of sight and all that remained of this brief interlude was a packet of letters tied with string left in Stocky's hand. He gave an uncertain grin and said, unnecessarily, I thought, 'He wants us to post this when we reach home.'

Baldy ran true to type and said with patently fake jokiness, 'He doesn't trust the P and T out here.' But Gills wasn't having any. Suddenly coming to life, he pronounced, 'There's something fishy in this.' He looked at me for confirmation and it was all I could do not to nod my head, or rather, waggle it side to side in good old Mallu fashion. I stayed impassive.

'Maybe a letter bomb in trout,' riposted Baldy. Now, I get jokes as well as the next Malayali does, but it took me a minute to get this one. The other two men stared blankly at the inordinately smirking Baldy. Ha, a compartment of Malayalis all under the Mensa quotient.

'He had a kind of look about him, that man,' said Gills. 'He looked desperate . . .'

'A desperado,' finished Baldy, who, I decided, either was or had a sad case of Comeditis. 'Quick, throw the packet out,' he instructed. Even as Stocky stretched out a panicked arm, Baldy then did a volte face.

'Don't,' he said sharply. 'Where is your faith in human nature?' he asked Gills severely. 'It's probably a second or third batch of invitations. Wedding invitations.'

'Of course,' breathed Stocky, relieved. 'No one posts wedding invitations all together at the same time from the same place. Everyone knows that.' And he threw a challenging glance around the compartment. I unbent and gave him a miniscule Jeeves-like twitch of the lips. He ignored it.

'I don't know,' muttered Gills grumpily, his illness quite forgotten, whatever it was. 'It could be poison pen letters that he did not want traced back to his local post office.'

My crack of laughter sounded too loud in the stifled interior of the box and the three men threw me a startled glance, which quickly turned as one expression to disapproving. This obviously wasn't women's business.

They then went back to the business at hand, men's business, of course. 'Can't be poison letters, so many of them,' declared Baldy emphatically. Stocky then said with an air of pathetic earnestness, 'I thought he had a kind face.' This, of course, is typical of the Malayali. Just when the general consensus swings one way, there will always be an intrepid attempt to bring it back to Confusion Point.

'I didn't see his face,' said Gills, committing perjury. At which the other two began to argue him down. They argued all sides of the matter in hand. They took all positions, some downright peculiar. I clean forgot my book, this was way too absorbing. The attendant brought us our meals (cream of some unidentifiable vegetable soup, too, and it was good) and they argued over dinner. They then settled down and went to sleep, all three snoring fit to explode.

Now, if the reader is wondering what my take on the packet was, well, any take I might have had had been aborted by the excess of attention paid to the letters. My three loco companions (I dare you to ignore that pun, dear reader!) were more than vocal in their opinions: the packet was harmless, the packet contained something heinous, the packet was an irksome task at hand. Really, I saw no need to add to this morass.

In the morning, no one, not one of them, talked about the packet tied with string. It lay there on the small table. They just kept throwing it fascinated glances as indeed I did, too. I suspect all four of us in that compartment were thinking deep thoughts about that packet even as we had breakfast, ate some heartwarmingly greasy banana fritters, drank endless cups of tea and stared out at the overwhelming green of the scenery. When the train drew up at Shoranur junction, the three men rushed for the door.

In the process, they forgot all about the small white packet wrapped in string, of course.

As assignments went, it was a fairly routine one. I was doing the area cartographers termed South Malabar, comprising Palakkad, Guruvayoor, Trichur and thereabouts, for a travel book. The idea at HQ was to send people to cover areas they belonged to. It turned out to be more than a routine trip though. At Palakkad, I was at the home of a Palghat Brahmin who was giving me valuable info on the life lived in the agraharams. When he mentioned that the Shiva temple, one of the hallmarks of a Tam-Bram village, usually had an *aal* tree out front, I ventured to say that I had found the tree with its wide concrete base, at the front of the Shiva temple in the Ramanathapuram agraharam, an especially splendid specimen. This huge tree had caught my attention earlier and I had spent almost an hour relaxing on its cement base, walking around the temple, taking photographs of the huge verdant canopy of its branches from all angles. Gopalkrishnan seemed amused at something. 'You took a close look at the tree?' he queried. I confirmed that I did. 'You couldn't have,' he retorted with a smile. 'Otherwise, you would have noticed the small plaque affixed to the cement base that proclaimed that it was your maternal grandfather who planted that tree so many years ago.'

A few days later, I was at Asia's largest elephant sanctuary, the Punathoor Kota, just a few kilometres off Guruvayoor. There were sixty-nine pachyderms taking R&R there, being fed huge rice balls, being bathed in the big tank, having their toenails clipped, just chilling. It was a fascinating sight and I was deeply appreciative of the Kota itself, an old manor house in the centre of the sanctuary, now lying in a sad state of neglect. Here and there, the old teak shone as if polished just a while ago. To one side of the house was a small Bhagavati shrine; the priest at the shrine and I got talking. He told me the history of the Kota and that's when I came to find out that almost a century ago the house and its surrounds had belonged to the P--- clan who sold it to a Brahmin. I didn't tell him I was a descendant of the same clan; later, my mother informed me that no trip to Guruvayoor was complete for the elders without a visit to what was still considered the family shrine, the Bhagavati temple at Punathoor Kota. The next time the ties-that-bind cropped up was just a day later. I had gone to Chavakad beach, a desolate strip of sand with a savage sea pounding away at concrete surf breakers. Water to one side, lush forest on the other, with a modest lighthouse in the centre, Chavakad was a lovely spot. I told my aunt so later that night at her place in Kollengode. In response, she told me a lovely story, the story of the origin of our clan, at Chavakad, near the beach. A local nobleman—childless, but of course—came upon a pair of twins seemingly abandoned near the water and he took the babies home, intending to adopt them... only to find an old crone who turned up at his doorstep claiming the babies were her own. With some difficulty he persuaded the old woman to give the twins into his care, promising to look after them like gold. The crone, who was Bhagavati in disguise, of course, told him archly, 'Well, so you must or you'll have me to contend with.'

My ancestor from times past built a small shrine for Bhagavati so she could always oversee her beloved twins, and I guess they all lived happily ever after.

Trichur was next. My great grand-uncle had been a diwan here many aeons back. A set of houses he had built for his family still retained their splendour, all huge white pillars, sweeping steps and wooden shuttered windows. What I was in search of was a road named after him; there was one, I had it on the best authority. No map seemed to show Diwan Narayana Menon Road though and the people I asked were of no help. I ended up chasing a red herring in the form of Diwanji Road. After a while I threw in the towel and glanced at the list the travel book people had given me, ready to move on to my next destination. It was the Lalit Kala Academy... on D.N. Menon Road!

While at the Town Hall, I was struck by an idea and went into the well-stocked library to see if the *Gazetteer* had something on Diwan Narayana Menon. The librarian seemed rather thrilled that someone from the family had come scouting for details and details he snowed me under much to my delight. As I got up to leave, thanking him, he stayed me. 'There's someone who knew the Diwan's family, your family, very well,' he said. 'Shall I arrange for you to go meet the old gentleman?' And so it came to pass that I was soon traversing the backlanes of Trichur town, winding this way and that, finally fetching up at the house of a local journalist. It was the journalist's very old father who knew the P---- family. Only, the man was senile, so not much could be got from him despite various attempts by his younger sister. When the name P---- finally seemed to hit home, he brightened, turned to me, addressed me as Ammu and started reminiscing. The Ammu he was talking of was the Diwan's younger sister, my great-grandmother. Which was why I was not in the least surprised to come upon Valiamama at my next port of call, the Pothundy Reservoir just below the hill-top resort of Nelliyampathy. There is a landscaped garden at the lip of the reservoir, which is a riot of colour in season. You climb up two flights of steep concrete steps and once you step on the tarmac up there, it's like a still life waterscape has come alive just for your delectation. The waters lie still and calm, celadon green at times, deep brown or a luminous silver at other times, with palm trees gracefully bending in homage along its edge, all of it ringed by blue hills with thin wreaths of mist weaving in and out of them.

The reservoir is fed by the Manchady, Kalchandy and Challa rivers; in turn, the reservoir feeds the Gayathri river at the dam site. When the rains come down, a blue-gray mist spreads itself lovingly on the surface; the weather was clearing after a spell of rains and everything looked just lovely. Including my favourite uncle.

Valiamama had been dead and gone some two decades now but still looked good, his kara mundu starched as always, contrasting with the soft crumple of his fine cotton shirt, the top of his Mont Blanc pen showing at the breast pocket. He smiled broadly on glimpsing me and I realised he had not been expecting me. Both of us had broken as pleasant surprises on each other. He beckoned and I hurried up to him. We had a lot of catching up to do.

What an assignment this one was turning out to be.

Sheila Kumar is a journalist and travel writer who writes for a clutch of newspapers and magazines. This army wife and NRK – non-resident Keralite – is passionate about the English language and lives a peripatetic life.

13 Silent Cats

Omchery

(*A room in a hospital where visitors and a receptionist sit. Two big pictures on the walls – a foetus in the womb and a six or seven-month-old baby. A young nurse is arranging papers as the telephone rings.*)

RECEPTIONIST (*attending the phone*): Jeevodaya Nursing Home, yes, it is there . . . yes, ultrasound test. You want to know whether she is pregnant or not . . . oh, alright. . . . You want to know whether the foetus is male or female? If you want to know just that, isn't it better to wait till the child is born? (*Laughing*) Knowing it beforehand . . . you could have made that clear earlier on, without beating about the bush so much . . . yes we do ultrasound test here. But the law forbids conducting tests just to know whether the foetus is male or female. Abortion? That option is possible only in the case of M.T.P. Medical termi . . . yes, just for that. To take care of the well-being of the pregnant woman. Tell me straight . . . You want to abort the foetus if it happens to be female, no? The law forbids that. Here, in front of the clinic, it is written on a board in big, bold letters. Better meet the doctor and talk. I'll fix an appointment with the doctor. (*Turning the pages of a diary*)

How many deliveries has she . . . oh, is it her first? Then why do you panic so much? Mmm . . . for the next one week, the doctor is not free. Twentieth is the earliest possible date . . . at 10.30 a.m. Okay? Tell me your name. (*Writes down*) Wife's name? Address . . . telephone . . . no, no . . . you have to ask the doctor about all that. You are welcome.

(*Puts down the phone.*)

(*At about the same time as the receptionist says, 'If you want to know just that, isn't it better to wait till the child is born?', a woman of about sixty enters along with a young woman under thirty. Waiting for the receptionist to end her conversation, the mother sits in the chair. Fear, sorrow and anger on the young woman's face, she stands listening to the receptionist's talk. When the receptionist puts down the receiver, there is another call.*)

NURSE (*picking up the phone*): Sir, yes sir. There is only one patient left for today. (*Looking at the mother*) Bindu Kumar?

MOTHER: Yes, she's is the one. I'm Biju Kumar's mother.

NURSE (*over the phone*): Sir, that patient, too, has arrived (*puts down the phone*). (*To the mother*) You will be called when it's time. Maybe it'll take some more time. (*To Bindu*) Sit down. (*Bindu stands expressionless, looking at the pictures on the wall. Sits down after some time.*)

NURSE: Mr Biju Kumar had rung up five minutes ago. He called thrice within the space of half an hour just to know whether you had reached.

MOTHER: He may call again. Please inform him that we have reached.

NURSE: He was in great tension. Husbands who love their wives should be like him!

MOTHER: The poor fellow is making so many calls because he is frightened. We had got an appointment for her in another hospital two weeks ago. But when the time came, she just got into bed and stayed put, pleading headache. I tried my best to get her to go along with me, but she wouldn't budge. When he came home, he raised such a hullaballoo. I can't blame him. Shouldn't she be aware of his great consternation?

NURSE: What consternation?

MOTHER: What if this one turns out to be a female too? He already has a girl. He is making so many calls today because he fears that his wife will find some ruse today also to not turn up here.

NURSE: Isn't she with her mother-in-law? How can she play such tricks then?

MOTHER: Oh dear, I can only talk to her. Can I belabour her?

NURSE: But the husband is there to take care of such things, right, auntie?

MOTHER: I have to get it over with somehow before I can go to my own house. My man's there all alone. He wasn't well when I left my house. My son phoned me up and told me I must come along immediately. How can I deny him? By bad luck, if this one also turns out to be a female, I must get that done too, before I leave, mustn't I?

NURSE: What 'too'?

MOTHER: If it is female, shouldn't we remove it?

NURSE: Of course, it has to be killed if it happens to be female.

(*The security man of the hospital approaches.*)

SECURITY MAN: Sister, did that crackpot come this way?

NURSE: So many crackpots come here. Which one?

SECURITY MAN: The woman who goes about singing lullabies for the child she said she aborted in this hospital? She used to sing *Omanathinkalkidav.*

NURSE: Oh, that one. Let her sing. How's it your problem?

SECURITY MAN: We'll lose our jobs. I was fined once because she managed to get inside. The authorities say that those who come to get abortions done are scared away by that woman's antics. Usually, she sings in front of the room where she had been admitted. She is not to be seen there now.

NURSE: If you see her anywhere, tell her to come here.

SECURITY MAN: For what?

NURSE: So I can see her. It is quite some time since I saw her or heard her sing.

SECURITY MAN: So it's not for nothing that people are talking . . .

NURSE: What do they talk about?

SECURITY MAN: That she is not the only crackpot around! (*Hastens away, laughing.*)

NURSE: He says that I am crazy, too.

MOTHER: Who was he talking about?

NURSE: A woman who comes here now and then.

MOTHER: What happened to her?

NURSE: Nothing. She comes here sometimes, and sings lullabies. Just that . . .

MOTHER: She got an abortion done here?

NURSE: Oh, I forgot about our chat. Don't you have siblings, auntie?

MOTHER: Of course, my mother delivered nine times. Did that woman have any health problems after getting aborted?

NURSE: Nothing. Jesus! If it was today, eight of them would have been murdered.

MOTHER: We are six girls. I am the youngest. Of the boys, one died early. The six females and two males are hale and hearty.

NURSE: Auntie, you escaped because there was no such test then. If the test was there, none of the six sisters would have seen this world.

MOTHER: In those days there was no need for any such thing. It's only after dowry came to be the rule that this killing of females began. Putting some ornaments on the ears and around the neck for the bride was more than enough then. None of the men would ever demand three hundred or four hundred sovereigns of gold or house or car as dowry.
NURSE: And there was no custom of burning the brides for insufficient dowry.
MOTHER: All six of us were married into decent families. Times changed drastically when the weddings of my children came about.
NURSE: How many children do you have?
MOTHER: Two boys and two girls. Both the girls were married into good families, paying handsome dowries. We gave them gold and their portions of the property according to the demands of the grooms' families. The elder one has two children, a boy and a girl. The second one doesn't have children. She took all kinds of treatments, offerings were done in so many temples, no use.

(*Bindu rises, walks up to the wall and looks at the pictures.*)

NURSE: Your daughter must be yearning for a son.
MOTHER: For her, anything will do – son or daughter! Last month she had gone to a hospital in Chennai. She insisted that I accompany her. I went along. A very famous doctor. He checked her up, gave medicines and asked her to come back after three months.
NURSE: Oh, you are so busy with all this, auntie! On the one side, efforts to get a child for your daughter; on the other, to kill a child before it is born.
MOTHER: This is all God's play. He won't give to the needy. He will go on giving again and again to those who do not need.
NURSE: It's an old bad habit of God, auntie. In olden times, when God used to give again and again to those who did not

need, they would gladly receive saying, 'God has given, so be it.' But now, if God sends unwanted ones, they are sent back without being received.

MOTHER: There is no use blaming people, my dear. As long as this dowry system is there, no one will readily accept female children saying, 'God has given them, so be it.'

NURSE: And God has no power to put an end to this dowry.

MOTHER: At the same time, all will compete with each other in demanding and taking dowry.

NURSE: And compete with each other also in killing the female child. Did your sons take dowry?

MOTHER: What do you think? Wouldn't it be demeaning not to accept dowry? People will only say that the groom has some serious problem if he says he doesn't need any dowry.

NURSE: That's true. People will say he's a leftover in the market.

MOTHER: My elder son is working in the office of the district collector. He got three hundred sovereigns worth of gold ornaments and the property-share of the bride. Biju is an engineer in the Public Works Department (PWD). He got gold ornaments and a car as dowry in accordance with his high-profile job. She had passed M.Sc. and was teaching in a college.

NURSE: If she was more educated, they'd have had to pay still more to get a suitable bridegroom.

MOTHER: Yes, that's what he is afraid of. When he marries away the girl he already has, he will be quite ruined. And suppose he has yet another? Are you married, my dear?

NURSE: Who, me?

MOTHER: Yes, you.

NURSE: No, auntie.

MOTHER: Why? You'd find it difficult to get a groom if you delay it further and further.

NURSE: Auntie, a time is going to come when there'll be no difficulty in getting grooms.

MOTHER: Why? Will there be a law prohibiting dowry?
NURSE: What is the use of having such a law? There should be dowry, auntie. Only that from now on, it's the girls who are going to demand and take dowry.
MOTHER: Dowry? For girls?
NURSE: A time when dowry will have to be given if one wants a bride.
MOTHER: Don't play the fool, dear.
NURSE: I am not joking, auntie. That time has already begun. Because of the contribution of people like you.
MOTHER: My contribution?
NURSE: Killing female children one after the other, before or after they are born. In many states in the country, there are only about two females for three males, or one female for two males. Soon boys will canvass heavily to get brides. They will bring recommendation letters from bishops, ministers and other such bigwigs, saying, 'please help this guy'. Thus, at a time when the demand for girls is the highest, I will marry.
MOTHER: You are a smart one, aren't you?
NURSE: I haven't finished, auntie. I will marry at least three men, one after the other, taking hefty dowries from each. If any one of them refuses to divorce and leave, I will burn him alive! I'll wait for four or five years more — by that time, birth of female children will altogether stop. My responsibilities to my family would also have finished by that time.
MOTHER: What responsibilities?
NURSE: My two younger sisters are in college. I have to see them through their education. I also have to look after my parents.
MOTHER: Don't you have brothers?
NURSE: Yes, two.
MOTHER: Don't they take care of the family?
NURSE: Yes, they do. They look after their own families. Both are married.

MOTHER: You are right, dear. Nowadays, all the boys are like this. Once they're married, it's them and their own affairs. To tell you the truth, it's like that in our case, too. I can tell you even though she's listening. These fellows will turn up once or twice a year, for Onam or Vishu. Like guests. And then, if there is some emergency like this, they'll ring up and demand that I reach immediately. The ones who rush in when parents are unwell are the daughters.

NURSE: It's the daughters who rush in, right? Suppose they had been killed off? (*Mother doesn't respond; sits looking steadily at the nurse.*) Let Bindu deliver one or two more daughters, auntie. Let there be granddaughters to love you and to look after Bindu when she becomes old.

MOTHER: In fact, I was really perturbed when they aborted her child the very first time. But I can't even say anything, seeing the troubles a female child brings with it.

NURSE: How many times did Bindu abort after the first child was born?

MOTHER: Twice. Got her tested both times. Both were females. Had them aborted.

NURSE: How many months pregnant was she at the time of the abortions?

MOTHER: The first one was at the fourth month . . . or was it the fifth? (*To Bindu*) How many months were you?

(*Bindu, who is looking at the wall, doesn't respond. The question reignites her grief. The wail of a newborn is heard from somewhere.*)

NURSE: The second one?

MOTHER: The second one was also in the fourth month. She prolonged it till then by weeping and wailing, arguing and quarrelling. This time too, we had planned to go to the previous hospital. Only then did we come to know that the authorities had proceeded against the hospital and sealed it for carrying out sex-determination tests. How can you do it here then?

NURSE: Didn't you see the signboard put up right in the front saying: 'Pre-natal Sex Determination Tests Not Conducted'?

MOTHER: The other hospital got into trouble because they didn't display a board like that?

NURSE: It was not for not displaying the board... you don't understand these things, auntie.

(*A woman closer to Bindu by age and looks, comes in from the interior. Grief and fear on her face. Walks slowly forward, stands in front of the wall, looks at the pictures, sings raptly the lullaby, 'Omanathinkalkidaavo', as if trying to lull a child to sleep. After singing a few lines, her throat gives way; she falters and stops. The mother stands up as if she has found herself in front of a mentally deranged person. The young woman stops singing, looks at the pictures for some time and turns her face away.*)

NURSE: It's quite some time since I saw you.

YOUNG WOMAN: Not that I didn't come. I come every now and then. Whenever I remember my child, I come here. Those monsters won't let me in. Today is the second anniversary of her parting. (*Pointing at the picture on the wall*) If she was alive, she would have looked like her. I went straight to that room, dodging those demons who devour infants. I went to that room where I was admitted to take her life. Sang the lullaby that I had hidden in my heart, to put her to sleep. The demons came running. Making me lie down on the stretcher, they tried to take me into the operation theatre. But I came here, to see my child's picture.

NURSE: You didn't complete the song.

YOUNG WOMAN: She has gone to sleep. I will sing the rest when she wakes up. (*Looking at the mother and Bindu*) Who are they?

NURSE: This is Bindu and her mother-in-law.

(*The young woman stares at the mother-in-law. The phone rings.*)

NURSE (*over the phone*): Sir . . . sir, sitting right here, sir . . . shall ask, sir . . . (*to Bindu*) There is some problem with the instruments, will take quite some time. If you don't need to do the test today, you can go home and come back tomorrow.

MOTHER: No, no, let it be today itself, even if it's going to be late.

NURSE (*to Bindu*): How now Bindu, can it be today?

(*Bindu does not respond; looks somewhere else.*)

MOTHER: Didn't I say? It should be today. I can't take the trouble again if it is put off for another day.

NURSE: They say it has to be today . . . sir. Yes, sir . . . I'll tell them. (*Puts down the phone*) You'll be called as soon as the instruments are ready.

MOTHER: Alright.

YOUNG WOMAN (*peering at the old lady*): You are in a hurry to kill the child. I will not let that happen now. The wail of my child whom you killed reverberates in my ears even now. The blue eyes behind her shut eyelids, the smile that bloomed on her tender lips. She was asleep. In the cradle of the womb, she was enjoying deep respite—the respite in-between two *jenmas*, dreaming about the next *jenma*, yearning for the marvel of light—you didn't allow it. I can hear her scream as life burned and smarted out of her, injected with toxic liquid . . . (*sobbing*) her wail, 'don't kill me, please'.

(*Stands with eyes closed, hand on her chest. The loud wailing of a child. Grief, about to brim over, on Bindu's face.*

The security man, who appeared previously, comes in again. Looks at the young woman angrily.)

SECURITY MAN: Haven't you been told not to come here?

(*The young woman looks at him without responding.*)

NURSE: She'll go. I'll see her off and be back in a minute. (*To the young woman*) Come with me, please.

(*The nurse leads her away with great affection.*)

MOTHER (*her fear not receding, to the security man*): She's soft in the head, isn't she?
SECURITY MAN: Yes, yes. Loose nuts since her abortion here, her grief for killing her child.
MOTHER: Are there any others who have lost their mental balance like this?
SECURITY MAN: There would be, how can there not be? Many women are forced to do this, like cattle for slaughter. Most of them are intimidated into it by their husbands and mothers-in-law.

(*The nurse returns.*)

SECURITY MAN: Is she gone?
NURSE: Yes, she's gone. Now you may leave.
SECURITY MAN: She may return anytime, by another route. Mud in our mouths, if the superintendent gets wind of it. (*Leaves.*)
MOTHER: What happened to that girl, dear? To lose her wits like this . . .
NURSE: It was her first pregnancy. It was found to be a female foetus when tested. The husband and his family insisted that they wanted only a male child. This lady was grief-stricken at the thought of destroying her child. Finally, all of them compelled her and she underwent abortion.

(*The telephone rings.*)

NURSE (*over the phone*): Jeevodaya . . . yeah . . . they have come . . . they are here . . . I'll call them . . . will take some more time . . . I'll call them . . . (*To the mother*) It's Mr Biju.

(*The mother takes the receiver.*)

MOTHER: Nothing's happening: It will be quite late... Anyhow, we'll return only after getting to know... After all, we've set out... mmm... you ask... I can't... Yeah, I'll ask.
(*To the nurse*) If it turns out that the child is female, can you, today itself, decide upon a date to carry out that thing? He wants to know.
NURSE: To carry out what?
MOTHER (*hesitantly*): To destroy it... operation...
NURSE: It is the doctor who decides that.
BINDU (*as if her silence, which was smouldering till then, has erupted under the gravity of her controlled emotions*): It's not the doctor who decides.

(*The mother gapes at Bindu, as if she's got a shock.*)

MOTHER: What did you say?
BINDU: That it is not the doctor who decides.
MOTHER: Who then?
BINDU: I, it's I who decides.
MOTHER: It is you who decides?
BINDU: Yes, it's I who decides. I have decided.
MOTHER: What did you decide?
BINDU: That I am the owner of my body. Till now my body was an obedient slave, a slave who submitted to the master. Conceiving in obedience, aborting in obedience....
MOTHER (*in a commanding voice*): Bindu!
BINDU: Didn't you see a slave, who has made obedience a habit, going out a little while ago, singing a lullaby? I'm not singing a lullaby, because my mind is harder.
MOTHER: Bindu, he'll hear!
BINDU: He must hear. I can do without telling him again.
MOTHER: Is she possessed by some evil spirit?
BINDU: Yes, by the spirit that has just left. My own spirit that has killed two of my own children. That ghost will go about all over the country possessing others.

MOTHER: Oh, this girl was such a silent cat...
NURSE: You didn't think this silent cat would break the pot? (*Taking the phone from the mother's hands*) Mr Biju, sorry. Will ring you back... no, there is no problem... should I call Bindu? (*To Bindu*) He wants to talk to you.
MOTHER (*anxious*): No need. We'll call him later, that'll do.
BINDU: That'll not do. He said he wanted to talk to me, right? I'll talk to him. (*Gets up and takes the phone*) Yeah, you want to talk to me? You heard all that I said? Very good. You've heard everything. I needn't repeat it to you. (*Laughing*) You didn't expect the silent cat to talk, did you? It's my fault that I was silent earlier... yes, I've decided. I'm not going to have this test. Mother? She should be glad too. I will tell her. (*To the mother*) Mother, Biju says he is not sad. But he doesn't say that he is glad either....
MOTHER: He'll be alright.
BINDU: So, we shall leave right now. The sister will inform the doctor. The sister is the one who made me talk... OK... OK... (*She puts down the phone*) Sister, may we leave? Thank you very, very much.

(*The phone rings.*)

NURSE: (*over the phone*) Sir, no sir... they've just left... the patient felt uneasy all of a sudden... I think she has some mental problem... Left saying they'll come again later on... I was about to come to you... yes, sir... I'll collect fees for fresh registration when they come next... yes sir... (*Puts down the phone.*)
NURSE: Go then, hurry.
BINDU: Thank you very much, sister. I heard what all you told mother while I was sitting here as a silent cat. That stirred my conscience. The poor woman who appeared here was my conscience that had lost its serenity. That poor woman was me, myself. That lullaby turned into a wake-up tune for me.

NURSE: The grief of the woman who killed one child caused the grief of the one who killed two children to flare up.

BINDU: It's her fear that removed my fear; it's her cowardice that gave me courage.

MOTHER: It's precisely for this reason that the authorities don't let her come anywhere near this hospital.

BINDU: The hospital people should experience fear now – they who carry on conducting the test, after putting up the board saying, 'It Is a Punishable Offence to Carry Out Sex-determination Tests. That Test Is Not Done Here'.

MOTHER: The hospital she was taken to last time was sealed for that. Let's go. (*As parting words to the nurse*) Don't forget to invite us for your wedding, dear. If you wait to get married after the number of females comes down drastically, you'll be like the one who waited and waited for the hen to develop udders to drink milk from! And the number of the likes of her (*points to Bindu*) will keep rising.

NURSE: If one Bindu goes back, ten Bindus will come, auntie.

BINDU: Not that they'll come; they'll be brought hands and feet bound to abattoirs like this.

(*The doctor comes out from the interior. The receptionist stands up with extreme deference.*)

NURSE: Good evening, doctor.

DOCTOR: Are there any more patients? Didn't you say the last patient had left?

BINDU: Good evening, doctor. I was that last patient, Bindu Kumar.

DOCTOR: Didn't the nurse say that you had gone?

BINDU: Yes, doctor. As I was going out, I noticed a board. Suddenly a doubt rose in my mind. I came back to ask someone about it. It's my good fortune that I saw you, doctor.

DOCTOR: What's your doubt?

BINDU: The board says, 'It Is a Punishable Offence to Carry Out Sex-determination Tests. That Test Is Not Done Here'. Who'll be punished? Is it the patient? I thought I'll proceed after clearing this doubt.
DOCTOR: Isn't it enough that you can get the test done?
BINDU: No, I must feel reassured that I'll not be punished if I undergo this test. I want to make sure that I am not punished for doing this.
DOCTOR: What's your occupation?
BINDU: For the last two to three years, minding my child and undergoing abortions every now and then. I was a lecturer in a college earlier. I availed of long leave to look after my baby when she was born. Then the two consecutive abortions and related problems. I had to give up the job. My mother-in-law was summoned to take immediate action if it was found to be a female child this time, too.
DOCTOR: Didn't you say you didn't want the test today?
BINDU: Yes, I'm not feeling too well. I was on my way back home, thinking I'll return another day. It's then that I noticed the board. I came back in to ask someone whether I have to undergo punishment under the law for committing this offence. It's by God's grace that I met you here, doctor.
DOCTOR: You were not punished when you underwent abortion twice earlier. The same law is prevalent even now.
BINDU: I was not punished then. But I got to know that the hospital was punished.
MOTHER: She got the abortions done earlier in the Mahatma Gandhi Nursing Home. The authorities sealed it.
BINDU: Didn't you just say that the same law is prevalent?

(*As the doctor stands staring at them without replying, the same security man who had gone out earlier comes rushing in.*)

SECURITY MAN: What the hell have you done? You've ruined my job.
NURSE: What happened?
SECURITY MAN: That woman! That madcap is going around singing lullabies. You didn't let me chuck her out when I tried a little while ago. Didn't you lead her away, saying, 'I'll see her off?' and you made me stand here. These people are all witnesses to it.
NURSE: Yes, I led her away and made her go out. I did so because I thought you'd harm her if you were to forcibly expel her.
SECURITY MAN: Did you say you forced her to go out? And yet she has just gone over to the front of the operation theatre, sung the lullaby and raised a racket.
NURSE: I had taken her outside the gate and sent her off. She must have returned.
SECURITY MAN: After singing, she got inside the operation theatre. They chased her away. But she is here, somewhere. The superintendent sent word that I must trace her, throw her out and then report to him. I went about searching for her. She is not to be seen anywhere. Whenever she comes to the hospital, she ends up here, doesn't she?
NURSE: She didn't come here. Go to the wards and check.

(*The security man glares at her and then goes out.*)

NURSE (*to the doctor*): It was that woman who got the gender determination test done here and then underwent laparoscopy too. It was her first pregnancy.
DOCTOR: I know.
NURSE: She comes to the hospital now and then. Goes to the room she was admitted in, and also to the operation theatre. Sometimes, she comes over to this room; standing here, looking at the picture of these infants, she sings lullabies.

(*The 'mad woman' appears at this juncture. As she approaches, she keeps looking back in fear. Spotting the doctor, she stands flabbergasted.*)

Everyone's attention is centred on her. The 'mad woman' walks slowly back, in obvious fear, and disappears. The wail of an infant from afar. Everyone stands motionless, looking at the spot where she had been standing. The light fades.)

– *Translated from Malayalam by A.J. Thomas*

Omchery is the pen-name of Prof N.N. Pillai, who has written eight full-length plays and fifty-two one-act plays, including *The Deluge, God Gets It Wrong Again* and *The Temple Elephant*. The playwright, who is also the principal of PG College of Communication and Management, Bharatiya Vidya Bhavan, Delhi, has won several awards like the Kerala Sahitya Akademi Award and the Writers' Society of Kerala Award.

14 Sitrep Seventies

Hormis Tharakan

There is in the Police Department, as well as in the government in general, the practice of preparing and sending reports to keep superior officers apprised of significant developments. Usually, these are in the form of daily, weekly or monthly reports. In times of crises, however, situation reports, often by the hour, are called for. This Situation Report (Sitrep for short) that I now prepare is a rambling chronology of the events in the seventies of the last century, a period of crisis for me, my family, my village, my state and my country.

It is perhaps necessary to place the story in its proper context by introducing myself, my family and my village. I grew up in a village called Olavipe on the banks of the Kaithapuzha *kaayal*, the name given to the backwaters that stretch along the western shore of Pallipuram island from Arookutty at the southern edge of the city of Kochi to Chenganda, where it links up with the larger body of water known as the Vembanad *kaayal* near Kumarakom. There was no road access to the village until 1970, when my youngest brother Michael, then heading the All India Catholic University Federation, held a summer camp in our village, and students from all over India joined the endeavour of the villagers to make a long-held dream come true. Olavipe is the most beautiful place in the universe for me and my siblings. (Unfortunately, I am aware that some of those who married into the family, including my wife, do not share this rosy view of the village!) My ancestors are reputed to have settled down in this quasi-island to save themselves from the fury of Tipu Sultan. As the Sultan's army advanced, they escaped from their ancestral village of Pazhuvil near Pazhur in Thrissur district, carrying an ancient statue of St. Antony from the village church. Tradition says they dedicated the church they built in Thycattusserry (the larger village, now a panchayat, of which Olavipe forms a part) in 1791 to St. Antony and placed the statue in that church. It is still there. We celebrated the bicentenary of the church with great fanfare in 1991.

Fifteen years later, a young priest in charge of the parish decided that the church needed to be expanded to cater to the needs of the ever-expanding flock. Along with several others, I pleaded with him to resort to restoration rather than expansion. He went ahead with the expansion, and to his credit, it must be said that he managed to replicate the facade of the original church faithfully. However, some of the priceless murals on the ceiling of the church, including one depicting God the Father, have been lost for ever. I am told that it is extremely rare for God the Father to be depicted in churches, one famous exception being Michelangelo's depiction of the Creation on the ceiling of the Cappella Sistina in the Vatican. Besides, the less said about the huge pieces (presumably based on the principle that big is beautiful) that have replaced the graceful statues that adorned the side-altars, the better.

It is a pity that much of the heritage of the ancient Syrian Christian Church of Kerala is now threatened by the zeal displayed by parish priests and parishioners to pull down old churches and erect 'modern' churches in their place. The church at Udayamperur, where the historic Synod of Diamper took place in 1599, was pulled down some decades back. It was at this Synod that Archbishop Menezez of Goa imposed the rituals of the Latin Church on the followers of the Syrian Church, causing much resentment and a vertical split in the Kerala Church. A few months ago, there was a controversy over the proposed destruction of the twin churches of indeterminate antiquity at Ramapuram near Palai. I do not know where the matter stands now. The Chowara Church had a mural painting on its wall depicting Tipu's army in encampment near the church, obviously done by a contemporary artist who had seen the scene he had painted. This mural was destroyed during 'restoration work' and has been replaced by a copy. All this points to the need for priests to be educated on the importance of preservation of our heritage. I was heartened to find that the Pope himself has in his recent Apostolic Exhortation, 'Sacramentum Caritatis', referred to this issue, when he said, 'A solid knowledge of the history of sacred art can be advantageous for those responsible for commissioning artists and architects to create works of art for the liturgy. Consequently, it is essential that the education of Seminarians and priests include the study of art history, with reference to sacred buildings . . .'

I do not think that temples in Kerala face any such threat. However, I was sad to see that the exterior of an ancient mosque in Kodungalloor (believed to have been built by Malik bin Dinar on instructions from Cheraman Perumal), where Tipu Sultan himself had in all likelihood offered namaz, has been completely altered. (Mercifully, the government of Kerala has recently allocated Rs 50 crore for a project called the Muziris Heritage Project to preserve heritage sites around Kodungalloor.) Tipu Sultan and his father Hyder Ali are two names that hold a great deal of fascination for me. No two other princes of eighteenth century India offered the kind of resistance they did to the British. I have just finished reading two highly interesting books on them – *Haidar Ali And Tipu Sultan And The Struggle With The Musalman Powers Of The*

South by Lewin B. Bowring (first published by Oxford in 1899 and reprinted by Asia Educational Services in 1997) and *History Of Hyder Shah Alias Hyder Ali Khan Bahadur And Of His Son Tippoo Sultaun* by M.M.D.L.T., General in the Army of the Moghul Empire, revised and corrected by His Highness Prince Gholam Mohammed, the only surviving son of Tippoo Sultaun, (published originally by W.Thacker & Co., London in 1855 and reprinted by Asian Educational Services in 2001). The first part of the second book was written (though published much later) when Hyder Ali was still alive and about fifty-four to fifty-six years of age. I wish we knew more about the author who was probably French, because his animosity towards the English comes through quite clearly as does the fact that he knew Europe, particularly France, very well.

Hyder, though he conquered Malabar, chiefly by surprising and overawing the Nairs with his cavalry ('which was a body of troops absolutely unknown to the Nayres, no foreign army having penetrated as far as the Malabar Coast, where no horses had ever been seen . . .'), following which the King of Cochin also submitted to him, crossed neither Kodungalloor, which had a Dutch fort, nor the Travancore Lines. These defences known as Nedunkotta in Malayalam and Travancore Lines in English had been erected along the northern boundary of Cochin to protect both Travancore and Cochin by Raja Kesavadas (Diwan Kesava Pillai) of Travancore on land ceded by Cochin. The wisdom shown by Hyder in not trespassing into the backwater country was lost on Tipu. On 28 December 1789, Tipu's army under his personal command launched an attack on the Travancore Lines on the pretext that 'the Travancore Raja had erected the defences on the territory of his feudatory the Cochin Chief, aggravating the insult by purchasing from the Dutch the forts of Kranganur and Ayakota'. Tipu gained entry into a part of the ramparts, but the Travancore soldiers made a stand when they were forced back upon a strong position. In Lewin B. Bowring's words: 'The whole of Tipu's army was soon in precipitate flight, he himself being carried away by the rush.... The bearers of Tipu's palankeen were among the fallen, and he himself escaped with the greatest difficulty... In the hurly-burly, he lost his sword and shield, which were taken away to Trivandrum, the capital of Travancore.'

To the best of my knowledge, this significant victory is not recorded as such in the history books of Kerala and not celebrated by the people of Kerala as it should be. The reason may be that Tipu Sultan, smarting under the defeat he had sustained, ordered siege-guns to be despatched at once from Srirangapatnam, recommenced the attack, effected a breach after one month's sustained effort, laid waste the country with fire and sword and marched up to Aluva (Alwaye), which is the gateway to the urban conglomerate of today's Kochi. The rest of the story is perhaps best told in Bowring's own words: 'The Diwan, Kesava Pillai, had, however, strengthened the garrisons at the principal posts and constructed stockades along all the backwater-passages on the coast so as to intercept the progress of the enemy. In the meanwhile, the monsoon set in, and the whole country was soon under water, so that no communication could be maintained except through boats. Tipu, despairing of accomplishing his purpose under these adverse circumstances, and hearing that the English were assembling an army at Trichinopoli, was compelled to retreat to Palghat, losing a large number of men on his way. The local chronicler grandiloquently compares his abrupt departure with the disastrous withdrawal of Napoleon from Moscow.'

It is quite clear from the foregoing that the Travancore Army, by a clever utilisation of the natural defences of the country and through their own valour, defeated Tipu Sultan twice, the second time decisively. In this victory, the British did not play a major role, as is commonly believed. Bowring has recorded that though five English regiments were available in Ayacota belonging to the

Madras establishment, 'the vacillation of the Madras Government and want of enterprise on the part of the commanding officers themselves, prevented their cooperating with the Travancore troops in the defence' of the Travancore Lines. (However, the British under Col Hartley and Gen Abercromby did play a major role in freeing Malabar from Tipu's sway the very next year – 1790. But that did not help the Malayali. The British kept Malabar under their direct administration.) No wonder that a century and a half later, Commandant Barboza of the celebrated Malabar Special Police recorded as follows:

'While inclined to be impulsive and sensitive to a degree, alive to injury and prone to resent ill-treatment, whether fancied or real, the Malayali, agile, energetic and adventurous, with his inherent sense of cleanliness and neatness, and his native intelligence, makes, when properly treated and imbued with real sense of discipline and esprit-de-corps, an excellent soldier. Faithful, cheerful and readily willing, he is second to none in India.'

The point I am trying to make is that my ancestors were wise in seeking refuge in the backwater country, which Tipu could not penetrate. There, in the shade of the new St. Antony's Church, they prospered very fast, and by the middle of the nineteenth century, the Parayil family, which somewhere along the way picked up the title of 'Tharakan', had become the uncontested leaders of the Syrian Christian Catholic Church in Kerala (designated the Syro-Malabar Church by the Vatican). In that capacity, they led the fight for the liberation of that church from the domination of the Latin hierarchy, represented by the Goa-based Padroado bishops under Portuguese patronage and the Verapoly-based foreign bishops sent out by the Propaganda Fide in Rome. Even before the end of the eighteenth century, the family had funded the trip of Paremmakkil Thoma Kathanar (the Gobernador or Apostolic Administrator) to Rome, in a quest for indigenous bishops. The mission succeeded only partially (Bishop Joseph Kariattil, who was the Gobernador's travelling companion and was consecrated Archbishop of Kodungalloor by the Queen of Portugal with the approval of the Pope, died in Goa before he could get back to Kerala), but it led to the penning of the first travelogue in Malayalam. The original manuscript of the *Varthamana Pusthakam* written by the priest covering his journey to Rome was jealously guarded by the family for several generations until it was handed over to the newly created (2001) St. Thomas Museum in Kakkanad, Ernakulam, a few years ago.

In 1861, a bishop named Rokos was sent out to Kerala by the Chaldean Catholic Patriarch, Joseph VI Audo. Although he was not an indigenous bishop, he was considered a welcome alternative to the bishops sent out to rule the Kerala Church by the Padroado (Goa). Rokos was given a grand reception when he landed in Kochi and taken in a procession of boats to the St. Antony's Church in Thycattusserry where he took up residence under the patronage of the Parayil Tharakans. Rome was not amused and issued an edict condemning the 'Rokos Schism'. The venerated abbot of the Carmelite Order, Chavara Kuriakose Elias, who was a friend of the Parayil Tharakan who headed the revolt, seems to have helped protect him from the fury of Rome. In a few years' time, the Kerala Church was given two indigenous bishops, one of whom was the nephew of the Parayils, his mother being a Parayil. The Syro-Malabar Catholic Church is now recognised as a separate *sui generis* entity by the Vatican, an Arch-episcopate (second in status only to a Patriarchate), its head (normally a Cardinal) having the powers to lay down its own liturgical practices.

The significant contributions made by the family to the church, including setting up of schools and donation of the land on the Periyar on which the magnificent Mangalapuzha seminary stands, were recognised by the Vatican in 1881 by awarding two Parayil Tharakan brothers the title of the Grand Knight of the Order of

St. Gregory. They were also given the title of Marquis of Parayil. The Pope continued to grant titles of duke, marquis, etc., to a select few even after the loss of the Papal States in 1870. As per the Lateran Accord of 1929, the Pope's powers to grant titles were recognised by the Italian government and Papal titles were recognised as equivalent to Italian titles. A historic letter from Pope Leo XIII issued from the St. Peter's Palace in Rome on 12 February 1989, in which he addresses Parayil Varkey Tharakan as *Dilecto Filio Marchioni Georgio Parrai* (Dear son, Marquis George Parrai) is in the proud possession of the family.

I had an opportunity to look at the concerned file relating to this award in the Kerala State Archives a couple of decades back. The brothers had sought the permission of the state government to accept the honour. This was referred by the Diwan to the new British Resident, who seems to have gone to Ooty for a holiday immediately after taking up his new assignment. The Resident wanted to know who these Parayil Tharakans were. The Diwan informed him that the brothers were the patriarchs of the largest land-owning family in the state. The Resident declined permission to the brothers to accept honours sought to be conferred on them by a 'foreign power', i.e. the Vatican. The next sheet of paper available in the file is an invitation from the brothers to the Resident to attend the grand function in which the Papal heraldry was to be conferred on them! Obviously, the Parayil Tharakans did not care too much for the representative of Queen Victoria.

The oral tradition in the family says that one of the two ancestors who had been invested with the Papal honours equivalent to that of a Marquis was invited to the Maharaja's formal reception for the governor of Madras who was on a state visit to Trivandrum. He went for the reception wearing the insignia of his new title. The governor, finding himself outranked, refused to take his seat unless the Marquis was also given a seat of honour along with him and the Maharaja. The Maharaja is said to have asked my ancestor after the departure of the governor, 'My dear Kochu Varkey, why couldn't you tell me beforehand about your funny new title?' I did some research to verify this. The title of Marquis is ranked below that of Duke and above that of Earl. The governor of Madras at the time when the Tharakan brothers were invested with the title of Marquis was possibly Sir Montstuart Elphinstone Duff, who did not have a peerage. The story could, therefore, very well be true. However, to my chagrin, the research also revealed that the only privilege accorded to those admitted to the Order of St. Gregory, including the Grand Knights, was that they could ride through St. Peter's Basilica on horseback! I do not think the Marquis de Parayi ever exercised that privilege. A century later, I had the occasion to interact closely with Cardinal Lourduswamy, who was in charge of the Oriental Congregation at the Holy See. I wonder what his reaction would have been if I had asked him to let me ride through St. Peter's on behalf of my ancestors!

There was a Parayil Tharakan presence in every legislature in Travancore and later in Travancore-Cochin. It was perhaps because of this aspect of the family, viz., its display of social responsibility, that the Parayil Tharakans are not generally seen as having been responsible for the agrarian labour unrest that led to the Vayalar Uprising of 1945. (Vayalar is a mere ten kilometres away from our village.) My historian brother Michael tells me that this has been certified by no less a person than K.C. George, the undisputed leader of the uprising, who wrote in his book *Punnapra Vayalar* that though the Parayils were the biggest landlords in the area, they were not against the demands of the workers. In fact, there is even a novel based on the Vayalar Uprising, in which the heroine who gave shelter to many of those who fled after taking on the army at Vayalar was a Parayil Tharakan girl!

This was the family that I was born into in 1945. Before I reached my teens, a communist government had come to power in Kerala, the first time that the communists had come to power anywhere in the world through the ballot, except in the tiny Republic of San Marino tucked away between Ancona and Rimini in Italy. However, the times were still feudal. We lived in a huge fin-de-siecle mansion built by my grandfather, which continues to be the rallying point for the family till today. However, the enormous riches that the previous generations had enjoyed were gone with the wind, and at least our branch of the family found the going tough. But still, we had a certain sense of security that came from the land that we still possessed and the influence we still commanded in the village.

My father, an only son, had lost his father when he was seventeen. My grandfather who built the mansion where I was born had apparently overextended his resources in building what must have been a marvel in the village and its neighbourhood, and in establishing a zoo with the rarest of animals. My father spent practically his whole life in litigation, fighting cases that the liablities on the property compelled him to defend. Bringing up twelve children and supporting their studies resulted in father's financial resources getting whittled down considerably. In spite of that, he managed to send all of us who finished school before he died, to the best colleges in South India – the Loyola College in Chennai or the St. Joseph's College in Bangalore. He had, of course, realised that land no longer offered the security that it did in his generation.

Loyola was known for its strict administrative regime; consequently, its students were known as the 'slaves of Loyola' among their peers in the colleges of Madras University. But the college did instil in us a sense of perfection. Not even a fused bulb on the hostel corridors was left unattended to for more than an hour. However, the system of functioning in Loyola led to students tending to stick together on a regional or linguistic basis. The Malayalis stuck together and so did other ethnic groups. The fact that Loyola had six messes to cater to every South Indian state's culinary preferences, plus those of North India and Europe, helped consolidate these dividing lines. Things were different in Madras Christian College where I went to do my MA in Economics. The atmosphere was more relaxed, even laid back. There were three halls on the campus and a system that encouraged competition among the halls, which in turn helped to overcome ethnic divides. Over and above all, there were girls on the campus unlike in Loyola!

I spent seven long years in Madras, staying on after my MA to do a newly started course in the Catholic Centre on Armenian Street by my former principal in Loyola, Fr. Sequiera, meant to prepare Catholic students for the UPSC exams held every year for candidates seeking entry into the higher Civil Services. I made it to the Indian Police Service in 1968, and returned to Kerala after completing my training at the National Police Academy in Mount Abu, just as the seventies were dawning. It was on the first of January 1970, that the Kerala government under Chief Minister C. Achuta Menon introduced the historic land reforms that put an end to all sorts of landlordism in the state and placed a drastically low ceiling on land holdings. The reforms also provided for ten cents of land to be given to every landless *kudikidappukaran* (serf). These reforms had a dramatic impact on the land-based relationships in Kerala. Several Namboodiri families that owned hundreds of acres of land which had been leased out on 'pattam' lost all those holdings overnight. Others also lost land in considerable degrees because of the low ceilings. All of a sudden, lakhs of kudikidappukars became proud owners of ten cents of land each. It was almost as if the stirring lyrics of a revolutionary song of the fifties had become a reality: *The fields that we harvest for our landlord will one day become our own.* To all intents and purposes, the death-knell of feudalism in Kerala was sounded that day. We handed over on the new year's day itself our excess land and the ten cents that we had to give to each of the not inconsiderable number of people living on our lands as kudikidappukars. In doing so we had to incur the ire of several who had decided to hold out and fight to the finish. However, all of them had to fall in line in due course. Many of us who lost land as a result of the land reforms of 1970 thought the legislation unreasonable and unfair. However, looking back after so many years, I have no doubt that these drastic measures prevented a Naxalite takeover in Kerala

In fact, the Naxalite movement was gaining considerable momentum as the seventies dawned. The agrarian revolution that started in Naxalbari on the West Bengal-Nepal border spread rapidly to other states, including Kerala. The first major action by the Naxalites in Kerala was the attack on Tellicherry and Pulpally police stations in November 1968, the month I joined the police. The involvement of Kunnickal Narayanan's family, including his young daughter Ajita and wife Mandakini, in such major actions stunned the general public. These attacks were followed in 1970 by targeted killings of landlords in various parts of the state, ranging from Nagaroor in the south to Tirunelly in the north. Names of Naxalite leaders like Philip M. Prasad and Verghese who organised tribals in Wynad caused dread amongst the landed gentry. There was a sense of panic and insecurity all over the state. There was pressure on the police from the government, the public and the media alike to produce results. Every successful police action against the Naxalites was extolled by the press. By the end of 1970, the phenomenon seemed to be under control, with most of the Naxalite modules busted and leaders like Verghese eliminated. There was a general sense of relief and the media was profuse in its praise for the police. All this was to change before the 1970s were over.

My first exposure to the Naxalite movement took place when, on the morning of 31 July 1970, I was informed that Kongad

Narayanan Nair, a landlord, had been killed by Naxalites the previous night. His head had been severed and placed on the parapet of the family pond. The dead man was closely related to a very senior officer in Kerala Police. It was clear that the killing was meant to be a chilling warning to the Kerala Police and to the bourgeoisie whom the Naxalites believed the police were supporting. There was panic in Kerala society as a result of this murder as well as a series of other similar killings attributed to or claimed by the Naxalites.

Balagangadhara Menon, a seasoned officer from the pre-Independence Cochin Police, who probably had some experience dealing with the Edapally Police Station attack carried out by the Communists in the early fifties, was my Superintendent of Police (SP). I reported to him in Kongad, although being a probationer on practical training I had no direct responsibility for the investigation of this gruesome murder. For the next few months, my regular training schedule was given a go-by as I plunged headlong into the investigation on the direction of my SP. Being a bachelor I had all the time in the world to spare and I had the opportunity to drink in as much excitement as a young police officer could ever hope to.

On the first day of investigations, I was sent to follow the trail of the killers. The murder had happened on the night of the thirtieth, shortly after the family members had their dinner. The man was simply taken out and killed. The remaining family members were tied up at the time, but they could give us a graphic description of the attack and the number of accused involved, whom we judged to be around twenty. The tracking dogs of the Kerala Police led us cross-country from Kongad to Pathiripala on the Palakkad-Ottappalam road, a good ten kilometres away. It was raining heavily, being the peak of the rainy season, and all of us—my men, the dogs and I—were equally and thoroughly drenched. They say in the Sardar Vallabhai Patel National Police

Academy, where IPS officers are trained, that you do not become an officer until you walk with your men when it rains. Maybe I became an officer that day.

The landscape that we walked through was stunningly green and lovely. As the unknown poet quoted by M. Hammick to describe the travels of Col. Marks Wilks through the kingdom of Mysore said:

> *The mountains wooded to the peak, the lawns*
> *And winding glades high up like ways to Heaven,*
> *The slender coco's drooping crown of plumes,*
> *The lightning flash of insect and of bird,*
> *The lustre of the long convolvoluses*
> *That coiled round the stately stems, and ran*
> *Ev'n to the limit of the land, the glows*
> *And glories of the broad belt of the world,*
> *All these he saw.*

The term 'mountains' is perhaps inappropriate for Mysore as well as Malabar, but the hillocks that we passed were equally glorious. The dogs stopped by a huge overflowing pond somewhere along the way and started barking. It took us several days in the pouring rain to drain out the water from the pond. Meanwhile, some of the accused who were arrested confessed that the weapons had been disposed off in the pond. Sure enough, we found the weapons that were used to kill Narayanankutty Nair at Kongad on the bed of this pond set in beautiful surroundings. The dogs of the Kerala Police had done their bit to help unravel yet another sensational case.

At the end of that first day, when we returned from Pathiripala, however, we did not know that the dogs had correctly identified the place where the weapons had been disposed of and that, therefore, we had achieved a significant breakthrough. We felt we were returning empty-handed, without having apprehended any of the accused. Early next morning, I was deputed to lead an expedition to look for Naxalites in the hills and jungles above Mannarghat that led up to the Nilgiris range. My SP had received reports that suspicious movements had been noticed in the hills. I had a platoon of men from the Malabar Special Police armed with .303 rifles.

We entered the jungle and started climbing from a point on the Mundur-Mannarghat road. Our guides were forest guards familiar with the terrain. They were very good, but their concept of distances in the forest differed considerably from ours. Locations they said were close by turned out to be several hours of walk away! We had our share of thrills during that day's search but had to return empty-handed once again. The thrills included the storming of a cave in Mookkuthimala, where we found clear evidence of very recent human presence, but no one to be apprehended. At another location, our guides spotted a group of men coming downhill camouflaging their movements. We took positions, only to be disappointed to discover they were bootleggers carrying illicit liquor produced clandestinely in the hilly terrain for delivery in the plains. Having moved at short notice, we had not carried the necessary wherewithal to stay overnight in the jungles. We, therefore, had to return to base camp before nightfall. Leeches were aplenty in the jungle in the rainy season. We had carried with us tobacco leaves, which are effective in clearing off leeches from your legs. However, towards late afternoon we found we had to move very fast to get back before it got too dark and, therefore, could not stop to clear the leeches clinging to our skin. And then we came across elephant droppings that were still warm. The guides informed us there was a herd of elephants very close by. We were not carrying the .375 Magnum, which is known as the Elephant Gun, but were confident, on the strength of our .303 guns, of stopping any herd of elephants that got in our way though we would have hated to use the rifles on the pachyderms or for that matter the absconding accused unless they tried to kill us. In the event, we did not come across any and I presented myself before my SP late at night to file an unexciting report.

The next day, detective inspector Gopala Menon of the crime branch, who had been deputed to assist the investigators, saw my feet ravaged by leeches and remarked, 'Let your mother not see this.' In fact, my mother was staying with me for a few days in Palakkad and did get to see my feet when I returned home late that night; she took it in her stride. She was a remarkable and hardy woman from Palai in the foothills of the Poonjar Ranges and was the daughter of the legendary Kallivayalil Papen; no one in his generation knew the hills of Travancore and Malabar better than he did. I remember telling Ichachen, as we used to call our grandfather, when I visited him during our half-yearly break in police training, about learning to ride. To my surprise, Ichachen asked if I had learnt to gallop! I had not. He went on to tell me how the gallop was the most exciting part of horse-riding. He had bought a horse from a police inspector in his youth and used to ride all the way from Vilakkumadom, where he lived, to Peruvanthanam on the Kotayam-Kumili Road, where he had his extensive estates. Ever since we could remember, he had a stately Chrysler, which we children thought the most superb automobile in the world. We daydreamed of Ichachen permitting us to drive it. Ichachen fell seriously ill the day I got engaged to Molly in February 1972 and died a few days later.

While we were looking for them in the hills and jungles, the Naxalites were actually moving about in the plains, losing themselves amongst the crowds in the small towns of Malabar. I was told that the real breakthrough in the investigation came when an MSP inspector heading a night patrol party came across a person sleeping in the open in a suburb of Palakkad town and routinely asked him why he was not spending the night at home.

It so happened that he had been part of the group that carried out the attack – in fact, the weakest link in the group. He was a head-load worker if I remember correctly, not ideologically committed to the cause, but who went along having been persuaded by one of his acquaintances, an active Naxalite. He broke down on being confronted by the inspector and told him that he would come out with the whole truth if he was not physically harmed. He gave the investigators a vivid account of how the crime was committed and furnished the names of those accused known to him. Thereafter, the hunt became easier, and one by one, almost all the accused, including Mundur Ravunny the mastermind, were arrested and prosecuted successfully.

This is how investigations often work out. A lot of hard work is put in by the investigators in pursuance of various leads without any concrete returns. Then suddenly, a lucky break takes place in a totally different direction without any great effort on the part of the investigators and everything falls into place. Investigation is often a frustrating and tedious affair. That lucky break does not happen in every case. Those cases that remain unsolved are confined to the dustbins of history and the unsuccessful investigator does not get any credit despite the fact that he may have put in as much or even more effort than the successful investigator.

The Kongad case taught me a great deal about police and policing. Although the investigation of the case was done by the district police under the able leadership of the SP, Balagangadhara Menon, two officers of the crime branch had been deputed by the police headquarters to assist the investigators. One of them was Inspector Gopala Menon, whom I have already mentioned. The other was Deputy Superintendent of Police, Muraleekrishna Das.

I met this man at the beginning of my career and since then, he has forever remained in my memory as belonging to a rare breed of police officers. Soft-spoken and gentle, he had already acquired a great reputation as an expert on Naxalism. He had a phenomenal knowledge of the Naxalite movement and of Naxalite leaders. In fact, I sometimes felt, while sitting with him as he spoke to detained Naxalites, that he knew more about the movement and its ideology than they themselves did.

Mundur Ravunny was the leader of the team that carried out the Kongad attack. He was a committed Naxalite leader who could perhaps be rated along with Kanu Sanyal and Charu Majumdar among the most prominent leaders of the Naxalite movement that swept many parts of India in the late sixties and early seventies. He and Das got along famously and it was a pleasure listening to their ideological debates at the MSP camp at Mangattuparamba near Palakkad where the investigation team was based. Das did not believe in third-degree methods. To a probationary officer on practical training, watching DySP Das at work was a refreshing change and practical guidance in the right direction. His interrogation consisted of carrying out a discussion, sometimes on the intellectual plane, with the accused/suspect. It was surprising how he used to extract a great deal of information that way. Perhaps the Naxalites hoped to influence and brainwash investigators by explaining their beliefs and principles in detail, which made them forthcoming in response to Das' searching queries. At the end of the day (which more often than not happened late into the night), Das would go around instructing the police guards that no Naxalite detainee, accused or suspect, should be touched. I was very sorry when this gem of an officer, who was called back from retirement to investigate the Kayanna Police Station attack, was arrested on murder charges in the infamous Rajan case. He was later acquitted. I was in Thiruvananthapuram when he passed away a few years back; I had the honour to place a wreath on his body.

The Rajan case had its origins in a Naxalite attack that took place during the Emergency period on the Kayanna Police Station in Kozhikode district. During the investigation, an arrested accused managed to set fire to the police jeep in which he was being transported, killing a DySP and inflicting serious burn injuries on an inspector. Several students, mainly from the Regional Engineeering College in Chathamangalam, were picked up by the police in this connection and questioned. One of them, Rajan, is believed to have died in police custody while under interrogation in a police camp at a place called Kakkayam. The body was never found. However, on a habeas corpus petition filed by Rajan's father, Eachara Warrier, Justice Subramanyam Potti of the Kerala High Court ordered that a case be registered and investigated against DIGs of police Jairam Padikkal, Madhusoodanan and others. Rajagopal Narayan, an exceptionally correct officer, later to become director general of police in Kerala, was put in charge of the investigation. He arrested the two DIGs and SPs, Lakshmana and Muraleekrishna Das, apart from several other police officers of various ranks. K. Karunakaran, who was home minister at the time of the Kayanna Police Station attack and subsequent investigations but had since then become chief minister, had to resign. Both he and Jairam Padikkal became immensely unpopular. Until then, Padikkal had a high reputation in the state as the best investigator in Kerala Police. He was the darling of the press. Overnight, he became a villain and his family was ostracised. They had to shift from Trivandrum to Ernakulam for the sake of safety.

For us police officers of Kerala, this was a most incongruous and difficult situation. The investigator and the investigated in this case were senior colleagues well known to us. So were their families. Most officers chose to distance themselves from the now disgraced officers lodged in the district jail in Kozhikode. I was by now on deputation with the union government, but posted in Cochin. I, therefore, had less reason to be concerned about the possible disapprobation of the state government if I interacted with the arrested officers. I consulted my wife. Though neither of us is particularly devout, she drew my attention to one of the most moving passages in the Bible, ending: 'When I was lonely, you kept me company; when I was in prison, you came to see me; now I welcome you into the home of my Father.'

I went and saw them in prison. It was a most pathetic experience though all of them tried to put up a brave front. I asked them if there was anything I could do for the families. Padikkal told me that his young son who had a serious problem of vision impairment had to have monthly eye-tests at a particular hospital in Trivandrum but was unable to travel because of the uncertain security situation. I promised him I would take care of the boy's travel from Ernakulam to Trivandrum. I was to go to Trivandrum the next week with my wife and mother. We took Mrs Padikkal and her son along in my personal car to Trivandrum. On the way, near Alapuzha, huge crowds of agitating students were stopping all passing cars. They wanted us to shout, 'Hang Karunakaran. Hang Padikkal'. I rolled down my window glass and asked them, 'Why not crucify them?' The sarcasm in my voice fortunately escaped the students and they allowed us through. I did not have the heart to look back at the lady and her son. Nor did I stop to think what would have happened if the crowd had recognised her in the backseat.

Yet another sensational case of the seventies was the one related to the killing of Verghese, a Naxalite leader who was at once much loved and much feared. The case is now subjudice and I shall, therefore, desist from commenting on it except to say that among those standing trial in this case is the eighty-four year old former director general of police in Kerala, Vijayan. He was the DIG of the Northern Range based in Calicut when I started my career in Palakkad which was under his jurisdiction in 1970. He was a caring, mild and friendly superior officer. A renowned sportsman in his youth, he now tries gamely to retain his spirit despite the misfortunes that have befallen him in his old age. But I know that the spring in his gait is gone. His wife, Thangam, walks in beauty and grace beside him as they endeavour to cope with the vicissitudes of life.

All this makes me reflect. I who started my career as a young police officer in Kerala in the incipient years of the decade of the seventies, full of hopes, full of dreams, am now retired and in a position to put my feet up and introspect. I wonder if any other decade in the recent past has borne witness to momentous events of the kind that happened in the 1970s – mind-boggling occurrences that shook the state and the nation, including the rise, fall and return of Indira Gandhi. No other generation of police officers, except those who were in service during the seventies, is likely (one hopes) to see the declaration of a national emergency. As these developments took place on the national scene, there were parallel and equally incredible developments in Kerala – the fall of titans like Karunakaran and of officers whom we young police officers considered icons. In the realm of our minds, the concepts of honour, valour, success and failure underwent paradigm shifts.

Where did we in the Kerala Police go so wrong that by the end of the decade many of our colleagues and seniors were in the dock? Hugh Trevor-Roper says in his study of Archbishop Laud—the all-powerful Archbishop of Canterbury under Charles I of England who was thrown out of power and executed on Tower Hill in 1645, and who continues to be a controversial figure in history, denounced or extolled according to the political persuasions of the biographers—that he was driven by a rigid social ideal obscured by human limitations which proved fatal to it (*Archbishop Laud*, Hugh Trevor-Roper, Phoenix Press). Is that what happened to us in the Kerala Police?

I am aware that there were people my age, like Ravunny, who had a different set of dreams in the seventies, perhaps a different set of ideals, who heard the spring thunder reverberating in the hills and plains of my state, my country. Muraleekrishna Das taught me to respect the revolutionary. There is a spark of virtue in every revolutionary, he told me, the urge to do good, the determination to fight perceived injustice. Unfortunately, the revolutionary does not believe that the law is adequate for impartial dispensation of justice and hence resorts to extra-legal methods, fully convinced that what he is doing is for the good of the people. In the ultimate analysis, however, is this not exactly what the policeman assigned the task of combating the revolutionary also does? Is the policeman also not convinced that the laws are inadequate for bringing the revolutionary to book? Does he also not resort to extra-legal measures, fully convinced that what he is doing is for the good of the people?

Sitting by the west waters of Olavipe, watching the sun set over the Kaithapuzha *kaayal* and ruminating over events long past but equally relevant today, this old cop tells himself – there are no easy answers.

Hormis Tharakan was Director General of Kerala Police before he took over as Secretary (R) in the Cabinet Secretariat, Government of India, in 2005. After his retirement in 2007, he was advisor to the Second Administrative Reforms Commission, Government of India, and later advisor to the governor of Karnataka when the state was placed under president's rule. He writes on strategic issues and police reforms and is currently engaged in setting up an institution for research into aspects of national security.

15 Fort Lines

Shreekumar Varma

There's an old saying in our family – 'In a vast jungle of circular paths, a hunter goes round in circles, while another finds new pathways, discarding old weapons for new – such is life!'

It originated from an uncle named Kunjunny Raja who lived three or four generations before my mother. He goes on to explain, 'Life is a series of circular paths; when you've completed one, another opens out and you're free to start from scratch.'

It presents a reassuring picture of life. When the time comes, you can always make a fresh start, stepping on to a different circle, armed with new choices.

Kunjunny Raja's life was a bag of intrigues and liaisons. A widely acknowledged poet during the mid-1800s, he used the pen-name 'Mahabali' and coined many aphorisms to explain himself. We now live in the house he built. It is close to the city's heart, though most of its rooms are kept shut in keeping with our less colourful lifestyle.

I sometimes think we're the same, he and I; we differ only in the language of our utterance.

The new dawn breaks on the concentric streets within the Fort. The temple complex is a vast matrix in the middle. Here, everything is touched by the temple in one way or the other. Brahmin housewives wake up early, washing slimy stretches of street beyond their front-doors and possessively patterning them with curling white *kolam* designs. They work silently, with a street artist's focus, as though anchoring the rising day to the damp ground.

Tea stalls have grumbled into wakefulness, sleepy boys pulling out and arranging wooden benches that were packed in just a few hours ago. Soon kettles of boiling water, jars of savouries and sweets appear amidst the smell of tea and kerosene smoke. A few men have already begun to walk their bicycles. I'm up with them for a change.

Going to the Shri Padmanabhaswamy temple is a morning ritual for those who live in the walled Fort Area. Not for me generally, but today's different. This is the first anniversary of my walking a different path, the 'normal life', as my mother puts it.

I gulp down my coffee, hurry through a shivering bath and manage to get out of the house before six. 'Pray well. You need all the blessings you can get. He won't let you down.' My mother looks fresh and tired, oiled grey hair in place with a sprig of tulsi tucked in above her ear, circles under her eyes, a tiny frown and an abstract smile.

I have to run. After seven, the general public must wait until after the Maharaja has worshipped and left.

There is a small group, a knot of devotion in a corner of the vast temple grounds. The early worshippers are mostly from our neighbourhood. We keep together, all bathed and silent with devotion, moving from shrine to shrine, throwing our hearts out at the main sanctum where He lies, grandly visible through three doors – head and outstretched arm, middle and feet. An old man with a dyed beard sighs loudly – 'Narayana!' A woman chants in a sing-song voice. There is the smell of cool freshness and oil spilt on ancient stone.

I shut my eyes, praying with the weight of a year behind my words. I don't expect miracles, only what I deserve. 'Today's the day,' I tell Him until a guard informs us it's time to leave.

The rest is in my hands.

My father is a double-worker. Many people in government service have that luxury – drawing wages from two or more sources. He teaches maths in the Poojapura Higher Secondary School, but often takes long leave to work as a conductor on private bus routes between Thiruvananthapuram and nearby towns. He says a conductor's job isn't different from a schoolmaster's – guiding and escorting people to their destination.

My mother doesn't see it that way. 'Teaching is a full-time job, it's a service. You shouldn't cheat children!'

If my father is in the mood, he takes the issue to its logical conclusion – 'When your highness stepped down to marry a penniless Menon, you should have thought of the consequences. And foregoing the family share for this ugly, ramshackle house! So much space. Unfortunately, that means more maintenance. If you stop being sentimental and agree to sell it, we'd be rolling in money. If you agree to let out a few rooms, I can retire and live as a landlord. But in the present circumstances I need all the jobs I get. I can't be worried about students losing a few hours of maths . . .'

If my mother is also in the mood, the argument takes wing and I leave the house to attend to my own affairs. Each generation has its own war to wage.

Instead of being sleepy, I'm fresh and alert. I try to brush up, somehow spending an hour in my room. I've spent a whole year preparing for today. It's burdensome, sacrificing a year for a day.

My mother will realise her dream if I do well today. No one we know has got into the IAS. 'Put your heart into it. You're sharp, I know you can do it.' She repeated this all year, placing her mission in my lap.

But I'm walking a tightrope. This is my last chance. If I don't make it today, I never will. Next year I'll be too old for the exam. I've arrived late at the starting line, skipping the heats. It's up to me now, inexperienced but ready, untested but sure. I shouldn't have to look back on the year in regret.

At breakfast, both are uneasily sure of my success.

'Whatever you do,' my father tells his plate of idlis, 'do it with conviction and it will get you through.' When my mother starts coughing, his concern shifts. 'Don't you have a check-up today? How will you go? I must sign in at the school at least today. It's been over three months.'

'I can't come either,' I add unnecessarily.

She shakes her head in mock despair. 'As if this is the most important thing! It's just a routine check-up. I'll go with next-door Ammini. I've been going to K-CERAS for the past three years.'

'If you can postpone it by a day . . .' I begin.

'You think I'm a child? It's just a question of catching a bus and going.' With that, she dismisses the subject.

In the vacuum that follows, my father clears his throat, looking at the wall behind me. 'It's time you returned to the proper route.' He drains his coffee with an appreciative sound.

'He's right. Until now you lived for strangers, forgetting your own life, forgetting us.' She comes up and strokes my head, her hand smelling of coconut oil and green chillies. 'You earned the curses of a lot of people. You must turn that into goodwill.'

A hunter goes round in circles, while another finds new pathways, adds Mahabali in a ghostly aside.

The hartal changed my life.

A year ago, just past nine, a time when the city is blinkered and traffic mad, and nothing can stop the flow. I was leading a mixed bunch of students and professional goons, cutting the flow with deadly efficiency, road after road. We were in a central place, the looming white Secretariat building in front, hotels, shops and offices behind, the bus terminus not far away. Only government buses were running.

Some of the goons had cycle chains slung over their shoulders casually, just for immediate impact. One of the students carried a hockey stick for the same reason. The cops had been advised to stay away for the first half-hour.

It's a different feeling; you sit in a theatre watching the hero bash up a dozen thugs. You hear the sound of his blows and the cries of his foes, and you feel the adrenalin flow and your breath catches – see how everyone respects him terribly after that!

My name is Jayesh, and it signifies victory.

Watch the buses emptying, auto-rickshaws scurrying away, fear on the faces of those college girls. Kerala is used to spread-out strikes. Everyone is prepared. They know when to ignore the call and when to take it seriously and do the disappearing act. When news cameras come out to record the result, they're supposed to find empty streets and 'cooperative citizens' huddled away. That's how our politics redeems itself.

The third bus we stopped before the Secretariat proved to be my undoing. We were progressing well until then. I've learnt the fine art of deafening myself. As usual, passengers came with their plaints. I remember a girl almost falling at my feet; her parents had wasted the academic year pushing her into a TV reality show, hoping to hear her sing in films. If she didn't reach the studio on time, she might as well be dead. 'Take an auto,' I advised her. But, of course, there were no autos on the road.

During the early years, I sympathised. Sometimes I paused midway through my aggression and listened. Now I know life goes on. We do our best, and they do theirs; tough luck to the ones who buckle first. But the tables turned that morning. How was I to know? If you believe in fate and the hand of God and the jungle of circular pathways patented by poet Mahabali, then this was the working of one of them – or all.

I stormed in and found my mother in the last row of the bus, looking helpless in the chaos. We saw each other in the same second. The air sizzled with the electricity of our silent contact, but amidst all the shouting, no one noticed. I backed away.

I turned my attention to the bus behind, waving this one away. The youngsters and goons were stunned. Some of them tried to badger me, but they knew my clout. I made it known that I didn't have to explain myself. Merely a month ago, I had lectured them, 'When it comes to the crunch, ignore parents, teachers, relatives and friends. Stand up for the cause!'

It wasn't my fault, it was hers. I had a rule that I'd keep my activism beyond the Fort Area, never crossing the lines. Why had she ventured out like that? I can face just about anyone else. I don't know if it's emotional weakness or moral strength; for her I redefined myself.

My mother gave me a couple of days to begin preparations. 'I want you to devote yourself to *me* from today.' As simple as that.

The bus trundles past the Fort Lines, throwing the sun in my face.

2.

Scene One

A hospital waiting area, shabby walls, lines of dull-looking patients. Prashant, a tall, earnest-looking youngster stands by a sign that says K-CERAS in bold letters and 'Kerala Centre for Education, Research & Sciences' in smaller letters.

Jayesh, a short, stocky young man, enters, looking agitated.

JAYESH: Where's she?
PRASHANT: No need to panic.

JAYESH (*aggressively*): Where's she?
PRASHANT: In the ICU. Where are you going?
JAYESH: I must see her!
PRASHANT: I'm a rep, I know the doctors here. She'll get good care.
JAYESH: Who's the chief? Let me talk to him!
PRASHANT: Visiting time is after four. I'll arrange a pass and you can see her through the glass. Right now, I'm waiting for the doctor's call. He'll give us the exact position.
JAYESH (*long pause*): She just came for a check-up.
PRASHANT: She fainted in the waiting room. I recognised her at once. Later, when I told her we used to be classmates, she insisted I shouldn't disturb you because of your IAS entrance.
JAYESH: You told me the doctor said it was serious.
PRASHANT: That's why I called you. Don't look so depressed. Let's hear what he says.
JAYESH: Where's that girl she came with?
PRASHANT: She's up there. They only give one pass.
JAYESH: Then get it for me!
PRASHANT: And when the doctor calls?
JAYESH: *Naasham*, I have my exam. (*Consults his watch*) In ten minutes! I can go now and get back by visiting time.
PRASHANT: You decide which is more important.
JAYESH: *Naasham*!
PRASHANT: Don't get tense. We'll wait in that tea shop until he calls. Come.

Scene Two

A small tea shop near the hospital. Jayesh and Prashant sit on benches facing each other. Both look uneasy.

PRASHANT: Maybe there's nothing wrong with her. (*Pause*) Learn to count your blessings.

JAYESH: What's that supposed to mean?
PRASHANT: What if I hadn't been around? You'd be sitting there writing your exam, with her in the ICU.
JAYESH (*intensely*): I should have gone ahead and written it. What a bloody waste!
PRASHANT: Your mother told me it's your last chance. Bad luck! (*Longer pause*) By the way, you know we're related?
JAYESH (*in disbelief*): You and me?
PRASHANT: Mahabali married twice. His first wife didn't have children. We're the second wife's descendants.
JAYESH: Granduncle Kunjunny!
PRASHANT: Grandfather, in my case. But his family didn't approve of her, so she was relegated to the wings. Just as it happened in your mother's case. (*Grins companionably at Jayesh*) When I helped your mother today, I was also helping my aunt. Isn't that funny?
JAYESH: That's funny, you as a cousin.
PRASHANT: I didn't know all this when we met on that famous day last year.
JAYESH: When was that?
PRASHANT: Remember the ANPUC hartal, how you pulled us out of the bus? There was a ghost sitting there, watching all of us.
JAYESH: Ghost? You crazy or what?
PRASHANT: Your mother dragged you back to reality that day. And the ghost has set the balance right. (*Jayesh looks irritated*) You were the author of several stories that day. You emptied half the bus and let the other half go. Just because your mother was on that bus.
JAYESH: Nonsense!
PRASHANT: Yes, it is. You can't do things like that. One rule for yourself and another for others. There were people who had urgent things to do. You just let them suffer.

JAYESH (*with hostility*): Don't bring that up...
PRASHANT: Why not? I was in the bus that day with my father. You threw us out. He was suffering a bad asthma attack. All the autos and cabs were off the road because of you. And when we took a state transport bus, you threw us out!
JAYESH: What happened to your father?
PRASHANT: Good of you to ask. He survived. Luck was on our side. A doctor driving out of a hotel near the bus-stop saw us and gave us a lift to the hospital.
JAYESH (*after a pause*): Anyway, I'm sorry...
PRASHANT: I should thank you, actually. That hospital was *this* hospital.
JAYESH: So?
PRASHANT: He took a liking to my father. He's the one who got me this rep's job. So if you hadn't stopped the bus...
JAYESH (*beginning to grin*): So something good came of it.
PRASHANT: Yes, I got a job, my father met a doctor who could finally control his asthma and your mother showed you the right path.
JAYESH: How the hell do you know that?
PRASHANT: Are you wondering why I went and saved your mother's life today? You threw my father out and I took your mother in. That's not poetic justice, is it?
JAYESH: But you got the job.
PRASHANT: Yes, I did. But how many people *didn't*, you know that? They begged and grovelled, and you simply turned away. That shouldn't happen.
JAYESH: Don't start preaching...
PRASHANT (*tightly*): More than you, I blame the state. It simply stands and watches! Watches while its own politics sponsors the disintegration of our education! It's not fair. Boys and girls are running around madly, grabbing at anything – even TV reality shows, if that gives them a key to success. They join parallel

colleges, crammed into unholy spaces because regular colleges are closed due to strikes.

JAYESH: Don't lecture me.

PRASHANT: They spend years notching up song and dance points at youth festivals because it gets them valuable pass-marks. Haven't you seen parents fighting bitterly over their children's points? They sue the authorities for higher points. That's how it's become. Name another state like this! No, it happens in the most literate state. It happens in the state most politically aware, where activism and concern for the masses are at their height. (*Pause*) It's all because of people like you! (*His voice rises.*)

JAYESH (*looking around*): That's enough.

PRASHANT: Don't like it, do you? You feel small and unmanly. And yet you kill the heroism of so many brave students when you drag them out of buses. You and your gangs! You people can only operate in numbers.

JAYESH (*noisily pushing back his chair*): I'm off! Let me know when the doctor calls.

PRASHANT: One final word. In memory of Kunjunny Raja, our common ancestor . . .

JAYESH: What's he got to do with it?

PRASHANT: Some of his children's children were revolutionaries. I grew up listening to stories of their passion and zeal. Now that revolution is like a set of deflated tyres; won't get us anywhere. When those people fought for a classless society, they didn't mean a society without classrooms. My childhood dreams haven't been vindicated, Jayesh, because of people like you! (*Jayesh gets up*) You helped my father in a way, so I helped your mother today. Don't worry, there's nothing wrong with her. The doctor's already given his verdict.

JAYESH: Where is she?

PRASHANT: Not in the ICU. She must have reached home by now.

JAYESH (*angrily*): So you deliberately...
PRASHANT: Don't blame me. Think of the people you deprived. How can you play the villain out there and then come home and be a good little boy, writing your IAS to fulfil your parents' wishes? Young people are killing themselves because their studies were nipped in the bud. (*Jayesh pulls back his arm as if to hit him*) If you're going to start a new life, might as well start with a new page. (*Jayesh stops and stands staring at him*) Here's something from our poet Mahabali. Let him have the last word as usual. (*Recites theatrically*)

> Like pregnant clouds that circle the sky seeking deliverance,
> we roam the earth, casting off sins, acquiring others,
> yearning to unburden ourselves!

Lights out. Curtain.

Chennai-based playwright and novelist **Shreekumar Varma** has written the award-winning plays *The Dark Lord* and *Bow Of Rama*, and novels *Lament Of Mohini* and *Maria's Room*, which was longlisted for the Man Asian Literary Prize 2007. He is an adjunct professor of Creative English at the Chennai Mathematical Institute.

16 Chinese Takeaway

M.V. Rappai

Even a casual visitor to Kerala cannot miss the static fish-nets hoisted on sturdy wooden structures along its coast. These fish-nets, known locally as *cheenawala* (Chinese nets), are proof of a long tradition of trade with China and the world in the past. However, these nets only partially reveal Kerala's role in ancient global trade. Historically, this type of static fish-nets became prominent only in the fifteenth century AD after Zheng He from China visited the Kerala coast. Yet, the story of Kerala trade dates back to the Old Testament period.

Some of the old Biblical stories refer to two or more spices available in present-day Kerala, further proving that in ancient times the Jews, Greeks, Romans, Chinese and Arabs were familiar with trade here, linking these ancient civilisations to the South Indian coastal trading ports.

Take the contemporary cultural and culinary traditions of Kerala for instance. The area of Kerala as we know it today, even though it remained a part of the Indian subcontinent and closely linked to its cultural traditions, always kept a separate identity of its own in different ways; this is true of its culture, food habits, etc. This may be largely due to the peculiar geographical features of Kerala, which is a comparatively narrow stretch of land mass bordered by sea on the western coast and mountain ranges on the east.

Traditionally, Indians are not well-known for keeping historical records, a fact that also restricts us from hazarding a knowledgeable guess about Kerala's ancient history. Yet, evidence in the form of inscriptions, travel accounts, cultural and traditional accounts of its people are still available. Known resources show that this coastal land played a key role not only in trade relations but also in the religious and cultural traditions of great ancient civilisations. From ancient China to Greece and to Rome, this coast played a pivotal role. Ports of ancient southern India along Kerala (the modern name of Kerala is knowingly used here; this place was known by different terms like Malabar Coast etc.) were significant as they served as an exchange venue for traders coming from various parts of the world. Therefore, these regions of the Indian subcontinent helped in facilitating trade with ancient China, and therefore, some writers term this as part of the Silk Route.

It may not be a mere coincidence that Kodungallur, known also as Crangnoor, became the hub for all famous ancient religions in different ways; the well-known disciple of Jesus Christ, St. Thomas, visited Kodungallur in the earlier period of Christianity itself (the existing Basilica and a thriving Christian community tell this story). The first known Islamic worship centre, the Cheraman Mosque, considered to be the first mosque to be established outside West Asia when Prophet Mohammed was still alive, was established here in AD 629. Apart from these, there are still a few Jewish families staying near Kodungallur. This place is also considered a well-known centre for Buddhism in ancient times.

The story of Muzires (Muziris), an ancient port town that thrived till around the end of first century AD, can certainly throw a lot of light on the interactions of various religious beliefs and the stories about a once-thriving transit trade along the Kerala coast. According to a number of historians, Muzires is the present-day

Kodungallur. However, other historians opine that Muzires might be another port town that existed slightly north of present-day Kodungallur and which lost its significance due to some natural calamities or the peculiar geographical conditions. The ancient Tamil literature of the Sangam period also contains many stories that revolve around Muzires.

This ancient port city was familiar to many trading communities of that time – Jews, Chinese, Byzantines, Scythians, etc. In ancient Indian history, too, Muzires figures prominently till the end of first century.

The monsoon winds or trade winds are closely linked to Kerala's history and life from time immemorial. They are known in different ways to the people of ancient Kerala. The scientific details of these winds are better known today, but the life of the people of Kerala is closely linked to them. The winds that blow south-west from April to October and north-east from October to April affect the socio-cultural and political aspects. The monsoon winds still largely decide the outcome of the agricultural produce of Kerala and India; this, in turn, fixes the economic life of the people.

Over 3,000 years ago, Kerala's maritime trade was a prosperous one with merchants across the globe making a beeline for its jewels, spices and condiments. Teakwood from Kerala is said to have been identified in the Moon Attur temple of Mesopotamia and it has also been traced to the palaces of Nebuchadnezzar in the sixth century BC.

There may be a paucity of adequate records for all these linkages. However, available records from a variety of sources suggest that the Phoenicians, Greeks and Romans knew that if they launched their vessels along the monsoon winds, they could reach Kerala's coast in fifty days. Later on, the Greek sailor Hippalus found in AD 44 that a ship setting out from the Gulf of Aden along the monsoon winds arrived at Kerala's western side in a little over a month. This discovery started to facilitate trade through sea for a long time to follow. Till mid-fifteenth century or till around the second voyage of Zheng He, the famous Chinese sailor, this trade continued and the Kerala coast acted as a major transit commercial hub for trade between China, West Asia and Rome.

A number of words used in present-day Malayalam language have an uncanny similarity to some Chinese words; it will be very difficult to dismiss this as mere coincidence. For example, there are two distinct set of words used in Malayalam. The first set belongs to the tools or instruments that Kerala received directly from its interaction with Chinese traders and other visitors – this list ranges from the *cheenachatti* (a half-moon shaped open frying fan used in all Malayali households for frying), *cheena bharani* (China clay pot for keeping preserved food, beverages, etc.), *cheenawala* and other such daily use items. The second set of words and phrases are those that are used in the everyday language; for example, *ni* is a commonly used term for 'you' in both Chinese and Malayalam. *Chechi*, a word to address an elder sister, is very close to the Chinese equivalent *jiejie*.

Likewise, the food habits of Keralites and many other inhabitants of modern-day South India can tell the story of the connections ranging from today's China to different parts of West Asia. Dosa, puttu and many other rice preparations, which are eaten mainly for breakfast are identical to preparations available in Ethiopia and China. Rice prepared inside a bamboo strip pierced delicately and cooked over steam or a low-heat coal fire remains a rare delicacy in different parts of Kerala and China. A variety of food items and their preparations tell the story of an ancient period when these three different areas interacted at different levels. Any Keralite who tasted some of the authentic Sichuan cuisine can vouchsafe for this fact. The Sichuan food from southern China forms a large chunk of Chinese food available all over the world.

The use of steamed rice preparations, chopped dried red chillis, etc., may be telling the stories of generations of sailors and traders travelling together along long stretches of the open and merciless sea during a time when only a rudimentary knowledge about the seas was available. If some of the mysteries of these long voyages are unravelled, one will be in a better position to connect the historical linkages between these three distinct geographical locations and their connectivity to the here and now from China to Greece and Rome.

This long-lasting link between different parts of South India and China resulted in the cultural and political rituals thriving in the soft underbelly of China, now largely comprising of East Asian countries. Jawaharlal Nehru summarised in his enduring work *Glimpses of World History*: 'The Chinese, of course, had always been close neighbours, sometimes interfering and conquering; oftener living as friends and exchanging gifts; and all the time influencing them with their great culture and civilisation.'

However, this long tradition of not so conflictual relations for a considerable period of time changed drastically with the advent of the western traders in the earlier part of sixteenth century. They not only took over the trade, largely based on exchange of goods under friendly terms, but also started a colonisation process in the whole of Asia. Certainly, there was an interlude when Islamic culture spread in these serene island territories for a while. But soon, this changed into a master and slave tie for western powers and these smaller, largely island, states. Indians, by and large, started to be viewed as the appendage of the British colonial masters. This has certainly had a long-lasting impact on India's relations with the countries in this region.

However, even during the early fifties, East Asia had a very vibrant South Indian community in different places like Malaysia, Singapore and others. Lately, these communities have lost their significant position in terms of trade and commerce in those regions. Keralites once enjoyed a key position in providing unskilled labourers to a number of countries in West Asia. Now, due to a variety of reasons, Keralites have partially lost this advantage.

In the post-World War II scenario, these relations underwent further twists and turns. The area stretching from the eastern sea board of India to the island chains abutting Japan became a favourite playground for the Cold War players. However, during the past decade, conditions have undergone drastic changes. A largely symbolic presence of British power in the Hong Kong islands, the last vestige of colonialism in Asia, ended in 1997. This has certainly given rise to new trade equations in Asia; during the last few years, the intra-Asian trade has critically surpassed Asia's trade with the western world. In 2007, the Greater China region has emerged as the number one trade partner for India.

These developments have had a positive impact on Kerala and India at large. Therefore, it is time for Kerala and its people to think about its future relations with the emerging world. If it has to recover even part of its glorious tradition of those yonder years, the state has to think seriously and position itself as a key player in this emerging global trade order.

The Chinese, Japanese and other visitors from East Asia form the largest chunk of tourist flow into different parts of the world. Of late, Kerala has become a favourite tourist destination in India. If one has to take advantage of this growing service industry, Kerala has to transform itself into a centre of excellence to provide various specialty services needed by this growing industry. These range from knowledge of concerned foreign language to cultures of these different regions.

The Malayalis have also started playing a crucial role in the growing information technology industry. Personnel from Kerala also form a significant part of the migrant workforce in the West Asia region.

If Kerala, and therefore India, are to play a decisive role in the emerging new world order, the planners and leaders of this state have to plot carefully now. In ancient times, the Kerala coast could play a vital role in global trade due to the availability of certain unique products and the capability of the people to provide the required service support. In those days Kerala could certainly use its favourable geographic location to its advantage.

However, the times 'they are a-changin' with the internet and other modern transportation facilities altering the terms of trade in various ways. Location no longer plays the significant role it once did and, therefore, service providers have to become more innovative in their methods.

Therefore, if Kerala is to recover even part of the importance it once enjoyed in the area of global trade, its leaders in education and related fields have to plan for the future. It will be hardly possible to remain competitive if we just stick to providing certain basic service skills. Rather, it is time to scout for emerging areas of business and trade wherein Kerala can develop its niche areas of excellence in fields such as management, foreign languages, delivery techniques, etc. If the state is willing to properly chart its future, it can ink out a glowing map.

M.V. Rappai, a defence analyst currently with the Institute of Chinese Studies, Delhi, specialises in security issues in Asia. A former fellow of the Institute of Defence Studies and Analyses, he has many research articles to his credit.

17 The Clove

Sarah Joseph

'Lie down. Open your mouth,' said the dentist.
Radha had a morbid molar tooth for so long because of her reluctance to open her mouth before a stranger. Combating the suffering from the severe toothache busied her for the past four days. Other teeth, ears, eyes and nose joined in to create one single pain. There was no other way but to consult a dentist. When she sat next to her child and opened her mouth to talk, the child had said, 'Amma, your breath smells bad.'

She did not like what the child said. Radha's face was slightly swollen; the swelling on her left cheek had become as round as a gooseberry. Unmindful of that, Madhavan Kutty pressed his teeth on her left cheek. He was in a good mood. On such days, they employed teeth and nails.

Unable to withstand the pain, Radha had shaken him off. Defiance had always thrilled Madhavan Kutty. In the darkness, he was incapable of thinking of her toothache. Instead, he thought she was trying to win him as usual through resistance. He pressed his lips on her mouth, not allowing her to make a single sound. He enjoyed watching her shudder for two or three minutes under his weight.

'Your breath stinks,' Madhavan Kutty laughed later, adding, 'but I like it.'

What he said was a lie. Such lies were the product of these crazy times. As the moments wind up, lies disappear. Radha wished she could call him some obscene name.

Meanwhile, desire sprang up and he firmly pressed his teeth on her left cheek.

'Ayyoo!' Radha screamed aloud.

'Stupid.' Madhavan Kutty turned away from her.

Radha felt indignant. Sex was such a bore!

The toothache had begun to take shape in her mind like slow-burning husk exploded all of a sudden. It was at that moment that crackers blasted in her left ear and boiled water gushed forth from her left eye without any warning. Somehow, she must see a dentist in the morning. There was nothing else to do but pull this tooth out. Pressing down her left cheek tightly and immersed in deep thoughts, she lay there till dawn.

'If you remove the tooth, your cheek would look hollow,' said Madhavan Kutty in the morning. 'It is better if the cavity can be filled.' That day he had inspection at his school.

Radha frowned at this remark and took an oath thrice that if possible she would pluck all her teeth out and spend the rest of her life without clothes showing him toothless gums. She mentioned she would never go for a set of artificial teeth.

'Why don't you try some short-cuts?' Madhavan Kutty asked.'

'Grind a clove and put it on the aching tooth.'

'Gargle with salted water.'

'Bite or chew a small twig of pepper vine smeared with salt.'

Radha set out in search of a dentist.

While getting ready she scolded her child as she could not find a *pottu* that would go with her sari.

'Where have you dumped everything? It is OK, don't bother. I think he is not lucky,' she said aloud.

'Who is not lucky?' asked Madhavan Kutty. He was correcting a composition book.

'That dentist,' replied Radha.

Madhavan Kuttty had laughed aloud.

The dentist's clinic was somewhere inside an ancient fort in the town. To reach his place she had to climb up and down several flights of stone stairs, pass many corridors shrouded in prehistoric darkness and wade unexpectedly through some open spaces. At last when she reached her destination, she was afraid that someone had erased the path she had travelled so far. To retrace her steps, she'd need help.

Holding a card, which had the number forty-five printed on it, Radha stood waiting at the end of a long line of patients who had taken appointments earlier. Shifting the weight of her body from one foot to the other, she had listened to those who were praising the doctor and watched with unease the never-ending line that kept forming behind her. Toothache and backache troubled her alike. By the time her chance came, she was exhausted by pain and boredom.

The dentist pointed towards a slanting chair as she entered the room. 'Lie down. Open your mouth.'

Radha's body was not as long as the slanting chair. The chair had been upholstered with a soft cushion material. Radha screamed the moment she pressed her fatigued back on the cushion. For hours she had been waiting in different postures.

A fan revolved above, spreading coolness. Droning like a beetle, it filled the silence of the room. A tall window was open, through which light fell on her. The room was green in colour.

'Open your mouth,' repeated the dentist.

Knim! A metal instrument dropped on the floor. As far as a dentist was concerned, it was not the face but the mouth that counted. He doesn't see the face or the body. Except your teeth, he doesn't take your physicality into consideration. If you present yourself as a set of thirty-two healthy teeth, he would feel aversion for you. His eyes may ask, 'Then why on earth are you here?'

'What is the problem?' the dentist asked Radha. Pressing his left hand on her forehead, he pushed her face backward with force.

'Bad breath,' said she.

The dentist stood before her now, his back against the window. Light fell on one half of his body and shadows on his other half. Like a photograph that had been taken using techniques of light and shade, everything appeared still within the frame of the window. He was thinking. Hands inside his trouser pockets, head slanted a bit, he stood motionless. His long nose was outside the frame. Since he held his shoulders high in an aristocratic way, Radha imagined a tie and hat on him to complete the picture. She put a pipe between his teeth. Even though it seemed funny, she felt very close to him at that moment, close enough to openly relate without hesitation everything about a tooth the roots of which were decaying. If needed she could develop a relationship stronger than the one that was possible between a panicky patient and a dentist.

Suddenly he was outside the frame of the window. A naked window and the light that streamed through it remained before her. She liked something about the way he moved. Slanting his body to some extent and keeping his hands inside his pockets, he had adopted an artificial gait.

'If only I could get hold of a mirror,' thought Radha.

Drawing apart the frilled curtains that lined one side of the room, the dentist vanished. Definitely, she must get a mirror before the dentist came back. How long had she been lying down on that elongated chair! The feeble sounds of a telephone conversation could be heard from one of the enigmatic rooms inside and she guessed the dentist was there. Imagining that she was at the other end of the phone, she started talking.

Hello! This is Radha. I am tired of sitting here all alone. I feel so sleepy. You know how siestas are without me telling you about it. Sometimes, like me, don't you sleep for two seconds, just two seconds, while plucking the tooth of a patient? I used to sleep for two minutes, just two minutes while I cook or iron clothes. A small snooze frees the mind and body much more than long hours of sleep. What do you think? Madhavan Kutty sometimes gives me booze that is weak. That puts me into deep slumber. He likes it very much. Hello! he says, then he would lift me up like a feather and put me down on the bed. My tongue would scold him but my speech got so garbled. I would beat him with hands I couldn't lift. How do you feel? Madhavan Kutty says this is the greatest bliss of wedded life. He gives me booze very rarely and carefully to avoid the boredom of repetition. Hello! Madhavan Kutty does not have any other woman except Radha.

'Oh! Are you still lying here?' asked the dentist as he hurriedly returned to the room. His hands were still inside his pockets and his high-flown foreign slang sounded quite out of place.

Radha felt astonished. Was she supposed to do anything else? Be anywhere else?

'What is your problem?' asked the dentist again.

'A tooth.'

'Open your mouth.'

Radha opened her mouth.

'Oh-ho.' The dentist went towards the window. He stood there looking outside for some time. Now he was a long dark shadow only marginally lit.

'You have a cavity,' he told her standing there.

None of the other teeth have problems.

Neither dirt nor decay.

Perfect lines.

Model teeth.

Strong gums.

But still, how come this tooth . . . ?

How did this happen? The dentist turned to express his wonder.

Sometimes it is like that, Radha thought. She said, 'That is my problem.' Because of the bad smell that came out of her mouth, she could not communicate with the world outside. It was very cruel.

Just because of this single tooth. This has bothered me too much. Rubbing against my tongue and cheek, the sharp edges of this tooth creates wounds that cannot be healed. Wounds that cannot be cured can be cancerous. Pluck this out!

Radha burnt with indignation. She appeared like a chimney that might explode if exposed to a single drop of water.

'Calm down,' advised the dentist.

With the end of a forcep thin like a thread he took a piece of cotton soaked in medicine and pressed it against Radha's aching tooth. Inside a mouth heavy with the strong perfume of clove and the frigidity it caused, the ablution was spicy hot, numbing and yet chilling. Now Radha could deal confidently with the outside world.

Radha longed to touch the dentist just once. *I love you.*

'Spit,' the dentist pointed to an ugly basin.

What does he think of himself? The world's handsomest guy? She spat into the said basin with contempt. *How on earth could he live being so dull? An uninteresting dentist!*

Radha stared at him. Suddenly she remembered Madhavan Kutty and his advice – 'Women should not stare at people'.

'Then how else should women look at others?'

'They should look slyly.'

Radha hit the dentist with a stealthy look.

Standing on his toes, he is lifting himself a bit to lower his body towards her. He has the fragrance of a forest!

'Your face will swell. I will prescribe a medicine for that,' he said.

Suddenly the outer shell of the toothache exploded, breaking her head apart. She collapsed into exhaustion. Anybody in pain could be fatigued at any time.

'Take this tablet three times a day,' he handed out a prescription. She remained exhausted.

'You may get up now,' said the dentist, rocking to and fro on his toes.

'Never,' thought Radha.

In the first place, it's been four days since I slept due to this unbearable toothache (now I can sleep). In the second place, even though it was a short one, this dentist and I have shared the hearty feeling and experience of 'smell'.

Hello!

The dentist leaned abruptly and touched her. Radha turned her face slightly to the left. The swelling on the cheek and the rotting tooth underneath it were out of his vision now. What he sees is a beautiful profile.

Four or five minutes pass without sound or movement. In the sixth moment the fragrance of a breaking forest avalanches towards her as if a tornado has suddenly broken out of the buzzing fan. The scent of crushed leaves, flowers and fruits! The smell of floating grime from wounds! The smell of wide open sources of sap! The smell of frightened animals running for their lives; the smell of earth that tears apart! It is difficult to enter a forest. The dentist's cheek grazes her cheek. His tongue, softer than a worm, crawls into her ear.

Radha jumps up. Facing him, she looks bluntly at him.

'There is no need to pluck the tooth out,' he said. 'Once plucked, it will not grow again.' Grabbing the prescription from his hand, Radha rushed out. She ran, pushing away some of the people who were waiting in the long queue.

At the end of the run, as she was panting, supporting her hands on a wall, she wondered why she had been running. She was afraid of someone. She was confused as she could not make out whether she was afraid of the dentist or herself. She felt dizzy thinking of the complex structure of her exit. She had even tried her hand at breaking the fort wall for a short-cut.

When Madhavan Kutty came back after the inspection at school, he asked Radha, 'How is your toothache?'

'Oh,' she replied carelessly. 'I put a ground clove on the tooth.'

'Ha ha ha,' Madhavan Kutty laughed aloud. The inspection at school had been good that day. 'Do you remember what a fuss you made about it in the morning? "I will pluck the tooth out immediately. I will beat it out right now",' he imitated her. 'Now tell me, what happened?'

'We can talk about it later, there is time. He is not going to run away anywhere.' After plaiting her daughter's hair, Radha rubbed the remnant oil on to her hands and legs.

– *Translated from Malayalam by Sangeetha Sreenivasan*

Thrissur-based author **Sarah Joseph** got the Kerala Sahitya Akademi Award and the Kendra Sahitya Akademi Award for *Alaahayude Penmakkal* (Alaaha's Daughters). Her *Ramayana Kathakal*, a subversive reading of the Ramayana, ties in with her organising of the feminist movement 'Manushi' in Kerala.

18 Music And Lyrics

Rama Varma

The music of Kerala dates back around two millennia when the boundaries of each of the South Indian kingdoms differed drastically from their current parameters. Separated by mountains from the rest of India on one side and serenaded by the Arabian Sea on the other, Kerala is called God's Own Country after the legend of Lord Parashurama reclaiming this land-mass from the ocean with a throw of his divine axe. Till 1947, when the British were forced to leave India, Kerala was made up of three separate kingdoms – Malabar up north, Cochin in the centre and Travancore down south. One of the most strategic locations in the whole of India where the three oceans, the Indian Ocean, the Arabian Sea and the Bay of Bengal meet—Kanyakumari—belonged to Travancore. Post-independence, however, petty political intrigues handed Kanyakumari to the neighbouring state of Tamil Nadu.

Malayalam, the language spoken in Kerala, is an amalgam of two unrelated languages – Sanskrit and Tamil. A glance at so-called 'classical' Malayalam versus insults reveals that the Sanskrit synonym is oft employed in classical parlance while the Tamil word with the same meaning as slur.

Music involves *geetham* (singing), *vadyam* (instruments) and *nrithyam* (dance). To begin with, there were lullabies, harvest songs, festive melodies for occasions like Onam and marriage . . . Alas, most of these songs were neither properly documented nor preserved, with the result that many art forms either died out completely or were corrupted beyond recognition because of other influences or misguided attempts at modernisation.

Just like western classical music owes much to the Catholic Church, many forms of traditional music in Kerala owe their roots to Hinduism. Hinduism came into power all over the country with a bang somewhere around the fifth century AD. There are two branches of Hindus – the Shaivites or followers of Siva and Vaishnavites or the followers of Vishnu. The Shaivite rulers were called Nayanars and the Vaishnavites, the Alwars. Unlike many Shaivites and Vaishnavites of the present (not to mention Catholics and Protestants or Sunnis and Shias), the tolerance displayed by rulers of either faction was legendary. One of the kingdoms that preceded Kerala extended all the way from Kancheepuram in present-day Tamil Nadu to Aluva in present-day Kerala.

Temple music and temple arts flourished in all these ancient religious abodes. And the music associated with temples in Kerala came to be called Sopana music (Sopana being a part of the sanctum sanctorum). Around the fourteenth century, the epic love poem written by Jayadeva, the *Gita Govindam*, swept the country and made its impact in Kerala, too. The *Gita Govindam* comprises poems with eight stanzas, called Ashtapadis, depicting the passionate interaction between Lord Krishna and his beloved, Radha, who was an older, married woman. Soaked in explicit eroticism, Ashtapadis became an instant hit even among the prudes of Indian society—and there are a lot of them—because of the breathtakingly beautiful use of the Sanskrit language (which more or less obscured the meaning of the words themselves much of the time), the quality of the poetry as well as the brilliant imagery. To this day, one finds small children in traditional Hindu families quaintly singing the most blush-worthy lines from Ashtapadis during their evening prayers, blissfully ignorant of the meaning!

Since a satisfactory system of writing down Indian music is yet to be invented and since most of these arts were passed down from generation to generation orally, many schools of music claim that their versions of Ashtapadis (and much else) are the 'authentic' one. It is up to the discerning music lover and scholar to pick a version that goes with their idea of what is right. I've even heard English translations of Ashtapadis sung in Europe. Stripped of the heavy Sanskrit that lends a rare dignity as well as regal stature, it sounded rather embarrassing, to put it mildly. Ashtapadis, in turn, inspired a marriage of music and dance in the form of 'Krishnanattam', which was an exquisite dance form depicting the various *leelas* of Lord Krishna – and the leelas of Lord Krishna were numerous, intriguing and colourful indeed. From 'Krishnanattam' was born 'Ramanattam', which in turn became the predecessor to Kathakali, one of the most celebrated art forms of Kerala.

Veera Kerala Varma Raja of the seventeenth century Kottarakkara is said to be the originator of Kathakali. Maharaja Karthika Thirunal Rama Varma of Travancore refined, embellished and modified this art form further and raised it to unprecedented heights. Pages and pages could be written about Kathakali, an art form where it takes a team of experts more than seven or eight hours merely to apply make-up on the dancer's face. Kathakali is a combination of music, poetry, dance and theatre, and most of the stories enacted in these performances are taken from the Puranas or from Hindu mythology. Any Kathakali performance can extend all through the night, but these days one comes across bonsai performances, tailor-made to suit the audience's ever decreasing attention span. The recent Malayalam film *Vanaprastham* did try to capture the travails of a Kathakali artist in period settings.

By the end of the eighteenth century, music in South India changed completely because of the advent of a handful of great masters in South Indian classical or Carnatic music. The word, in Indian languages, is Karnataka Sangeetham. 'Karna' means 'ear,' 'ataka' means 'pleasing to' and 'sangeetham' means 'music.' So Karnataka Sangeetham means 'music that is pleasing to one's ears' and not 'music from Karnataka', as it is sometimes mistaken for. Another term for Indian classical music, in Indian languages, is 'Shasthreeya Sangeetham' or scientific music. Because of the exoticism deliberately propagated by some of our artists abroad, many westerners are shocked when they come to know that Indian classical music, both Carnatic down south as well as Hindustani up north, is, in fact, 'scientific music'. Solid and clear, mathematical and aesthetic, with very clear guidelines as to when and where one could do what and how, when it comes to improvisation and not at all exotic despite the very real spiritual content contained within.

Despite the pioneer of South Indian classical music, Purandara Dasa, having come a few hundred years earlier along with luminaries such as Annamacharya, it wasn't until the end of the seventeenth century that the trinity of Carnatic music—Thyagaraja, Muthuswamy Dikshithar and Shyama Shasthri—appeared on the scene. They had an amazing colleague in Kerala's Maharaja Swathi Thirunal Rama Varma (1813-46). Even over 160 years after his demise, the Maharaja's accomplishments in the field of music are unparalleled. He remains the only person to have mastered both Hindustani as well as Carnatic music to such an extent that he went on to compose many brilliant songs in both systems. Rather like Mozart having made his mark in sonatas, duos, trios, quartets, concertos for various instruments, symphonies and operas, he made his mark in various forms of composition such as *thaana varnams, pada varnams, jati swarams, swarajathis, keerthanams, prabandhams, padams, javalis* and *thillanas* in the Carnatic style, and *dhrupads, khyals, thumris, horis, tappas, tharanas, bhajans* and *ragmalas* in the Hindusthani style. His court attracted musicians of all styles from all over the country during a time when the world was a much larger place than it is now and communication much more difficult. After his demise there was a great decline in the musical scene in Kerala.

During the twentieth century, many of his compositions were resurrected and at present a festival of music—Swathi Sangeethotsavam—is organised every year from January 6th to 12th at Kuthiramalika Palace, Thiruvananthapuram, Kerala. Another annual festival of music and dance takes place in Thiruvananthapuram in October, organised by the Soorya society. While many of the forms of folk music have died out, efforts are being made by various cultural bodies to document and preserve the ones that survived. One of the most fascinating art forms of Kerala, Ottan Thullal, was an invention of the genius of Kunchan Nambiar, a poet in the court of Maharaja Marthanda Varma in the eighteenth century. The essence of human foibles that he captured in his brilliant and free-flowing verse is so universal that one feels they were composed today. The tragedy with Kunchan Nambiar's poetry is that much of its brilliance and earthy flavour gets lost in translation. Legend has it that once when the king erected a lamp-post in the marketplace, court poets went into gush mode, praising him and thanking him profusely for bringing them light, comparing him with the sun and so on. The king happily handed out gold coins to them while Nambiar remained a silent observer. The king asked him: 'So Nambiar, don't *you* have anything to say?' and pat came the two lines, without rhyme or meter, '*Deepa sthambham mahaashcharyam! Enikkum kittanam panam.*' (The lamp-post is amazing! I, too, want money.)

South Indian rhythm and percussion is one of the most sophisticated and brilliant ones in the whole world. When orchestras of more than 150 drums such as the chenda, maddalams, thimilas and so on play together in a temple courtyard, starting at an excruciatingly slow tempo and building up to a shattering crescendo, they literally root one to the spot. The Thrissur Pooram, which takes place at the Vadakkunnadha Swami temple in Thrissur every year in April/May (the dates of most Indian festivals change yearly according to the Hindu calendar), is a perfect occasion to enjoy this spectacle. The edakka, used in Sopana music as well as for the music accompanying Kerala's own classical dance form Mohiniattam, is akin to the talking drums of Africa. With modern times came the radio, followed by films, television, and internet. Preceding cinema came dramas and their songs, mostly depicting the plight of peasants and popularising revolutionary zeal, produced by Kerala Peoples Arts Cooperative. Many of these songs, composed more than sixty years ago, are still very much alive and kicking, along with Kerala's own version of communism. Katha Prasangam, with its mix of mythology and social satire, came into being, which was a secular form of 'Harikadhakalakshepam', where a person would tell a story heavily interspersed with songs.

However, a dominating force during the second half of the twentieth century till the present, be it in Kerala or the rest of India, has been film music. Most Indian films have five to ten songs. In the 1940s, the actors themselves sang while the scene was being filmed. By the 1950s, playback started, with the piercing female voices going higher and higher till most of the actresses had to use a similarly shrill voice to dub the spoken dialogue, too, during the movie to match the singing pitch. While the female voice stayed more or less unidimensional all over India, male voices in the Hindi film field fared better, with a host of talented singers like Mohammed Rafi, Mukesh, Kishore Kumar, Manna Dey, Hemant Kumar and Talat Mehmood singing in their own distinct style.

Not so in Kerala. The single voice of K.J. Yesudas and others trying to sound like him took over not just Malayalam films but the very essence of Kerala during the past three decades and more. The thousands of Malayalis who find this boring are silenced by the millions who have given this singer god-like status. The latest craze among the public is the Malayali imitation of the Indian imitation of the 'American Idol'. The combination of pushy parents, rude judges, garish sets, desperate performers, many of whom give the viewers the feeling of 'if he can sing, so can I!' and, of course, the big bucks involved make a heady concoction for vicarious entertainment.

Despite the Malayalam film industry churning out dozens of comic films year after year, comedy in film music hasn't fared too well during the past three decades. To remedy this has come a bunch of brilliant young men with parody songs, many of which have more spark than the originals they spoof. 'Hotel Keralafonia' and 'I Am A Malayali' are in cyber circulation. Meanwhile, members of the older generation shake their heads at the electronic assault and wonder if this indeed is God's Own Music!

Prince **Rama Varma** of the Travancore royal family is a well-known Carnatic vocalist and veena artist. A direct descendent of Maharaja Swathi Thirunal Rama Varma, he has performed in many prestigious venues, including the Queen Elizabeth Hall where his maiden CD was released. The annual Swati Music Festival held in Thiruvananthapuram is his initiative.

19 Houseboat Story
A Travelogue In Disguise

Jayanth Kodkani

Once again Mukundan wiped his brow with the white handkerchief, shifting uncomfortably in the backseat of the Ambassador. The scenes and scents of the world moving past him brought back faint images of his childhood. Narrow, palm-fringed roads wove past shops lined with stacks of banana chips in glass jars. Somewhere the smell of salt-water and fish filled the air and jerked his thoughts as much as tea-coloured puddles from last night's rain that the car skimmed over. Another village street, another row of shopkeepers waiting to sell banana chips . . .

When I called the yard at Kumarakom after arriving at Ernakulam—just waking up with a yawn—the voice at the other end told me, 'The drive should take around three hours. The boat will wait for you.' The stickiness outside had me fish out my soppy handkerchief and roll down the windows of the Ambassador for some breeze. The monsoon was yet to arrive, but the landscape was green and astir.

I wouldn't have imagined that my first trip to Kerala would be absorbed in the story of Mukundan, my friend in college who

I had met only once later, some years ago on a train to Goa. A white streak was conspicuous in the unruly mop across his brow. He didn't want to talk much about the past and he didn't seem to read as much as he did when we were young. I gathered he had married Vasundhara, a coy girl from his hometown who cooked good fish curry; lived in Delhi, Pune, Mumbai and Bhopal but had never been home in the recent years.

I told him, 'My boss always says, "aah these Keralites, they are everywhere. But no matter where they are, they want to go back home every weekend!"'

His smile drooped and his eyes dimmed. 'You know,' he said, 'I'm haunted by a Kathakali dancer who chases me everywhere – up the stairs and down the corridors of my flat. When I stay late in office, I can hear the bells on his feet outside the door.'

Like many of us, Mukundan had scribbled his thoughts in free verse in college, but that his images would come to simulate those in the movies was beyond my comprehension.

He had a story to tell me. A few years ago he had met Karen, a British tourist, in Mumbai and they had spent days together visiting pubs, cafés, the Flora Fountain, the Elephanta Caves, Chowpatty and the Jehangir Art Gallery. One evening in an Irani café when his cup of tea had gone cold, he spilled out his secret thought to Karen. In response, she threw back her head and laughed. Two evenings later, in the taxi back to her hotel, she held his hand in hers and said, 'You have the magic in you.'

'She may have as well said "Eyes of a Blue Dog" like in the Marquez story,' Mukundan told me. That evening he bought his son a toy plane and Vasundhara some flowers and went home grinning like a schoolboy.

The next day Mumbai seemed to be in slow motion . . . reflecting his mood. Karen had planned it out – she was to break from her friends on their next stop and fly to Kerala from Chennai where they could meet. 'Why not a houseboat at Kumarakom?' she had suggested. 'It would be like home.'

After I paid off the taxi-driver near a culvert somewhere in the middle of the countryside, he pointed towards the edge of a creek down a slushy pathway. A furlong away, two big houseboats stood moored near an adjacent path leading to a village.

The *kettuvallom* (boat), knotted in coir and resting on jackwood planks, stood serene like an elephant waiting to lead a procession. A strong smell of bamboo and coir hung heavy as I jumped in with my luggage.

'Lucky you're the only one travelling today.' Two hairy men—one in trousers and the other in a lungi doubled-up at the knees—smiled at me. Not good for your business though, I wanted to say, but held myself after looking across to see the neighbouring boat populated by families, garrulous women and screaming children, all carrying pieces of luggage.

They were the oarsmen-cum-guides, I gathered, as the men led me to a compact bedroom with bulbs inside lanterns, a small writing table and beside the sealed glass-window, a reclining seat of wood. It looked like an extra-modest hotel room but near the lower rim of the bed, a plank on the floor creaked noisily every time my step fell and reminded me of where I was. The narrow aisle outside was still filled with warm air. Just then, another smiling lungi-clad man, the cook, offered me some lime juice which did little to quench my thirst.

At noon sharp, with me alone on the deck, the motor sputtered and the boat squished ahead, the waters slapping its bottom. As it took its first curl, we passed through a narrow lane of water flanked by backyards of homes that threw up sights of daily life – women washing utensils, a boy playing with a hoop, a young man repairing his bicycle . . . I thought of Mukundan again as the soft current took us ahead. Just the evening before he was to meet Karen at Kumarakom, Mukundan's son fell from the stairs at his apartment in Mumbai and broke his leg.

'She called me the next day at home and I told her about the boy. Never mind, I'll wait here for three more days, she said. I couldn't stay back in Mumbai any longer. My routines at hospital, home and office were making me a bit uptight. Two days later I called the hotel in the evening and was told she might be back for dinner. I kept trying and close to midnight, got her on the line. She said her friends had rejoined her and she had to end her holiday the next morning. Won't you stay for two more days, I pleaded. She said she was sorry. When do we meet then, I asked. On my next visit perhaps, she said. Will you write to me? How do I talk to you? Don't you want the magic again?'

After a long pause at the other end, Karen had told him, 'I've never seen the houseboat myself. I will, maybe with you, some other time. That will be our little dream.'

'But shouldn't we keep in touch? Shouldn't we let the magic work?' Mukundan had begged.

'I will someday. And tell you my own story . . .' Karen replied and hung up, leaving a deafening silence.

Mukundan had missed the last train to Virar. He had loitered for an hour on the platform trying to call the hotel again.

Karen didn't come back to him.

Suddenly from a stretch dotted with fronds and hyacinth, the waterway flared, opening to the magnificent Vembanad. I stepped on to the piece of the sundeck and peered at the country's longest lake. More sublime than the sea, perhaps languid, in the April afternoon, it lay there like an expanse of elsewhere that travellers long to discover.

The boat veered around towards the dense shoreline of an island.

'That's heavily wooded,' the navigator said. 'We're not going there, the water's too deep around it.'

Before I could ask him where we were headed, he pointed towards another faraway shoreline. 'We'll dock there for lunch and for the evening.'

An hour went by and soon we could see the land looping the waters. The other houseboat carrying the noisy family swayed past us. I strolled into the bedroom and almost saw Mukundan sitting on the edge of the cot. Would things have been different if Mukundan could, indeed, make that trip to Kumbakonam? What was Karen waiting for? What was her story? Mukundan didn't know.

Out on the deck, the cook began laying out the lunch spread. Rotis, rice, fish, *aviyal* and a basket of fruits appeared before me.

'Pour me some water,' Karen said and Mukundan spilled some on the table at a restaurant in Mumbai. He was always clumsy when faced with such situations. 'Relax, she would say,' Mukundan had recalled.

Back in the bedroom, through the crack of the window covered by an embroidered curtain, I saw some islanders carrying wicker baskets. Mukundan would have known where they were going. He might have had tales to tell of boat-making, of Fort Kochi, of Chinese fishing nets, of the Ayemenem of Arundhati Roy and the spiceland of Rushdie's *The Moor's Last Sigh*. All if he had made it that morning to Kumarakom. Did Karen really wait for him? Did she mean home for houseboat? I'd never know.

In the evening, soon after we had tea and biscuits, and the boat curled towards the land again, there was a sign of rain. The first pellets fell heavily on the palm-leaf canopy over the deck and soon it was pouring. A pole-punted boat appeared abruptly along us and the old man rowing it, yelled out something to the crew in a mutual code. The navigators sprung into action, pulling down the covers, heaving the jangling anchor into the water and fastening the ropes.

An hour later, the rain eased but a thick cover of darkness fell. On the grassy patches nearby, clouds of mosquitoes began their evening peregrination. The lights flickered and I walked into the room again.

Mukundan would have asked the question again after he saw her face against the glow of the lantern-bulb. Karen might have arched her back and smiled a nothing smile. Or they would look into each other's smouldering eyes. And then, she would ask him a thousand questions. His pulse would quicken if she started to tell him her story. And if there was something he hadn't expected, face ripe with disbelief, he would draw the curtains of the window and stare outside. I sailed with that story for the best part of the night, not even sure when I had dinner. Mukundan, and Karen too, would have made imaginary trips in the houseboat for years. They may have stayed in the confines of the room, their desires dissolving into wet kisses or simply mulling over the improbability of the relationship in a world that loved to define frontiers.

On the deck, the crew was watching some sleazy movie on television. Their stuttering cackles pierced the night.

A journey, they say, is a discovery of an experience we've never had and probably will never have. Only for Mukundan, it is still a figment. The houseboat as fiction, as a metaphor for his little secret. A secret drifting along its own path and stopping only when ordinary life crackles into conscience like the dawn.

The morning's rays were already glistening in the water when the cook walked up to the table with a steaming cup of tea and some idlis. We were on the last lap of our trip. 'Hope you enjoyed yourself,' the grinning crew asked me as the boat began to move up a creek to end the trip.

It was 9 a.m. and a taxi was waiting near the culvert to ferry me back to Ernakulam. The air was warm and humid.

Once again Mukundan wiped his brow with the white handkerchief, shifting uncomfortably in the backseat of the Ambassador...

I haven't progressed beyond that paragraph. The story may be written some day. Better still, if I get to meet Mukundan again. Else, it might get embedded in the images of the houseboat ride.

Jayanth Kodkani, a senior journalist with *The Times of India* Bangalore, has written extensively on socio-cultural topics and co-edited *Beantown Boomtown: Bangalore In The World of Words*, an anthology on Bangalore. He has also translated short fiction in Kannada.

20 A For Anglo

Stephen Padua

To many it is an eye-opener to learn that the majority of the microscopic Anglo-Indian community, not only in Kerala but also throughout India, is predominantly of Portuguese origin. During the British rule, descendants of the British outnumbered those of the Europeans in India. But after 1947, with the changing scenario in India, many of them migrated to the UK, Australia and other lands. The community, which is today spread through the length and breadth of the country, comprises of the descendants of the Dutch, French, Germans and other Europeans.

Article 366 (2) in the Constitution embraces all such descendants:

> *An Anglo-Indian means a person whose father or any of whose other male progenitors in the male line is or was of European descent but who is domiciled within the territory of India and is or was born within such territory of parents habitually resident therein and not established there for temporary purposes only.*

It was at the formation of the Anglo-Indian Defence Association in 1882, that the term 'Anglo-Indian' was for the first time introduced as an official description of the Indo-European races.

A description in the Madras District Municipalities Act V of 1920 stated that an Anglo-Indian is a person who is not a European but is of European descent in the male line or of mixed Asiatic and non-Asiatic descent, whose father, grandfather or a more remote ancestor in the male line was born in Europe, Canada, Newfoundland, Australia, New Zealand, the Union of South Africa or the USA.

About 180 million people in the world speak Portuguese. It is the official language and lingua franca in Portugal, Brazil, Angola, Mozambique, Cape Verde Islands, Sao Tome, Principe and Guinea-Bissau. Portuguese is the official and working language at the Organisation of the United Nations. The chiefs of the states of Brazil, Cape Verde, Guinea-Bissau, Mozambique, Portugal, Sao Tome, Principe and Angola met on 1 November 1989, in Brazil and resolved to create an International Institute of Portuguese Language.

Portuguese was the official language of the erstwhile Cochin state for nearly two centuries. It was the lingua franca in all the sea ports and the dependencies of the Portuguese people in the East well after they left Indian shores. It was the medium of communication not only among the Indians engaged in trade and commerce and Eurasians and others who identified themselves with the Portuguese, but even among the Dutch, English, French and other settlers. Today we know that many vernacular words in Malayalam, Oriya, Hindustani, Bengali, Assamese and other Indian languages are of Portuguese origin and many Indian words through the Portuguese have found their way into the European vocabulary. Some examples are *armario* (almirah), *bankit* (banquet), *chuname* (processed lime), *camisa* (shirt), *cruz* (cross, *jaca* (jackfruit), *padre, verandah*, etc.

When the Dutch defeated the Portuguese in 1663, the descendants of the Portuguese in the native states of Cochin and Travancore had to flee to villages where education along with medical aid, transport and employment suffered. Being subjects of the maharajas of the native states of Cochin and Travancore, the Anglo-Indians there were not given any special treatment by the British government with regard to education and employment on par with their more fortunate brethren in other British provinces. The poor Anglo-Indian children in other British provinces could avail of the destitute grant in Anglo-Indian schools and, with the minimum of qualifications, get preferentially employed in departments like customs, railways, posts and telegraphs. Only in 1945 were half-fee concessions and a handful of scholarships granted to Anglo-Indian students in Cochin state, whereas the Anglo-Indian students were denied even those concessions in Travancore state. A two percent reservation in government services was granted to Anglo-Indians and Jews together from 1936 onwards in Cochin state. A number of Anglo-Indian schools were sanctioned to be run by the community only in 1945.

The first-standard-onward schools were started in September 1945. The first among them was named after Frank Anthony, the president-in-chief of the Anglo-Indian Association, all-India, New Delhi. The state association was an active provincial branch of the all-India association. Curiously enough, it was only later that Anthony made the erroneous claim that there were only a couple of Anglo-Indians in the state and that all others were 'firangis'.

The school at Edachochin was inaugurated on 23 September 1945, by Sir George Boag, the then diwan of Cochin. The next school, Holy Family EP School, Chathiath, was opened on 11 November of the same year.

The following schools were also started:
- Loretto Anglo-Indian Lower Primary School, Saude
- St. Francis Anglo-Indian Lower Primary School, Bolghatty
- St. Anthony's EP School, Vallarpadam

- Cruz Milagrez EP School, Ochanthuruth
- European Primary School, Elamagunnapuzha
- Luiz Anglo-Indian Lower Primary School, Kadukutty
- Don Bosco EP School, Padiyur
- Sacred Heart Anglo-Indian Lower Primary School, Moolampilly
- St. Sebastian's Anglo-Indian Lower Primary School, Palluruthy
- Infant Jesus Anglo-Indian Lower Primary School, Ernakulam

Even though the government's sanction was obtained to start these schools, the community had neither site nor building, no resources to provide the basic infrastructure, necessary furniture, etc. These schools were started in porticos of the local leaders of the community. The pioneers of the movement like Joseph Pinheiro, L. Lopez, J.L. Fernandez, Mathew D'Coutho and David Rodrigues had to cross several hurdles to provide sites, buildings and equipment to the eleven schools.

The Government of the Maharaja of Cochin was kind enough to sanction a lumpsum grant of Rs 300 to each school as per their order on 16 April 1946. But this sum could not be drawn by the schools as a result of the changeover of the education portfolio from the diwan to the minister.

During the first three years, the schools had to run without a single rupee as grant-in-aid from the government. This issue threw up a massive rally at Ernakulam on 7 January 1947. To the good fortune of the community, K. Balakrishna Menon became the education minister in the T.K. Nair ministry of Cochin in 1947. By government proceedings order on 27 December 1947, the government sanctioned ordinary grant-in-aid to the Anglo-Indian schools managed by the Central Board with permission for English as the medium of instruction and to teach English as an additional subject.

Article 30 of the Constitution guaranteed the right of the minorities in running educational institutions of their choice. It was the aim of the Central Board to conduct the schools on the model of the Anglo-Indian schools of British India when they started in 1945. However, the circumstances in the villages where most of the schools existed were not favourable to the growth of English-medium schools. With the opening of the schools, the Central Board of Anglo-Indian Education was also formed in 1945 to manage the schools.

With the starting of the Anglo-Indian schools, a new system of education came into vogue. The medium of instruction was English and the teaching methods were new and different from those prevalent in the country. Foreign languages like French and German were introduced. Western ideas of liberty, equality and fraternity percolated down to the grassroots. A fillip was born to the thirst for an independent India. The old order began to crack.

The late MLA **Stephen Padua**, 1914-1994, was general-secretary and later president-in-chief of the Union of Anglo-Indian Associations and chairman of the Central Board of Anglo-Indian Education. He represented the community in the Kerala Legislative Assembly for three consecutive terms from 1970 to 1986. This is an excerpt from his forthcoming autobiography to be published posthumously.

21 A Matter Of Faith

Vinod Joseph

'Mary Mathew,' the nurse called out.

Mary, who sat in the waiting area, nervously fiddling with the strap of a brown handbag in her lap, got up, hurriedly readjusted the drape of her saree over a shoulder and went in.

'Sit down,' Dr Cherian told her, averting his eyes. Even before she made herself comfortable, he slid a sealed envelope across the table towards her. Mary had no choice but to pick up the envelope. 'The test results,' Dr Cherian added unnecessarily.

Though Mary took the envelope, she did not open it. Instead, she scanned the good doctor's face for any sign of hope. There was none. Her shoulders sagged.

'Go on, read the report,' he insisted.

Mary bit her lower lip in an effort not to cry. She tore open the envelope and scanned the report. She knew what the report would say, the expression on the doctor's face having killed a faint lingering hope that the chemotherapy had worked. *Recurrent cancer in the abdomen, metastases, bowel still partially blocked* – the words flashed before her eyes.

'I had told you after the hysterectomy and debulking that we managed to remove only fifty percent of your mother's cancer,' he said softly.

'I understand, doctor,' Mary murmured. They had detected the cancer very late, as it usually happens in cases of ovarian cancer and Dr Cherian had never made any promises.

'Do you think more chemo will help?'

'It might. I won't advice you to stop the treatment permanently, but . . .'

'So, let's do it then. Let Ammachi undergo some more chemotherapy.'

Dr Cherian was silent for a moment. Then he said, 'Your mother's . . . sixty-five?'

'Sixty-four. She's sixty-four years old,' Mary supplied the information as though her mother's age might enable a unique form of treatment that could save her.

'Yes, sixty-four. And she's very weak. Maybe the charitable thing would be to . . .' he let the sentence hang.

'Not have any more chemo? You mean she doesn't have a chance?'

'It's all a question of how much longer she'll survive. I suggest you take her home and see if she manages to build up her strength. If she does, then we can consider more chemo.'

Mary was lost in thought as the bus took her back to Idukki. If only Mathew was around. What was the point of being married and having a husband if he wasn't around at a time like this? But Mathew was in Saudi Arabia and his annual leave wasn't due for another six weeks. Mary shrugged. She would call up both her brothers and her sister tonight after Ammachi went to bed. She had no right to decide on her own on further chemo. For a while, Mary toyed with the idea of explaining everything to Ammachi and asking her to decide. No, that wouldn't do, she scolded herself. Ammachi was so weak after her surgery and two months of chemo that she was in no position to judge.

Mary had to take a ten-minute walk to reach her home from the bus stand. On the way she passed Rosamma teacher's house.

Rosamma teacher and Joy sir were standing in their verandah and waving to her. Mary tried to lift her hand and wave back, but the effort was too much for her. She just walked on.

When she got home, Ammachi was asleep. The children were yet to come back from school. Chinamma, their full-time maid, made her some tea. A few minutes later, the phone rang. It was Rosamma teacher.

'Is everything okay? What did the doctor say?'

Mary started to sob over the phone. 'I'll come over,' Rosamma teacher said.

'No, I'll come to your place once the children come back from school. We can talk freely there. Ammachi will wake up anytime.'

Mary made her way to Rosamma teacher's house after the children had their evening snack and went out to play. She was not really close to Rosamma teacher or Joy sir. In fact, Mathew positively disliked them; 'They are nosy people,' he said. It was true. Rosamma teacher and Joy sir were infinitely curious about everything and everybody. They had a word of advice for everybody, even if it was not sought. And they subscribed to the Charismatic way of praying, their house reverberating to the sound of singing, chanting and clapping every night. But ever since her mother was diagnosed with cancer, Mary had come to rely on the couple for support, the only ones in the neighbourhood who had the time and willingness to listen to her troubles.

'What did the doctor say?' Rosamma teacher asked without any preamble.

'There's no hope at all.'

They were silent for a while. Then Joy sir said, 'You must go to Potta. Only Jesus can save Ammachi's life. He is the best doctor in the whole universe.'

Mary shook her head. Rosamma teacher and Joy sir had made that suggestion earlier. Mary had always dismissed passionate prayer displays with mild contempt. Don't harass God and he won't harass you, she had always philosophised. Her father's death after a sudden heart attack when she was fifteen had only made her more self-reliant. Mathew and the rest of her family, too, shared her scorn for people who spent hours in prayer everyday. Even her mother, who used to go to church daily till she fell ill, did not have a high opinion of such ardent prayer sessions.

'Let me think it over,' Mary said.

'What's there to think about?' they asked. 'Let's pray. Let's pray that Jesus may guide Mary in her hour of need and show her the right path.' Rosamma started to kneel after stealing a quick look at Mary's face. Before her mother fell ill, such melodrama would have brought a smirk to Mary's face; now it brought tears.

All three of them knelt down in front of the framed mug-shot of Jesus Christ that dominated the drawing room.

'Our father, who art in heaven, hallowed be thy name. . . .' Rosamma teacher's Christ had a slightly severe look unlike the picture in Mary's house where he looked more pleasant.

That night Mary decided to go to Potta. Or rather to Muringoor where the Divine Retreat Centre was now housed after it was moved from neighbouring Potta. What did she have to lose anyway? And maybe, *maybe*, Ammachi might get better. Her sister was coming over from Bombay for a ten-day visit in a couple of weeks' time and she could look after the kids when Mary was away. One of her brothers was coming over the next day from Thiruvananthapuram where he lived, but he wouldn't be able to stay for long. The other brother was in Dubai and God alone knew when his employer would be kind enough to give him leave to come home.

Mathew voiced his strong disapproval over her decision when he called up a day later. 'What's got into you?' he asked. 'You were always so rational. Potta of all places!'

True, she had always been rational, but then rationality did not explain everything, did it? Why did Ammachi have to contract cancer? And even if she did, why didn't they detect it earlier? They had taken her to their family's general physician a year ago when she complained of stomach pain. The GP had not even asked her to undergo a basic test. Instead, that idiot had merely prescribed painkillers. Go easy on the tapioca and fish, Ammachi, he had said in his usual jovial manner. If only they had done a biopsy a year ago . . . How could she explain such a continuous run of bad luck? Maybe Rosamma teacher and Joy sir were right. Maybe it was all the work of Satan.

The air-conditioned bus that took Mary to the retreat centre at Muringoor was run by a private operator. It collected fifty-odd people from outside the church compound every Sunday morning after the eight o'clock mass got over, and reached Muringoor village late in the afternoon. Thousands of people had started to gather for the six-day retreat, which would be held in English, Malayalam, Hindi, Tamil and a few other languages. Mary once again became apprehensive about her decision to attend the retreat. Her apprehension only grew as she paid the very reasonable fees of a few hundred rupees that would cover her board and lodging for the entire retreat. She clutched her bag nervously as she walked to her allotted bunk bed, one among the thousand-plus bunks inside a humungous hall. The chatter around her came from people of all shapes and sizes. There were the rich ones who smelt of foreign perfumes, middle class people who smelt of Lux or Cinthol soap and the poor ones whose bodies managed to exude a sweaty odour despite the various pedestal fans in the cavernous hall. There were people like Rosamma teacher and Joy sir who wore their faith on their sleeve, some with blank faces, and some whose frowns and other body language made it clear that they were there only because they had been pushed or cajoled to attend.

I'm going to keep an open mind, Mary told herself as the retreat began with a mass conducted by one of the Vincentian priests who had founded the retreat centre at Potta. Mary felt a sense of calm as she listened to the prayers. True, she did not pray as loudly as the old man standing to her right. She did not show any exhilaration on her face or radiate hope unlike the teenage girl in front of her. She did not look bored and irritated like the middle-aged woman to her left. You are in the hands of God, the priest said. Look at the birds in the air. They neither plough, nor sow, nor reap, yet they are fed and are happy. You are a lot more important than the birds of the air. So why should you worry at all? It made perfect sense to Mary. The fact of the matter was that she had a lot more on her plate than she could handle.

The next day Mary did not feel so calm. What she was doing went against all her instincts and sense of logic. If God gave her a brain and two pairs of limbs, He expected her to take care of herself. And now she had come running here instead of staying at home with her children. Abandoning her children for a week was definitely not going to please Jesus, was it?

The morning session consisted of speeches by priests and other leaders, interspersed with songs and prayers. What was it that the very young speaker was saying? How often do you talk to your father and mother? God is your heavenly father. You ought to talk to your heavenly father as often as you can. Has your father or mother ever complained that you talk to them too often? God loves you a lot more than your own parents do. He sacrificed His only son for you. And yet you wonder if you ought to talk to Him!

How did that speaker manage to read her thoughts? This was the precise dilemma tormenting her! Now she knew that it was perfectly right to leave her children with her sister and spend a whole week conversing with her father in heaven.

On Tuesday, Mary felt calmer and more relaxed. Things were falling into place. God cared for her, her mother and the rest of their family so much, and everything happened according to God's plan. Mary noticed a change in the people around her as well. They were all happier. The food was simple but wholesome Keralite food. Prayers started at six in the morning and went on till nine or nine-thirty in the night. But Mary didn't mind. She was there to pray and praise the Lord and pray and praise the Lord she would.

Forgive all those who sin against you and then try to forget what happened, a priest advised the congregation. Was there anyone she hated? Mary wondered. Anyone who had done them harm? Oh yes! Their family GP who had goofed up was a prime candidate, wasn't he? Mary decided to forgive him and felt deliriously happy about it.

Mary heard her first testimonial on Wednesday by a man who had accumulated gambling debts and had a drinking problem. He had tried for many years to shake off his addictions unsuccessfully. His wife and children had deserted him. And then he had arrived at Potta. 'Look at me now,' he said. 'I am back in the saddle of life. I am reunited with my family, I have a job and it has been over five years since I took my last sip.'

Tales of miracles started to fly thick and fast. A blind man had got his sight back. A woman who had lost the use of her right leg was now skipping about. Jesus could heal, Mary was told. Jesus is the best doctor in the world, Mary now believed. The conclusion was obvious. If Jesus cared for Ammachi, he might heal her if it was part of his plan. Mary had no clue what God's plan was, but she started to pray for a miracle. Didn't Jesus say, if you have faith as small as a mustard seed, you can say to a mountain, 'Move from here to there' and it would move? Nothing will be impossible for you!

On Wednesday evening, they were told that the next day would be a day of fasting. The sudden announcement did not upset Mary though she wished she had advance notice. On Thursday, they got nothing but black coffee in the morning and no breakfast or lunch was served except for people who claimed to be very weak or very ill. When the first meal of the day was ladled out in the evening, Mary was famished, but also refreshed. It had been so long since she had fasted or made a sacrifice for God. From Thursday evening onwards, Mary started to pray as loudly as the others. She felt no self-consciousness in clapping her hands or saying Hallelujah over and over again in the loudest voice possible. When her father was alive, she had never felt embarrassed about calling out for his help when she needed him. Why should she feel embarrassed to go crying to her heavenly father?

When it was announced that a blind man attending the retreat with them had his eyesight restored, Mary was as delighted as everyone else. But they were not surprised. Jesus had performed miracles in the past and if people of sufficient faith gathered together, he would do so again. The retreat would draw to a close on Saturday morning. Mary was sure Jesus would give her a sign that her mother had been healed before she left. But by Friday evening, there was no miracle and Mary started to feel disappointed. Maybe it wasn't part of God's plan. Maybe the Lord was testing her to see if she would hold fast even if her mother died. Well, she would take it in her stride. Maybe she'd ask God why He didn't spare her mother. She was entitled to do so, wasn't she? He was her father, wasn't He?

Mary composed herself and went to sleep. In her dream she saw Ammachi walking briskly to church; she was dressed in her usual white *kavani*, but the *kavani* radiated a brightness and sparkle that was unearthly. Mary was walking fast trying to keep up with Ammachi who was laughing aloud. Mary woke up in a sweat. She knew that a miracle had happened. She got out of the bunk bed, went down on her knees and praised God. It was four in the morning. She tried to go back to sleep, but sleep eluded her. Thank you Jesus, Praise the Lord, Mary whispered to herself over and over again. Soon, Ammachi would be able to walk to church everyday as she used to do until she was diagnosed with cancer.

The next day before the retreat ended, volunteers went around with buckets collecting money. Mary did not have much money with her, but as she dropped a five-hundred-rupee note in the red bucket, she promised herself that she would send them a cheque once she got home.

When Mary reached home, she found her mother looking much better. It was obvious that she had been cured. 'Look at Ammachi! Don't you think she looks so much better?' she demanded of her sister, who looked sceptical. So were her brothers when she called them up and breathlessly told them of the miracle. Doubting Thomases, all! Her mother, however, believed her. '*Mole*, I actually started feeling much better as soon as I woke up this morning,' she told Mary.

Mary called up Rosamma teacher and shared the good news with her. Rosamma teacher immediately rushed over to see the miracle for herself. Ammachi looks fully cured, she pronounced.

'I think we should take her to Kochi for tests,' Mary's sister suggested.

'How dare you question Jesus?' Rosamma teacher shouted. 'Don't you have faith?'

Mary's sister had the grace to look shamefaced. She did not argue her case any further until Rosamma teacher left. But after that Mary's sister started to argue again. 'What's the harm in having a doctor confirm that Ammachi is cured?' she demanded.

Mary tried to explain to her sister the sort of experience she had gone through. Once the best healer in the world had laid his hand on Ammachi, there was no need for any other doctor.

But Mary's sister was insistent on taking Ammachi for a test. And she would have had her way, too, if Ammachi had not put her foot down.

'I've had so many tests and treatments! I refuse to step into a hospital ever gain. Jesus has cured me and that's the end of it,' she declared to Mary's relief.

Mary's sister went back to Bombay. The next few weeks were full of happiness for Mary. Mathew came back from Saudi Arabia for a month. 'Why do you have to keep going back? Don't we have enough for our needs? Won't God take care of us all?' she asked him.

Ammachi felt better as the days passed. The entire family prayed together for an hour every night. The mood of piety infected Mathew as well. 'This will be my last trip back to the Gulf. The next time I'm back, I'll be back for good.'

'Let's go to Potta once again,' Mary suggested one day. 'And let's take Ammachi with us.'

Such a thought would have been unthinkable a year ago. To come home on a month's leave and spend one-fourth of it at a prayer retreat! Mary's mother-in-law was the only one unhappy with their plan, but she had no defence against divinity.

Two days before they were to go to Potta, Mary's mother complained of dizziness and fatigue. 'Don't take her to Potta. Even if she has been cured of cancer, she is bound to tire,' Mary's sister told her over the phone from Bombay.

'But a trip to Potta will cure her fully,' Rosamma teacher countered. Mary, too, was inclined to side with Rosamma teacher. However, Mary's mother vomited a few times and said she didn't have the energy to make the trip. Mary and Mathew made the pilgrimage on their own. When they came back a week later, Ammachi was not much better. 'God's only testing us,' Mary thought.

Ammachi only got worse after Mathew went back to Saudi Arabia. Mary's sister who came back from Bombay and Mary's brother who came over from Thiruvananthapuram insisted on taking her to the hospital for more tests. This time Ammachi was too weak to resist. When they came back, they looked accusingly at Mary. 'If only we had continued with the chemo instead of relying on a miracle, Ammachi might have had a chance,' they grumbled.

Mary ignored the accusations. She knew that God had a plan for her and her mother. She attended Charismatic prayer meetings in and around Idukki whenever she could. Thankfully, Ammachi continued to be in good spirits even though she became weaker and weaker. She spent all her waking hours reciting the rosary over and over again. Mary joined her whenever she could take a break from household chores.

One Sunday morning after mass, the parish priest came in to give Ammachi her final rites. As the priest slipped a coin shaped rice cracker, which represented the body of Christ, into Ammachi's mouth, a blissful smile spread across her face. That evening, Rosamma teacher and Joy sir went over to Mary's house as usual. They sat around Ammachi's bed and prayed. Ammachi was partially awake and at times her lips moved in sync with the prayers. When they finished praying, they noticed that Ammachi's body was unusually still. Joy sir took her hand and felt for a pulse. He shook his head. Mary and Rosamma teacher burst into sobs.

'I'm so happy,' Mary said. 'Ammachi died with a prayer on her lips.'

'And that too on a Sunday. What more can you ask for?' Joy sir added.

A week after her mother died Mary made a third trip to Potta on her own to thank God and to pray that her mother be given a fast-track ticket to heaven without having to spend any time in purgatory.

London-based lawyer **Vinod Joseph** is the author of *Hitchhiker*, a novel on missionary-run schools, reservations and religious conversions. He has also written many short stories, some of which can be read at his website: winnowed.blogspot.com.

22 My Urbanisation

A.J. Thomas

I was born in 1952, in a little village called Moonnilavu on the River Meenachil, in the foothills of the Western Ghats in south-central Kerala. Those were the post World War II years and the infamous wartime rice shortage had overstayed into the early part of the next decade. Rice, Malayalis' staple food, had to be given a go-by; the brown rice, with which 'at least a little rice water' (as the common plaint goes) was to be made, had to be smuggled in on head-load from Thodupuzha, a good twelve miles away, under the cover of darkness as there was a prohibition on the movement of rice from one area to another to discourage black-marketing. There was no question of starvation on account of the unavailability of rice. However, there was the versatile tapioca, sweet potatoes, yams, colacasia, and other root-tubers and rhizomes; there were enough of raw jack-fruits for making the popular *puzhukku* (mixture), tummyfuls of which people ate, and the ripe jackfruits of the *varikka* (firm kernel) and *koozha* (succulent kernel) varieties; there were also mangoes, papaya, pineapple, grapefruit, plantains, guava, rose-apple and other fruits. Besides, Malayalis had reluctantly switched over to millet and bajra, stubbornly (and nostalgically) using them to prepare food items similar to the traditional forms of rice-meals – *kanji* (rice gruel) and *choru* (cooked and strained rice). My mother, who yearned for a little *rice-water* (contrary to the common yearning of pregnant women who throw up at the smell of rice cooking), had to go without it. She was lying in labour in a room in which were kept eighteen ripe jackfruits of the varikka variety and ultimately gave birth to me breathing in the heady fragrance of *varikka* jackfruits on a starving stomach!

However, I was brought up, till age ten, in a hamlet called Mechal, five miles north-east, up the mountain slope which had not seen a wheel, be it a bicycle or a bullock cart, until the late 1990s. I saw the long-nosed Bedford buses and the Willyz jeeps back from the World War II frontlines and reeking of raw petrol, only when I came down to the village. What I paid most attention to were the gigantic (to my child's eye; my comparison was of course with the wheels of the toy-carts made of the outer bark of a raw jack-fruit or the inner stem of the plantain tree) wheels of the buses and the jeeps from which fumes rose and engine oil leaked; I used to wonder what would happen if I somehow fell before them. I used to imagine—with a lump in my throat—the jeep, halted atop a slope, rolling down and crushing me.

Mechal had a lower primary school and a church belonging to the Anglican Mission, which had converted the predominantly tribal population of Mala Arayars in the Hill Reserves of the local prince, the Raja of Poonjar, who was related by marriage to the Royal House of Travancore. Henry Baker, the legendary British missionary, had spread the message of Christ as well as basic education in the hills. But, somehow, no roads were built. Hence, Mechal remained a pristine island at least six kilometres away from civilisation from all directions. The Anglican Bishop who came to bless the congregation once a year along with his wife and daughters, would be carried in a litter. So would any one who had to be taken to a hospital in a fatal condition, like people attacked by the tigers or bears that often visited the hamlet, victims of assaults, accidents, contagious diseases like cholera, smallpox, etc. or a mortal illness. All those who had to do something with the outside world had to rely solely on their two legs!

Students who had to go to high school, those who went to churches and temples, those who worked in offices far away, those who came on leave during their military service and returned, those who went to the plains to participate in political rallies and marches, those who went to the police outpost in the village in the plains to make a complaint against rowdies and transgressors, the murderers who wanted to make a getaway, the thieves who wanted to sell their booty in the market, the black-marketeers of the prohibited coffee or cannabis, the policemen who came to enquire about the cases, the occasional lovers who eloped, the Muslim house-to-house-hawker-traders of dried fish, mirrors, plastic combs and glass bangles, the missionaries of the local evangelical churches who went about preaching, the madmen who roamed up from the plains, the porters—carrying huge head-loads of tea-leaves picked from the tea estates further up the mountain slope in Chakkikkavu, farm produces like paddy, dried tapioca, dried pepper, arecanuts, coconuts, and logs of wood used both as timber and firewood, charcoal produced on an industrial basis in kilns in the jungles—all had to depend on their two legs, braving scores of flash-flooding brooks, streams and mountain rivers, the vagaries of the weather, elemental storms and lightning, or scorching sun, to negotiate the crucial six kilometres down the mountainside to connect with the outer world.

We were very close to death all the time; by drowning in the rapids falling from the single-plank makeshift bridges that spanned the rivers and streams speeding down-slope, or by cholera or any other epidemic. There were also the brigands and outlaws who roamed free and engaged in gang-wars – carrying muzzle-loaders, country-bombs, long knives, daggers and staves. The mother of a classmate of mine was thus shot dead by a hooligan who, in fact, had aimed at her husband. There were sporadic attacks by cattle-lifting tigers that camped in the cave at the base of the peak, Maankallu Mudi (the Deerstone Peak). The rabid jackals and dogs howled and wailed through the night, keeping us awake; pierced through the night hunters hustled about with loaded guns and staves, and blood-curdling cries. Fear of the ghosts of those who died in violent incidents, accidents and pestilences, kept our tender minds always on the boil.

The trade union activities in the tea estates in the mountains and valleys to the north and northeast, Chakkikkavu, Pazhukkakkanam and Pullikkanam, began with the activists of the Communist Party of India of the pre-split days. One of my uncles, a second cousin of my father, was the local hero of this newfound adventure. He was ex-communicated from the Catholic Church, which he spurned in his youth when hot blood coursed through his veins. Rebellion in the form of an upturned, fierce moustache, the twirled ends of which shone bright-black, framed against his middle-parted, step-cut hair that resembled terraced fields. This was supplemented by a menacing dagger tucked into the folds of his mundu, with its deer-horn hilt from which the silver-steel rivets shone, and buttressed by mugs of palm-toddy downed on hot afternoons in the shady pepper grove. For good measure, he had floated an amateur theatre group and staged plays that were sometimes mere propaganda stuff.

Mechal was nearly an earthly paradise, where I lived in the lap of nature for the first ten years of my life. Whatever I have earned later in life is certainly the interest of this valuable deposit of the ten-year uninterrupted bliss of an absolute union with nature. My mother was a natural poet who never wrote even a single line and had only the bare minimum literacy in lieu of formal education. But she communed with nature and its beings with a sense of equality and oneness that I could emulate.

When I left this primeval haunt at the age of ten and migrated back to my home village, Moonnilavu, the situation was only slightly better. The rowdies and hooligans and the rough, Spartan homesteaders who took offence at the slightest instance of someone swearing upon someone else's father and stabbed the other to death, characterised the land. The common school, however, was the breeding ground of cross-cultural interchange. I sat on the same long-bench beside the son of the Brahmin priest of the temple, the son of the local princeling who belonged to the next highest caste – Kshatriya or the Warriors, the landlord's son who was a Christian, the son of the washerman who belonged to the lowest caste, and the son of the sole Muslim trader, who was outside the caste system, like us Christians. All ate the same kind of packed lunch of rice and curry; the Brahmin and Kshatriya would have vegetarian food, while the rest ate fish and occasional meat curries along with the rice, besides vegetables like string-beans and brinjal curry or mango curry cooked with jack-nuts or dried shrimp. But the sense of equality, both in triumphs and in misery, was the same.

There was only one family in the entire settlement that boasted of an English newspaper – our local landlord's cousin; he subscribed to *The Hindu*. He would board the daily morning bus to Palai Town, nineteen kilometres away, to his club for the daily card games that he regularly lost, and boarded the last bus back. We had the battery-driven valve-radios—big boxes—that gave us news of Nehru and Chou-en-Lai of China declaring the Five Principles of Good-neighbourliness, its deterioration leading to the Indo-China War of 1962 (we, class V students, marched to the Vakakkad School of the same parish, shouting 'Up-up Nehruji, down-down Chou-en-Lai' in my maiden introduction to agitational strike), the assassination of President Kennedy on 22 November 1963, Nehru's death on 27 May 1964, and the

Indo-Pakistan War of 1965. Then came the transistor revolution; now, news and music could be heard from all corners!

I saw occasional aeroplanes flying like silver crosses shimmering in the sun; the rare jet planes were obvious by the trails of white smoke, their rumble reaching us after the plane had disappeared. I remember the first-ever rocket launch by India on 21 November 1963 (a day before Kennedy's assassination). We all knew that we were witnessing a momentous incident. We were taunted that the rocket would fall on our heads, though it was happening at least two hundred kilometres to the south, at Thumba, near Kovalam, Thiruvananthapuram. We saw the brilliant orange trail lighting up the night sky and the downward fall of the spent rocket, which fell into the Arabia Sea. (Former President Dr A.P.J. Abdul Kalam was in the core group of scientists who sent that first rocket up into the sky.) That was the first step of the fantastically successful Indian Space Programme.

There were also sightings of at least two comets between 1965 and 1968. The first comet looked like a stationery flowerpot of bright orange colour in the north-eastern sky for nearly a week; the second looked like a shimmering highway before dawn in the south-eastern sky around Eastertide.

I saw my first movie in 1968, when I was sixteen. That was the day I ventured out to Palai, our nearest town. It was also the year I began to use footwear – rubber slippers – the only kind available to commoners. We did not have electricity until I left my village in 1970.

What I remember of the community life in my village is coloured by church and temple festivals, glittering processions, with the richly rhythmic *chenda* (the local drum) percussion recitals, deafening and blinding fireworks that instilled the fear of god into the pragmatism-hardened minds of the tough rural materialists, and the Kathaprasangam (narrative-performance), ballet or drama performances that made the 'night festival' memorable. The night festival was also rendezvous time for clandestine lovers – young and otherwise! Bodies entwined in tapioca farms under the filtering moonlight, the sudden appearance of a *choottu* torch and the separating bodies of assorted lovers, the gossipmongers in the teashops next morning...

Love was something of a 'no-no' within accepted morality. Young men and women or teenagers never 'loved' in actual life. When they were of marriageable age, parents arranged a match and they married. After marriage, conjugal activities were very much under the control of the mother-in-law of the family. Love was something to be discussed only in stories and films.

Those days, reading love stories, watching romantic dramas and films (mythological, morality or family-oriented) were also strictly prohibited for proper Christians, as love-stories, films and dramas, as well as acting in them, were 'the devil's business'. Post-pubertal boys and girls were frowned upon if caught talking freely; the natural assumption being they were lovers and that the next step would be pregnancy! When surreptitious love letters were intercepted, the ensuing ruckus sometimes had the girl's kin attacking and even murdering the boy or his family members. This tells the sad state of love in the times of yesterday's harsh morality!

Sex was the most precious thing, to be valued; priests harped on the theme of 'purity' in their sermons and retreats. Anyone who broke the 'Sixth Commandment' was worse than a murderer or a thief. The preponderance of suppressed sex bred inhuman violence. The cult of violence, prompting perfectly ordinary and normal people to draw out a dagger and stab somebody at the slightest provocation is prevalent in those areas even today.

The family was noted for rigid morals that bred exemplary fidelity between spouses (with the rank cruelty that was spawned by the rigid sexual codes fostering suppression notwithstanding) and a great amount of sibling loyalty among children in the early stages, and rivalry once they grew up, mostly over property division. However, most of the families saw great cooperation among their members and pride in family name and prestige, counting it in the numbers of priests and nuns it produced in Christian families. Like in the case of all propertied people, land decided loyalties. Most people were direct and plain in their dealings, with an innate sense of honesty and accountability, which would be stretched when dire straits yawned. In deprivation-ridden families, the siblings stuck together and roughed it out. Normally, the elder ones took responsibility to look after the younger ones, or to run the house if the father could not sustain them.

It is to be mentioned here that the spirit of abstinence and asceticism that ran through the Catholic Church, right from the times of the Desert Fathers, through the colourful and highly edifying lives of the saints it spawned, like St. Francis of Assisi or St. Theresa of Avila, was inherent in the strict code of conduct of the Christians of our region, too. St. Alphonsa (the recently canonised saint of the Catholic Church), the Clarist nun who made an offering of her sufferings to Christ and became a saint in the process, had taught in a school in nearby Vakakkad, where my father was briefly her student. The same spirit resulted in hundreds of young men and women getting the call of God, (which is technically known as 'vocation') and setting out to the different parts of the country and the globe, on the 'mission' of spreading the word of God and carrying dedicated service in various fields. At Bharananganam, where St. Alphonsa lies interred (her tomb is now a world-renowned pilgrimage centre), there was a 'Vocation Guidance Centre'. Organisations like 'Cherupushpa Mission League' ('Cherupushpam' means 'Little Flower', the sobriquet for St. Theresa of Lissieux) did intense work in aiding and guiding youth who fervently wished to 'go on mission', which was the noblest option for young Catholic men and women of the region in those days).

However, such a society, obsessed with the observance of strict moral codes in a fanatical spirit, was not at all sensitive to creative self-expression. The only aesthetic activity was 'critical' appreciation of films, music, and literature, which amounted to a sort of accounting. Acquisition of knowledge aimed primarily at earning a livelihood and the eventual piling up of material wealth were the highest virtues. At a time when in the hinterlands of Kerala's cities and towns, a modernist leftist sensibility—supported by western rational and liberal approaches—was raising literary and aesthetic standards almost on a world level, I was undergoing such a cultural conditioning in a conservative pocket.

Leaving Moonnilavu, the tiny village by the small river Meenachil, after a two-year-long debacle involving a pre-degree in a college in Aruvithura, I migrated to West Bengal, to Bandel, fifty kilometres upriver from Kolkata, on the Ganges (Hooghly) for pursuing a pre-university course. I lived in a boarding school run by the Salesians of Don Bosco as a priesthood aspirant. The natural beauty and grandeur and the sense of history and antiquity the place instilled in me inspired me to write my first few poems in English. It was literally a transplant, roots and all, and it took some time in the quiet atmosphere of the monastery at Bandel to place myself in the changed circumstances, where I got glimpses of what was happening in the wider world. I was lucky enough to undergo a film appreciation course, ironically in the monastery (at a time when films were taboo in my local Catholic community back home), following a pioneering textbook by Gaston Roberge. The priest who led the course showed us *Pather Panchali* many times over, and the famous Candyman sequence from it at least twenty-five times! Visits to the Calcutta Zoo, India Museum and the Birla Planetarium enhanced my horizons. The dizzying changes I underwent there proved a forerunner for my experience of the development of the countrysides of Kerala in the 1970s when I returned from Calcutta after three years. Though no sweeping changes had descended on our little village, drastic changes had come over in the wider areas in the midlands and coastal regions.

At first, people could not understand what was happening. Those who had gone to the Persian Gulf sporadically to do different kinds of odd jobs for the Sheikhs had taken their relatives and others to the desert havens to reap real gold. The 555 and Rothmans brands of cigarettes and Old Spice aftershave lotions were mere harbingers of the tsunami of cultural invasion that Kerala was to undergo soon. The meagre-salaried, stiff-collared, brittle-egoed, office-goer or teacher saar was out-purchased by the 'upstart' urchin who had run away from home and returned wearing Ray-Ban glasses and flashy suits, who tossed a freshly-ironed hundred rupee note to the local fishmonger and snatched away the seer-fish that used to be sold for Rs. 25! The local toddy and arrack shops soon stood in coy admiration of the 'Foreign Liquor Shops' that sprouted up soon all over the state. But the real Scotch that eluded our middle-classes was available only with the 'Gulfee'! Our urbanisation had begun thus.

Dr **A.J. Thomas**, an Indian-English poet and editor of the Sahitya Akademi journal *Indian Literature*, is the recipient of the Katha Award, the AKMG Prize and the Hutch-Crossword Award, for translating M. Mukundan's novel, *Kesavante Vilaapangal* (*Kesavan's Lamentations*). He has translated extensively from Malayalam poetry, fiction and drama, and has several books to his credit.

23 No Sex Please, We Have Cable

Suresh Menon

Malayalis hate geographical imprecision. The railway station at Irinjalakuda, my birthplace, is referred to locally as 'Kalletumkara'. Only foreigners (that is, those born outside Irinjalakuda) call it by the name on the board. Likewise with Kochi airport, the prettiest in the country. The foreign Malayali, to show his familiarity with Kerala, will refer to it as the Angamali airport; but the true-born calls it the Nedumbassery airport. Kerala, one of our few states to have an architectural style of its own, welcomes the visitor to a gently-spreading building with traditional sloping roofs and pillars. A hoarding inside promises hair to the hairless. This is appropriate. We are a people obsessed with thick hair and body weight. *Entha mudi, entha thadi*—what hair! how fat!—is the highest compliment we pay one another. Kerala might be the first state with one hundred percent literacy, but the visual precedes the intellectual and we make no bones about it.

Well laid out shops (five book-stalls!) manned by tidy, well-groomed men and women who are extremely polite and speak excellent English provide a much warmer welcome than the odd-flower handed out by bored daily wage earners in other airports. It wasn't always like this. When my parents, sister and I went on our annual vacations first from Calcutta and then from Bangalore, we got off at the Thrissur railway station, some twenty kilometres away.

'The train stops only for three minutes in Irinjalakuda, and if we calculate one minute for each of you to get off with your luggage, then someone is bound to be left behind,' an uncle, son of a Namboothiri (therefore, full of self-doubt and doubts on others' behalf), would say.

No one doubted his word though. After all, he hailed from Irinjalakuda, birthplace of Madhavan Namboothiri, a fourteenth century astronomer and mathematician who developed many of the ideas of calculus three centuries before either Isaac Newton or Leibniz did. Namboothiri lived near the place where the railway station is today.

The drive into Irinjalakuda hasn't changed. Narrow roads, excitable drivers, too many trucks and buses make it a unique adventure. One bus decides to kiss and make up with our taxi after a brief argument at an intersection. I can still hear my wife's scream ringing in my ears. It is early in the morning and many shutters are still down, shutters with the images of movie stars. I counted eighteen of Mohanlal's before the first one of Mammooty, both megastars (one level above mere superstars). There is a message here. Popularity is a garish shutter. It is more authentic than any PR handout. There are other stars, too, some I don't recognise. Every music shop announces itself with a sketch of the singer Yesudas. Some of these teeter on the verge of likeness.

Unprovoked, lines from a poem, by nineteenth century poet Thomas Hood, that I learnt in school pop into my head:

> *I remember, I remember*
> *The house where I was born*
> *The little window where the sun*
> *Came peeping in at morn . . .*
> *. . . But now 'tis little joy*
> *To know I am farther off from Heav'n*
> *Than when I was a boy.*

If an artist were to paint Kerala, green would be the predominant colour. Green for the vast fields and trees and water bodies. Variations on the green theme (with bright pink for variety) for the modern houses indicate a son or nephew or husband in a Gulf country. Later, at a bakery, a happy salesman tells us what to buy because 'this is what everybody from the Gulf buys'. We avoid these on principle.

My wife Dimpy and I spot Sukhasthan almost simultaneously – she remembers from photographs and I from my last memory of it a quarter century ago. This is the house where I was born in a room I have been terrified of ever since. It had one window that looked into a large *nadappura* (hall, for want of a better word) on its west side. It had a toilet with all varieties of coloured bottles in it. Through most of my childhood, the door never shut properly and I had nightmares of being surprised (by a host of female relatives) while using the toilet. An air of something I couldn't recognise as a child always hung over the house. Years later I realised what it was – sexuality. A cousin explained that in his house, too, people were always either doing it or thinking about doing it or talking about it or discussing how others did it. I had the same impression, although it took me a while to put a label on it. In the Kerala of old, they had sex. Now they have television.

There was a room upstairs with a window on its east side (it is only in Kerala that one talks of cardinal points. I have no idea where east is in my Bangalore home). This window faced the Iyyankavu temple, a Devi temple a few hundred metres away. If anything, I was even more scared of this room because my grandmother once told me that if I looked out of it at night, I would see dancing witches. (Immobile witches were bad enough.) On the few occasions I went upstairs, I did so with my eyes tightly closed. I was also told that if I ate an orange pip with the seeds in it, an orange tree would grow in my stomach. Elders delighted in planting such ideas in young minds. If that didn't work, there were the stories of Kuttichattan and ghosts and devils to put you off sleep.

My late grandfather, a college professor and a prominent citizen going by the foundation stone he laid in a public place on 11 November 1969, sold Sukhasthan a decade ago. He was a handsome, energetic man who sometimes took me with him to watch the coconuts being dropped from the trees in the family plot. Even at seventy, he was agile enough to block some of the more bouncy coconuts with either foot and flick them gently into a basket. He continues to haunt my consciousness for another reason – his habit of getting up at five in the morning and opening the metal front door with all the delicacy of steel balls being dropped on a tin roof. It woke me up, as I believe was the intention. This was in case my grandmother throwing the bucket into the well didn't wake me up. That sounded like a cannon shot going off on my pillow. I thought there were sixteen bolts to the door, but notice this time that there are only eight. There is a character in Joseph Heller's *Catch 22* about someone who saw everything twice. Perhaps in my childhood I heard everything twice.

The current owner of Sukhasthan, Louis Maliackal, symbolises some of the changes that have taken place in Irinjalakuda. A tall, cheerful man with a ready smile, he receives us without reservation and opens both his house and his heart to us. 'I have done many things. Run a taxi service, some farming, and sent my younger graduate son off to Dubai,' he says, leaving us in no doubt that he considers the last to be his greatest achievement. He has reorganised the house; the room where I was born exists only in my memory now. It has been converted into a store room. I was born red in the face, according to family legend, because the midwife accidentally scratched my nose. For years, relatives pointed to the mark while they recalled this. One week ago, my mother told me this was a made-up story. Myth-making was a cottage industry in my family.

Maliackal has partitioned Sukhasthan between his two sons – gone is the car-shed where uncle Ramachandran inspired my first ambition, to be a car driver. Gone, too, is the *nadappura* where uncle Chandran inspired my other great ambition – to be a cricketer. I remember my cover drive hitting a grand uncle on the chest during a family function. My heart leaped into my mouth, but his stayed where it was, which was a bit of luck for all concerned. Sadly, neither of my ambitions came to fruition, although I once rode a two-wheeler and did step on to some of the major cricketing venues of the world, but as a journalist. Where the shed and hall stood, a two-storey modern building is under construction.

This kind of social mobility is seen everywhere. This is probably a good thing – economic prosperity has ensured there are no beggars. Also, there is, very little of the Gulf influence of the sort I once saw near Ernakulam where a falooda-coloured residence bore this legend on its gate – 'fully air-conditioned'. Irinjalakuda's magnificent churches appear to be prospering, with far more people going there than to the Koodalmanikkam temple, which was the great social and religious centre when I was a child. It is the only temple in the world dedicated to Bharat, Lord Ram's brother. Legend has it that four images of the heroic brothers—Ram, Lakshman, Bharat and Shatrugan—were washed ashore, discovered by a local chieftan Vakkey Kaimal and installed at various sites. Bharat is also *Sangameswara* because Irinjalakuda was located at the confluence (*sangamam*) of two rivers, the Chalakudy and the Kurumali, both of which have changed course. The architecture of Kerala temples is unique, and although there might have been a Jain influence on the Koodalmanikkam, the gopurams and ponds are in keeping with this unique tradition.

According to legend, the image of Bharat radiated with such brilliance that devotees brought in a gem (*manikkam*) for comparison. The gem is said to have merged (*koodal*) with the image and hence the name Koodal-manikkam.

I was advised by Diwakara Menon, a widely-travelled eighty-four-year-old settled in Irinjalakuda, to wear a *mundu* (dhoti) and a shawl while entering the temple. This was how I remembered it from the old days, too, although as children I think we were allowed to wear shorts. Keeping a mundu up requires enormous will-power – some of the tension on my face in the video of my marriage is caused by the effort to keep the mundu in its place – only the true Keralite can accomplish this.

But obviously Menon had not advised some others, whose idea of bowing to tradition was to let their shirt dangle by the sleeve. The poojaris would be my cousins a few times removed – Koodalmanikkam is the only temple where this hereditary right is still observed (the remaining belong to Dewaswom Boards and are government jobs). My great-grandfather was the chief poojari there for over fifty years; when his son completed his fiftieth year in charge recently, there was a public reception. Anian thirumeni, as he is known (*anian* for younger brother, *thirumeni* an honorific), combined in him two great passions – religion and films. He knew the slokas as well as the themes of the latest movies.

'This is a plum job; people are willing to pay up to one lakh to become poojaris,' someone told me. The reason is not so much economic as practical. There are only three prayers a day and the eleven-day festival in March-April is the only busy period. It is a cushy job; however hard-working the Malayali is outside Kerala, within his own state he sees work as the last resort of the unfortunate.

The temples have changed little, but some of the prayers have. Most of the conversations (and some of the prayers, too, no doubt) revolve around the cricket in Australia. I follow the

Adelaide Test and Rahul Dravid's progress through the comments of the latecomers. This is new. Cricket was a heartily despised sport in the Kerala of my grandparents. 'Only madmen play it,' I was told then. Madmen and the local chieftains (sometimes the same thing). The local chieftains forced respect because of their birth; the economically powerful have since replaced them as the patrons of the city. The economic revolution went hand in hand with the social revolution, and where you come from is no longer as important as what you have achieved. This is comforting. Two generations ago, the 'low-born' addressed their social superiors as *thamburan* (lord) out of respect and habit. Then they hit upon the idea of naming their children 'Thamburan', so that the 'high-born' would have to ask for a 'thamburan' to do their menial work!

Starting from the temple, and beyond the main bus stop (Irinjalakuda is reputed to have had the first bus service in mid-Kerala), I walk with my wife, pointing out in advance what we are about to see. The big banyan tree, Dean's bakery, the Ayurvedic shop where the ladies of the house bought their hair tonic, the saree centre where tailor Thankappa Menon sat, and then closer to the temple, goldsmith Manikkan's place and taxi-driver Velayudhan and his brilliant smile.

Some of the people are gone, but in many cases their children have taken over the establishments. This continuity makes me uncomfortable. 'Why change when you don't have to change?' asks Diwakara Menon. He points out the way to my *tharawad* (ancestral home). This no longer exists, having made way for a modern building. Dimpy and I visit the oldest member of the family, my grandmother's sister who is ninety-four and sharp as a bell. She chats with us and walks us to the door when we leave. Customs must be observed; I hadn't met her since she was a spring chicken of seventy or so. Her daughter and niece stay with her—the latter had earlier welcomed us in the traditional Kerala outfit—the nightie.

Why do so many Malayali women spend their days in a nightdress? I have no idea. Perhaps they see their favourite heroines dressed thus on the TV screens; perhaps it is the most comfortable dress to wear – I see them at vegetable shops and movie theatres in that outfit. It brings a lump to my throat, but I dare not throw up anywhere.

The oldest movie theatre in Irinjalakuda—known as 'Konny' in the sixties, then 'Sindhu'—is now called the 'Sindhu Marriage Theatre'. Was it that long ago that it would announce the start of its shows with the popular songs of the day? There was something catholic about going to the Iyyankavu temple in the evening with a movie song blaring from the theatre nearby. The other theatre, then called 'Pioneer', now 'Prabhat', continues to screen the latest movies. The video culture hasn't taken over completely.

I feel like Rip Van Winkle waking up after a couple of decades to find that nothing has changed. The narrow stretch between the main road to the temple and Sukhasthan is unlit at night, and at least one of the newer buildings—a bar—gives it a surrealistic feel. There are autorickshaws parked in front of the bar, most of them without drivers. Perhaps the drivers have nipped in for a quick one. The road smelt of urine a quarter century ago; it continues to do so today. The mix of urine and alcohol adds a spring to our steps as we try to get away as fast as we can.

'The Municipality is asleep; there have been no lights here for a long time,' explains Maliackal unnecessarily.

The real changes are far more subtle. There are elderly people and very young people, but a good proportion of those in between have left Irinjalakuda. Diwakara Menon, who returned after sixty years, finds it depressing that many of the elderly are forced to live alone. His daughter is in Ohio and son in Chennai – they are on the phone with him regularly. 'I decided some three decades ago that I was returning to Kerala and living in this house,' he says of Kovilakam, his wife's ancestral property. He bought out her brothers' and sisters' share after Partition and lives a simple, but packed life, reading, looking after his herbs and plants, and his dogs and cow. 'I don't have a single minute to waste,' he says, 'My days are full.' He looks down upon the TV zombies who fill their days watching endless soap operas and then discussing these endlessly.

Many people find comfort in constancy. I find it worrying. It is just another word for stagnation. Diwakara Menon's explanation—why change when you don't have to change—is too facile. His wife Vatsala recalls how she and her siblings went to school in a bullock cart that was 'brightly painted and had windows'. Clearly, there is something to be said for going to Christ College, Irinjalakuda's best-known college, on a motorcycle. Or by bus to St. Joseph's College, where an aunt studied. Physical changes are inevitable. It strikes me that perhaps in the fifties and sixties, Irinjalakuda was ahead of its times. Then, while other cities caught up, Irinjalakuda remained where it was, merely constructing buildings where farms once stood.

Those who lived in Sukhasthan are scattered. My parents and an aunt live in Bangalore, my grandmother and two aunts live in Coimbatore while an uncle lives in Chennai. When I think of them and of the elderly living alone in Irinjalakuda, the words of Vikram Seth's beautiful poem come to me:

How rarely these few years, as work keeps us aloof,
Or fares or one thing or another,
Have we had days to spend under our parents' roof:
Myself, my sister and my brother.

All five of us will die; to reckon from the past
This flesh and blood is unforgiving.
What's hard is that just one of us will be the last
To bear it all and go on living.

To go on living is to change. By refusing to change, Irinjalakuda is working against nature. But suddenly, it doesn't matter. And I realise why. Over the years, those who left, worked hard at keeping their native place the way they remembered it. They wanted an unchanged, unchanging place to come back to. For them, the city has changed. For those like me, who went back there hoping for change, nothing seems to have changed. It is the perversity of nature. Our nature.

I might never go back to Irinjalakuda. But I have regained my innocence. I know there are no dancing witches or scary rooms in the house where I was born. Nor will an orange tree suddenly grow out of my mouth. Only after such knowledge can there be forgiveness.

Suresh Menon is a popular columnist and a widely-travelled cricket writer. His passions include literature, sports and music.

24 The Gift

Nimz Dean

Late nights and dawns—when salt-tinged tanginess filled the air—were my favourite times to walk along the beach. The backwaters tickle my feet when I walk too close to the shoreline. As wavelets ripple with silver-scaled fish, I almost hear dolphins singing and fancy that little mermaids are riding up to me.

But today, the sea seemed different. It seemed . . . angry.

Moody gray waves lashed at my ankles, almost toppling me over. Shrieking, I lost my balance and the small camera, given to me by my Dubai uncle, dropped into the sea and was instantly sucked in by its undulating darkness.

Upset, I waded towards the shore only to be hit by a wave so boisterous that it whacked me backward and threw up a strange object at me. At first I thought it was my camera returned to me by a benevolent sea god. But a closer look revealed that the flyaway object was, in fact, a small box.

I sat on my haunches with a dreamy smile, my fingers running up and down the grainy wood. The lid was inlaid with intricate carving and the box itself weighed no more than my fist.

Should I open it now? Or later at home? Would there be a message from a faraway friend? At last, I could contain my curiosity no more. With trembling hands, I pried open the box.

I was a little disappointed to see that there was nothing inside. Nothing!

I replaced the lid and... just held the box, this box of mine.

At home, the newspapers had already arrived. A strange new word dominated the headlines – 'tsunami'. The word leapt at me. I asked my father, 'How does one say the word?' He told me the 't' was silent. But I learnt that nothing else about the word was silent. And I thought to myself, what a horrible way to learn a new word.

Thousands had died in the neighbouring state of Tamil Nadu, the rest of India and the whole world. Thousands had died, including children my age.

So that's why the sea was so rough today!

Then my glance fell upon the box, the box from the sea. I was struck by an uncomfortable thought. Did this box that came bobbing down to me belong to a tsunami victim? Had it swum out of its owner's losing grasp and into my own prying fingers?

I ran back to the beach and placed the box on seaweed. As the box wobbled away into the distance, I heard the waves whisper.

'Let's go back, little box.'

At thirteen, **Nimz Dean** is the youngest contributor to the anthology. This story by the Bangalore-based student won a commendation in the 2007 Commonwealth Essay Competition.

25 Building Brand Kerala

Shashi Tharoor

A focus on the development of Kerala strikes me as particularly appropriate, because in some ways the great danger is that our state seems to have been left behind in the race for growth and transformation that India is running these days. In 2008, I found myself amongst a large number of management experts and policy-makers in Trivandrum, inaugurating a conference of the Trivandrum Management Association devoted to 'energising Kerala'. I was intrigued and curious that so many experts seemed to agree that Kerala is in need of energising. But that is odd: the only place in the world where Keralites seem to need energising is Kerala. Look around the planet, and you see Keralites everywhere, working extremely hard, from menial jobs in the Gulf to professorships in the States, displaying their entrepreneurial energies and achieving remarkable successes. So what is it that holds them back here, in their home state? Is it resources, policies, attitudes, politics? All of the above?

Before we answer that question we should, perhaps, step back a bit from Kerala and look at the national picture. As you well know, one of the key political debates in our country has been the 'globalisation' debate, or globalisation versus self-reliance: should India, where economic self-sufficiency has been a mantra for more than four decades, open itself further to the world economy? Here in Kerala, I know not everyone fully understands that in most of the rest of the world, people axiomatically associate capitalism with freedom, while India's nationalists associated capitalism with slavery. Why? Because the East India Company came to trade and stayed on to rule. So our nationalist leaders were suspicious of every foreigner with a briefcase, seeing him as the thin edge of a neo-imperial wedge. Instead of integrating India into the global capitalist system, as a few post-colonial countries like Singapore so effectively were to do, India's leaders were convinced that the political independence they had fought for could only be guaranteed through economic independence. So self-reliance became the slogan, the protectionist barriers went up, and India spent forty-five years with bureaucrats rather than businessmen on the 'commanding heights' of the economy, wasting the first four and a half decades after independence in subsidising unproductivity, regulating stagnation and trying to distribute poverty. (Which only goes to prove that one of the lessons you learn from history is that history sometimes teaches the wrong lessons.)

It took a financial crisis in 1991 to prompt India to change course, and now that seems truly irreversible. A measure of the extent to which the globalisation debate has ended in India came for me when I spoke in Kolkata alongside the Chief Minister of West Bengal, Buddhadeb Bhattacharjee, a stalwart of the CPI-M. And he said: 'Some people say globalisation is bad for the poor and must be resisted. I tell them that is not possible. And' – this is the crucial part – 'even if it were possible, it would not be desirable.' So when a communist chief minister speaks that way about globalisation, one can accept that this debate is largely over in India. (Even dare I hope, in Kerala.)

But a second front has been opened by the anti-globalists, who have raised a further question: does the entry of Western consumer goods bring in alien influences that threaten to disrupt

Indian society in ways too vital to be allowed? Should we raise the barriers to shield our youth from the pernicious seductions of MTV and McDonald's? My own view is that the best answer to this question was given more than sixty years ago by Mahatma Gandhi himself, when he said he wanted India to be a house with all its doors and windows open, so that the winds of the world could blow through the house, because India was strong enough to stand on its own two feet and not be blown off its feet by these winds. There will always be more masala dosas sold in India than McDonald's. There is no risk that 'Baywatch' and burgers will supplant Bharatnatyam and bhelpuri. I believe our experience with globalisation so far has demonstrated that we can drink Coca-Cola without becoming Coca-colonised.

There is also a further debate, what economists call the 'guns versus butter' debate, or perhaps we should speak of 'guns versus ghee' – the case for expenditure on defence against spending on development. With the twenty-first century having begun amidst new threats of terrorism and renewed talk of nuclear confrontation, there is an ideological battle looming between advocates of military security (freedom from attack and conquest) and those of human security (freedom from hunger and hopelessness). It is difficult to deny that without adequate defence, a country cannot develop freely, according to its own lights; it is equally impossible to deny that without development there will not be a country worth defending.

We hear a new buzzword these days about our country: 'Brand India'. It's an idea, says the subtitle of a book by a London-based author, whose time has come. Can we accept this notion, and from it, can we dare to extract a Brand Kerala?

But what is that idea whose time has come? A brand, the marketing gurus tell us, is a symbol embodying all the key information about a product or a service: it could be a name, a slogan, a logo, a graphic design. When the brand is mentioned, it carries with it a whole series of associations in the public mind, as well as expectations of how it will perform. The brand can be built up by skilful advertising, so that certain phrases or moods pop up the moment one thinks of the brand; but ultimately the only real guarantee of the brand's continued worth is the actual performance of the product or service it stands for. If the brand delivers what it promises—if it proves to be a reliable indicator of what the consumer can expect, time after time—then it becomes a great asset in itself. Properly managed, the brand can increase the perceived value of a product or service in the eyes of the consumer. Badly managed, a tarnished brand can undermine the product itself.

So can India be a brand? Can Kerala? Let's start with India first. A country isn't a soft drink or a cigarette, but its very name can conjure certain associations in the minds of others. This is why our first prime minister, Jawaharlal Nehru, insisted on retaining the name 'India' for the newly independent country, in the face of resistance from nativists who wanted it renamed 'Bharat'. 'India' had a number of associations in the eyes of the world: it was a fabled and exotic land, much sought after by travellers and traders for centuries, the 'jewel in the crown' of Her Britannic Majesty Victoria, whose proudest title was that of 'Empress of India'. Nehru wanted people to understand that the India he was leading was heir to that precious heritage. He wanted, in other words, to hold on to the brand, though it was not a term he was likely to have employed.

For a while, it worked. India retained its exoticism, its bejewelled maharajahs and caparisoned elephants against a backdrop of the fabled Taj Mahal, while simultaneously striding the world stage as a moral force for peace and justice in the vein of Mahatma Gandhi. But it couldn't last. As poverty and famine stalked the land, and the exotic images became replaced in the global media with pictures of suffering and despair, the brand became soiled.

It stood, in many people's eyes, for a mendicant with a begging-bowl, a hungry and skeletal child by his side. It was no longer a brand that could attract the world.

Today, the brand is changing again. As India transforms itself economically from a lumbering elephant to a bounding tiger, it needs a fresh brand image to keep up with the times. The government even set up, with the collaboration of the business association, the Confederation of Indian Industry and the India Brand Equity Foundation. They were tasked with coming up with a slogan that encapsulated the new brand in time for the World Economic Forum's 2006 session in Davos, where India was the guest of honour. They did. 'India: Fastest-growing free market democracy' was emblazoned all over the Swiss resort. Brand India was born.

But though it's a great slogan, is it enough? Coca-Cola, for years, offered the 'pause that refreshes': it told you all that you needed to know about the product. Does 'fastest-growing free market democracy' do the same? India's rapid economic growth is worth drawing attention to, as is the fact that it's a free market (we want foreigners to invest, after all) and a democracy (that's what distinguishes us from that other place over there, which for years has grown faster than us). But isn't there more to us as a country than that?

In fairness to the smart people who coined the phrase, the more attributes you try to get in, the clunkier the phrase and the less memorable it becomes. It's easier for smaller countries that aim for one-issue branding. The Bahamas came up with the great message – 'It's better in the Bahamas'. Puerto Rico sold itself as a 'Tropical Paradise', and there's 'Surprisingly Singapore'. But what do we want the world to think of when they hear the name 'India'? Clearly, we'd prefer 'fastest-growing free market democracy' to replace the old images of despair and disrepair. But surely there are other elements we want to build into the brand:

the exquisite natural beauty of much of our country, encapsulated in the 'Incredible India!' advertising campaign conducted by the Tourism Department; the glitz and glamour of Bollywood and Indian fashion and jewellery designs; the unparalleled diversity of our plural society, with people of every conceivable religious, linguistic and ethnic extraction living side-by-side in harmony; and the richness of our cultural heritage, to name just four obvious examples. Yet it would be impossible to fit all that into a poster, a banner or even a TV commercial. (And we'd still have left out a host of essentials, from ayurveda to IT).

So the challenge of building Brand India continues. But one essential fact remains: what really matters is not the image but the reality.

Which brings us to Brand Kerala. Despite all the strengths of Kerala—its liberality, its pluralism, its literacy, its empowerment of women, its openness to the world—it's difficult to deny that the state has acquired a less than positive reputation as a place to invest. 'Keralites are far too conscious of their rights and not enough of their duties,' one expatriate Malayali businessman told me. 'It's impossible to get any work done by a Keralite labour force – and then there are those unions!' He sighed. 'Every time we persuade an industrialist to invest in Kerala, it ends badly. The late G.D. Birla put a Gwalior Rayons plant in Mavoor – it has long since closed. The Doshis of Mumbai started the Premier Tyre factory in Kalamassery – you know the fate of that plant. The late Raunaq Singh set up the first Apollo Tyres plant in Chalakudi, but all the expansions of Apollo Tyres since then went to other states such as Gujarat, as neither Raunaq or his son Omkar could deal with the politically charged trade unions.' He shook his head. 'I am a Malayali,' he declared, 'but I would not advise anyone to invest in Kerala.'

It was with his words ringing in my ears that I stepped gingerly into my home state in 2007. Newly freed from my career as a UN official, I wanted to see what I could do for Kerala's development, in particular by opening the eyes of foreign investors to what the state had to offer. What I saw and heard here convince me that my friend's pessimism is, at the very least, out of date.

For one thing, the attitude of the workforce is not what it was. It's always been a curious paradox that Keralites put in long hours in places like the Gulf, where they have earned a reputation for being hardworking and utterly reliable, while at home they are seen as indolent and strike-prone. Surely the same people couldn't be so different in two different places? And yet they were – for one simple reason: the politicised environment at home. It's a reputation that has come to haunt Kerala.

Several people told me the story of how BMW had been persuaded to install a car-manufacturing plant in the state, thanks to generous concessions by the government. But the very day the BMW executives arrived in Kerala to sign the deal, they were greeted by a 'bandh': the state had shut down over some marginal political issue, cars were being blocked on the streets, shops were closed by a hartal. It had nothing to do with BMW or with foreign investment, but the executives—or so I was told—beat a hasty retreat. The plant has now been set up in neighbouring Tamil Nadu. Kerala's political and business leaders are aware of this story.

When he was kind enough to launch my book, *The Elephant, The Tiger And The Cellphone,* in Kerala, the chief minister gently chided me for my criticism of hartals, saying that it was through such popular struggles that the people of Kerala had advanced. But even if that were true, the advances of yesterday have already happened; the advances of tomorrow require work, not hartals. Yet few are aware of the counter-narrative. Antony Prince, a Malayali settled in the Bahamas, is president of a major ship-design company there, GTR Campbell (GTRC). GTRC had built many ships around the world and its contracts had helped revive

China's Xingang Shipyard. Why not try and do the same in his native land, Prince wondered. Ignoring all the friendly (negative) advice he was given, he decided to get one of his huge 'Trader' class double-hull bulk carriers built at Kerala's Cochin Shipyard. This was a major undertaking: GTRC's Trader class ships are 30,000 tons deadweight, have cargo holds of 40,000 cubic metres in capacity, and are meant to sail over a range of 15,500 nautical miles, so the task would have challenged a more experienced shipyard. But as the work unfolded, Prince realised he need not have worried. Not only was there not a single strike or work stoppage, but the shipyard workers took pride in having been given such a major assignment. They finished the job to GTRC's complete satisfaction — ahead of deadline. Five more ships will now be built in Cochin; it's the shipyard's largest-ever order.

But the potential is even greater. Working with GTRC had transformed Xingang into a world-class shipbuilder; there is no reason why the same cannot happen in Cochin. Prince was enthusiastic about the prospects. 'The officers and workers in the Cochin yard have proved that they can do it, launching the first vessel on schedule, with first-rate quality and meeting international shipbuilding standards,' he said. 'I hope the message will spread.' It should. The interesting point is that shipbuilding is a highly labour-intensive industry; some thirty percent of the input is human labour, which is what makes it ideal for a country like India. The workers at Cochin Shipyard—unionised to a man—demonstrated that labour remains India's greatest asset, even in Kerala. It is not, as skittish investors had long feared, a liability.

A visit to Trivandrum's Technopark confirmed my impression that the sceptics are behind the curve. CEO after CEO told me in glowing terms of their satisfaction with the work environment in Kerala, the quality of the local engineering graduates, and the beauty of the lush and tranquil surroundings. Indeed, Kerala's past failures at attracting and retaining heavy industry are now working in the state's favour. One Technopark firm, US Technologies, told me of having bid for a contract with a Houston-based company which had drawn up a shortlist of Indian service providers and placed the Trivandrum-based company last. The American executives making the final decision flew down to India to inspect the six shortlisted Indian firms. After three harrowing days ploughing through the traffic congestion and pollution of Bombay, Bangalore, and Delhi, they arrived in Trivandrum, checked into the Leela at Kovalam beach, sipped a drink by the seaside at sunset – and voted unanimously to give the contract to US Technologies. 'If we have to visit India from time to time to see how our contract is doing,' the chief said, 'we'd rather visit Kerala than any other place in India.'

As they say in the US: Sounds like a plan! It is time that Indian investors took notice as well. God's Own Country no longer deserves the business reputation of being the devil's playground.

So what are the qualities that we can infuse into a 'Brand Kerala'? What is it of Kerala that we must cherish, and of which we remain proud, wherever we are?

First, the natural beauty of Kerala, which is bred into our souls. Hailing from a land of forty-four rivers and innumerable lakes, with 1,500 kilometres of 'backwaters', the Keralite bathes twice a day and dresses immaculately in white or cream. But she also lives in a world of colour: from the gold border on her off-white mundu and the red of her bodice to the burnished sheen of the brass lamp in her hand whose flame glints against the shine of her jewellery, the golden *kodakaddakan* glittering at her ear. Kerala's women are usually simple and unadorned. But they float on a riot of colour: the voluptuous green of the lush Kerala foliage, the rich red of the fecund earth, the brilliant blue of the life-giving waters, the shimmering gold of the beaches and riverbanks.

Yet there is much more to the Kerala experience than its natural beauty. Since my first sojourn as a child in my ancestral village, I have seen remarkable transformations in Kerala society, with land reform, free and universal education and dramatic changes in caste relations.

It is not often that an American reference seems even mildly appropriate to an Indian case, but a recent study established some astonishing parallels between the United States and the state of Kerala. The life expectancy of a male American is seventy-two, that of a male Keralite seventy. The literacy rate in the United States is ninty-five percent; in Kerala it is ninty-nine percent. The birth rate in the US is sixteen per thousand; in Kerala it is eighteen per thousand, but it is falling faster. The gender ratio in the United States is 1,050 females to 1,000 males; in Kerala it is 1,040 to 1,000, and that in a country where neglect of female children has dropped the Indian national ratio to 930 women for 1,000 men. Death rates are also comparable, as are the number of hospital beds per 100,000 population. The major difference is that the annual per capita income in Kerala is around $300 to $350, whereas in the US it is $22,500, about seventy times as much.

Kerala has, in short, all the demographic indicators commonly associated with 'developed' countries, at a small fraction of the cost. Its success is a reflection of what, in my book *India: From Midnight To The Millennium*, I have called the 'Malayali miracle': a state that has practised openness and tolerance from time immemorial; which has made religious and ethnic diversity a part of its daily life rather than a source of division; which has overcome caste discrimination and class oppression through education, land reforms, and political democracy; which has given its working men and women greater rights and a higher minimum wage than anywhere else in India; and which has honoured its women and enabled them to lead productive, fulfilling and empowered lives.

More importantly, Kerala is a microcosm of every religion known to the country; its population is divided into almost equal fourths of Christians, Muslims, caste Hindus and Scheduled Castes, each of whom is economically and politically powerful. Kerala's outcastes—one group of whom, the Pariahs, gave the English language a term for their collective condition—suffered discrimination every bit as vicious and iniquitous as in the rest of India, but overcame their plight far more successfully than their countrymen elsewhere. A combination of enlightened rule by far-thinking maharajahs, progressive reform movements within the Hindu tradition (especially that of the remarkable Ezhava sage Sree Narayana Guru), and changes wrought by a series of left-dominated legislatures since Independence have given Kerala's 'Scheduled Castes' a place in society that other Dalits (former 'Untouchables') across India are still denied. It is no accident that the first Dalit to become President of India is Kerala's K.R. Narayanan – who was born in a thatched hut with no running water, who as a young man suffered the indignities and oppression that were the lot of his people, but who seized on the opportunities that Kerala provided him to rise above them and ascend, through a brilliant diplomatic and governmental career, to the highest office in the land.

Part of the secret of Kerala is its openness to external influences—Arab, Roman, Chinese, British; Islamist, Christian, Marxist—that have gone into the making of the Malayali people. More than two millennia ago Keralites had trade relations not just with other parts of India but with the Arab world, with the Phoenicians, and with the Roman Empire. From those days on, Malayalis have had an open and welcoming attitude to the rest of humanity. Jews fleeing Roman persecution found refuge in Kerala: it is said they came to Kerala following the destruction of the temple of Judea by the Babylonians before the birth of Christ, and there is evidence of their settlement in Cranganore in AD

68, this time after Roman attacks. Later, fleeing the Portuguese, the Jews settled in Cochin 1,500 years later, where they built a magnificent synagogue that still stands. (It is instructive that the Jews knew no hostility, let alone persecution, in Kerala until the Portuguese came from Europe to persecute them.) The Christians of Kerala belong to the oldest Christian community in the world outside Palestine, converted by Jesus' disciple Saint Thomas (the 'Doubting Thomas' of Biblical legend), one of the twelve Apostles, who came to the state in AD 52 and, so legend has it, was welcomed on land by a flute-playing Jewish girl. So Kerala's Christian traditions are much older than those of Europe – and when St. Thomas brought Christianity to Kerala, he made converts amongst the high-born elite, the Namboodiri Brahmins. Islam came to Kerala not by the sword, as it was to do elsewhere in India, but through traders, travellers and missionaries, who brought its message of equality and brotherhood to the coastal people. Not only was the new faith peacefully embraced, but it found encouragement in attitudes and episodes without parallel elsewhere in the non-Islamic world: in one example, the all-powerful Zamorin of Calicut asked each fisherman's family in his domain to bring up one son as a Muslim, for service in his Muslim-run navy, commanded by sailors of Arab descent, the Kunjali Maraicars.

It was perhaps a Malayali seaman, one of many who routinely plied the Arabian Sea between Kerala and East Africa, who piloted Vasco da Gama, the Portuguese explorer and trader, to Calicut in 1496. (Da Gama, typically, was welcomed by the Zamorin, but when he tried to pass trinkets off as valuables, he was thrown in prison for a while. Malayalis are open and hospitable to a fault, but they are not easily fooled.)

In turn, Malayalis brought their questing spirit to the world. The great Advaita philosopher, Shankaracharya, was a Malayali who travelled throughout the length and breadth of India on foot in the eighth century AD, laying the foundations for a reformed and revived Hinduism. To this day, there is a temple in the Himalayas whose priests are Namboodiris from Kerala.

Keralites never suffered from inhibitions about travel: an old joke suggests that so many Keralite typists flocked to stenographic work in Bombay, Calcutta and Delhi that 'Remington' became the name of a new Malayali sub-caste. In the nation's capital, the wags said that you couldn't throw a stone in the Central Secretariat without injuring a Keralite bureaucrat. Nor was there, in the Kerala tradition, any prohibition on venturing abroad, none of the ritual defilement associated in parts of North India with 'crossing the black water'. It was no accident that Keralites were the first, and the most, to take advantage of the post-oil-shock employment boom in the Arab Gulf countries; at one point in the 1980s, the largest single ethnic group in the Gulf sheikhdom of Bahrain was reported to be not Bahrainis but Keralites. The willingness of Keralites to go anywhere to do anything remains legendary. When Neil Armstrong landed on the moon in 1969, my father's friends laughed, he discovered a Malayali already there, offering him tea.

But Keralites are not merely intrepid travellers. Kerala took from others, everything from Roman ports to Chinese fishing-nets, and gave to the rest of India everything from martial arts (some of which appear to have inspired the better-known disciplines of the Far East) to its systems of classical dance-theatre (notably Kathakali, to which I will return, Mohiniattam, and the less well-known Koodiyattom, recently hailed by Unesco as a 'masterpiece of the oral and intangible heritage of humanity'). And I have not even mentioned Keralite cuisine and traditional medicine, in particular the attractions of Ayurveda, the great health system of ancient India, with its herbs, oils, massages and other therapies, now revived and attractively presented at dozens of locations around our state.

In other words, Kerala has a great deal of energy already. There is an old verse of the poet Vallathol's which my late father loved to recite: *Bharatam ennu ketal, abhimaana-pooritham aavanum, andarangam; Keralam ennu ketalo, thillakkanam chaora namukke njerumbugalil.* (When we hear the name of India, we must swell with pride; when we hear the name of Kerala, the blood must throb in our veins.) It is, in some ways, an odd sentiment for a Malayalali poet, for Keralites are not a chauvinistic people: the Keralite liberality and adaptativeness, such great assets in facilitating Malayali emigration and good citizenship anywhere, can serve to slacken, if not cut, the cords that bind expatriate Keralites to their cultural assumptions. And yet Vallathol was not off the mark, for Keralites tend to take pride in their collective identity as Malayalis; our religion, our caste, our region come later, if at all. There is no paradox in asserting that these are qualities that help make Malayalis good Indians in a plural society. You cannot put better ingredients into the national melting pot.

Keralites see the best guarantee of their own security and prosperity in the survival and success of a pluralist India. The Malayali ethos is the same as the best of the Indian ethos – inclusionist, flexible, eclectic, absorptive. The central challenge of India as we enter the twenty-first century is the challenge of accommodating the aspirations of different groups in the national dream. The ethos that I have called both Keralite and Indian are indispensable in helping the nation meet this challenge.

So these are the qualities that I hope Kerala can build upon. Not everyone is equally admiring of the 'Kerala model'; economists point out it places rather too much emphasis on workers' rights and income distribution, and rather too little on production, productivity and output. But its results in terms of social development are truly remarkable; and as a Keralite and an Indian, I look forward to the day when Kerala will no longer be the exception in tales of Indian development, but merely the trailblazer.

To play a major role in the twenty-first century – to fulfil its undoubted potential – India needs to solve its internal problems, and so does Kerala. Our country must ensure that we do enough to keep our people healthy, well-fed, and secure – secure not just from jihadi terrorism, a real threat, but from the daily terror of poverty, hunger and ill-health. Progress is being made: we can take satisfaction from India's success in carrying out three kinds of revolutions in feeding our people – the 'green revolution' in foodgrains, the 'white revolution' in milk production and, at least to some degree, a 'blue revolution' in the development of fisheries. But the benefits of these revolutions have not yet reached the third of our population still living below the poverty line – a poverty line drawn just this side of the funeral pyre. We must ensure they do, or the ascent of India will ring hollow, at home and abroad. In Kerala's case, we can no longer remain a state whose economy is kept afloat by remittances and tourism alone. We have to develop the knowledge industries that can attract more resources to Kerala and generate new jobs. And we have to become a service economy too, providing services in Kerala and not just in the Gulf.

Part of the challenge lies in training our people. I am proud to tell you that the Technopark in Trivandrum now houses a world-class training institution – the Afras Academy for Business Communication (AABC). The reason for this is simple. When I visited the Technopark in 2007, CEO after CEO told me that Kerala graduates are smart, they know their science, their maths and their IT, but can't speak English properly; they don't have the confidence to articulate their ideas in English; and if they do so, they do so in an accent incomprehensible to non-Keralites. This is a major handicap in our globalising world, and it is to overcome this that AABC offers world-class, state-of-the-art instruction in business communication and presentation skills. The need for such an institution was well reflected in the decision of both the governor and the chief minister to inaugurate the facility in 2008.

I believe that the India that will succeed—and therefore also the Kerala that will do so—is one open to the contention of ideas and interests within it, unafraid of the prowess or the products of the outside world, wedded to the democratic pluralism that is our civilisation's greatest strength, and determined to liberate and fulfill the creative energies of its people. Such an India, such a Kerala, is one that nurtures and rewards entrepreneurs and helps them to change the lives of Indians.

Shashi Tharoor, columnist and novelist, was the UN under-secretary for communications and public information 2002-07. His books include *The Great Indian Novel, Show Business* and *Riot* as well as *Kerala: God's Own Country* and *Bookless In Baghdad*. This article was originally a speech made by him at the 2007 New Indian Express Conclave held in Kerala.

26 Happy

Omana

In the little corner of Thrissur where I was born, I was not the only orphan. Fortunately for me, my parents died *after* I had joined school. So, I have the memory of two full years of going to school, sitting there while the teacher came in, her hands full of chalk. My younger brother never got to go to school.

The four of us, ranging from eleven years to two, moved in with my uncle after my parents' deaths. The four cents of land our hut stood on, automatically passed on to my uncle, my father's brother. My chief job from then on was to look after their young ones. It was not that my aunt was cruel in any way, but she had her children to think about. They had to be bathed, fed and sent to school. The good thing is we never starved, there was enough rice gruel to go around.

When I turned twenty, I got a few proposals. Mainly from labourers whose first wife had eloped with a migrant worker from Tamil Nadu or were widowers and had small kids that needed to be taken care of; my aunt was always insisting I choose from them.

'You are so dark and all skin and bones! What do you expect?' she said. Though she was right, my mind rebelled at such a settling in life. She was also angry, though secretly relieved, that my elder brother had run away from home by then. One fine morning when we all woke up, he wasn't lying on his mat. After a week, someone said that he had seen him hanging around at the railway station.

Months passed, my cousin sisters got married. Their grooms were not labourers as they had a dowry, however small, to offer. I was the chief cook at the wedding feasts and when a couple of women asked how come my cousines were getting married before me since I was the oldest of the lot, I only smiled and continued to pound the chillies. What can one say?

Then my uncle died. He had been our only ally in the dark. With his death, something in me snapped. I saw my future turning an unknown corner. What was there to live for? After the funeral, property matters were revised and it was apparent that we, the nephews and nieces, had nothing to our name. We might as well have dropped from the sky!

In the evening, there was a light shower. I walked out as if to take the clothes from the washing line, but kept on walking. By and by, I reached a brook. It was one of those small water bodies by the wayside that lock in rubbish and deflated tyres. I stared into it with great fascination. As I stared, a ripple swam up into my mother's face in the waters. I saw it as a sign and, tucking my half-sari's end into my waist-band, jumped in.

The water was sour in my mouth, there was even a rotting fish-head floating near me. I soon realised my folly; the water was not deep enough to drown me!

I floated in the filth for a while, the cold water seeping into my brain and laughing at me. Shivering, I got out finally and made for home. I changed and went back into the kitchen where rice was in the pot I had left it in, still waiting to be cleaned and washed. I picked up the pot with an air of defeat.

'There's a letter for you,' my aunt called out.

It was from my brother. 'I am settled here now,' he had written. 'You can also come.'

In Bombay, for two months, I stayed in a small slum in Colaba where my brother had holed up with ten other men. Since I was the only woman, I kept house for them. A Malayali woman who lived nearby told me there was a house that needed a servant; the saar there lived alone, his wife and kids were back home in Kerala. At first, my mind went blank; back in Kerala, I would've died before sweeping someone else's courtyard. At least the courtyard I had swept until then belonged to my own uncle! But then I looked around – I had only that small rectangle where I slept to call my own. When my brother said he would take me there, the woman said no. She insisted that she herself would take me there.

She rang the doorbell, her eyes intent on me. Just before the door opened, she lowered the edge of my sari, showing more of my blouse.

The man who stood there spoke in Malayalam. He looked dismissively at me and said that he wanted someone younger. For cooking? For cleaning? For washing his clothes? I was twenty-four then. Never have I been younger than I was then!

After many such attempts and negotiations, I finally landed a job that required me to look after a baby for a couple who were both working.

Today, almost thirty decades later, I am still looking after someone's child. I'm passed on by one set of parents to another. My brother, who is married and has a son, comes to negotiate terms with my new employers every time. Each time, he asks for a fee that is at least a thousand rupees higher. My salary goes straight to him. This is my decision. After all, they have a child and home to take care of. My needs are thankfully taken care of by my employers – I am given clothes and food, what more can I ask for? He comes by every month and my employer hands the money to him directly.

I have even been to Dubai once when my employers went there for a while. I have been with this family now for a long time. I have seen many types of families, many types of fights, all types of parents and the cracks within a home's walls... At times, I look around at the expensive crystals on the shelves (kept there for me to dust) and the golden liquor in their bottles and think that the reason I stay on is not the money. Not strictly. It is because I see myself in these children.

When tiny fingers clasp mine while their parents are at a party far from home, I understand my life better. At fifty-four, I do sometimes wish I had a family of my own... you know, a husband and two children—a girl and a boy—who will call me amma and tell me that I'll catch a cold if I sit out in the open for such a long time. But every child I have looked after has called me amma. Let me count... yes, at least eight children now have at one time or the other called me amma and clung to me in the dark and told me when they were hungry or what they were scared of. One has asked me when my birthday was. One wanted to know my surname. Another combed my hair and fed me as I fed him. There was a grandmother who was upset on her visit to find that her grandson called me 'amma' and tried her best to rid him of the 'wrong' habit before she left. A little girl, barely three, got her mother to gift me Nivea cream on Diwali as she wanted me to smell like her mother did!

One day, a strapping young man of twenty-five came looking for me to invite me for his wedding. Imagine, *me*! He said he remembers me bathing him when he was small. He also told his bride about this right in front of me on the wedding dais, and stupidly, I started to cry. It is like the smell of mud when it rains here in Bombay . . . some things just make me think of home, though there is nothing missing in my life here.

Yes, I do remember my corner of Kerala now and then. It comes to me in flashes of dreams. Father's funeral. Aunty scolding. The filth-filled brook that did not have enough water to climb over my head.

Most of all, I miss the sound of Malayalam—spoken in seriousness or jest—and remember how good jokes sounded in my own language! What I do now is I teach my children some Malayalam words. When they ask me 'sukhamano?' I laugh. To be asked that in my language makes me happy and at that moment I *am* happy. I reply to them in all honesty, 'Sukhamaanu.'

Omana works as a domestic help outside India. The memoir here is a translation from Malayalam as recounted to Shinie Antony.